THE BROKEN BLOOD

A NICK DRAKE NOVEL

DWIGHT HOLING

For Riley Ann Holing

1

———

Sunrise came and sundown went. Dry lightning marbled the sky as the heat of a summer's day clashed with the chill of the night. A thunderbolt struck an ancient juniper tree shaped like a cross.

Loq watched it burst into flames and wondered if it was an omen as he waited at the end of a dusty road that gave way to a trail that climbed hunchbacked hills before being swallowed by dark mountains. He pictured his ancestors dancing around a bonfire in preparation for war and the firefights he'd survived during his multiple tours in Vietnam.

It didn't matter, he finally decided. Whatever the burning tree foretold—good, bad, or indifferent—nothing was going to change his mind. Only death could force him to give up his mission.

Loq wasn't there on official US Fish and Wildlife ranger business. This was personal, and that made it all the more dangerous. His greatest enemies weren't the people he was chasing. It was impatience as well as hesitation. Both were always risks when it came to rescuing a loved one, especially when they didn't want to be saved.

Another thunderbolt brightened the sky and illuminated a horse and rider making their way down the trail. Loq started singing to himself as they approached. He sang of growing up in the Klamath Nation. The horse was one hundred yards away. He sang of geese and swans blackening the sky over the blue lake his people lived alongside. Sixty yards away. Of plump redband rainbow trout crowding the rivers. Thirty yards. Of bald eagles perched atop fir trees calling to their mates. Twenty yards. Of racing his big sister on horseback across fields of bunchgrass and sagebrush. Ten yards away.

The gray stallion stopped. He didn't toss his head or whinny. Loq finished singing.

The rider sat on a red and black woolen blanket without shifting his weight or pulling on bitless reins made in the old way by twisting horsehair and dogbane. Two long braids tied off at the ends with strips of tanned deerskin fell down his chest. A buffalo bone necklace gleamed as white as the flashes overhead. Silver conchos shone at the ankles of his moccasins. So did the receiver of the lever-action Winchester balanced across his thighs.

"Are you alone?" he said.

"As you asked," Loq said.

"Where's your White boss, Nick Drake?"

"He's not my boss and I don't know where he's at, except it's not here."

"Of course he's your boss. You work for the government. All the bosses are White, from Jimmy Carter on down."

"Look at the pickup parked behind me. There's no Fish and Wildlife emblem on the door. No badge is pinned to my shirt, no government-issued sidearm strapped to my hip. It's only me here. Not President Carter. Not Nick Drake."

"Do you expect me to believe you've been on your own the week you've been tracking us?"

"You already know that. You're the one who's had eyes on me from the start, how you knew where I was two days ago to send the message to meet you here tonight."

"Only because you made sure I knew. You wanted me to see you."

"I'm here. Say your piece."

"Stop following us. You're making a trail for the alphabet police. FBI, BIA. You're putting all of us in danger."

"You've already put yourself there, but I don't care about that. All I care is that you've put my sister in danger too. That's why I'm here and that's why I won't stop until I speak with her."

"Carrie Horse said you'd say that."

"Because she knows me. She's my sister."

"Carrie said to look beyond the blood you two share. That you share blood with all of us, no matter our tribe. She has joined our war, a war that is right and just and blessed by the elders."

"Not by any of the old ones I've spoken with. Not the elders of the Klamath Nation. Nor any of the Northern Paiute and Shoshone tribes I've asked about your *just* war, Killian Daley."

The rider finally shifted his weight causing the gray stallion to shake his head, blow steam out his nostrils, and paw the ground.

"That's not my name, only something Whites call me as part of their subjugation of our people. Use my real name."

"Kills in Daylight?" Loq's long mohawk rippled as he shook his head. "You don't deserve a warrior's name for bombing the Bureau of Indian Affairs office in Pendleton and shooting it out with FBI agents in Warm Springs after killing their informant."

The rider scoffed. "I feel sorry for you, Loq. You've swallowed their lies. They're demonizing me, painting me as some kind of merciless evil savage to frighten White people and turn our own people against me. It's as old as slavery and colonization."

"You didn't do those things?"

"Look at our history. It's filled with cases of Indians being framed for crimes in order to exterminate us and steal our land. The FBI is lying. The BIA too."

Loq sang a song of patience to himself before saying, "You wear a Lakota choker that honors *tatanka* and Jicarilla moccasins and sit your horse on a Navajo blanket, but you are none of those people. I hear you grew up as a rich kid in New York City and your birth father might've been Oneida, but your Park Avenue parents didn't want to find out when they adopted you."

"You can try and disrespect me by parroting the oppressor's propaganda, but know this: I fight for all our people. The only way we'll win the war so that every tribe has sovereign nation status is to fight as one."

"The only way you'll win anything is to let my sister go."

"Carrie is free to leave whenever she wants, even though it'd mean being arrested again. She'd never see a trial, never see a prison. They won't let her become a symbol of our oppression. She'll disappear like so many of us have. Not locked in a cell, but buried in a deep hole dug in the middle of nowhere."

"Carrie's in more danger staying because the FBI will never stop chasing you. We both know how that will end. If you're innocent, then you'd be better off turning yourself in and hiring a good lawyer."

"I'd never see a courtroom. They'd assassinate me first because they're cowards. No, I'll gladly give my life for the cause of liberation. Carrie's also committed to it and volunteered to serve as warrior or martyr, if need be."

"Even at the cost of leaving her two children and our mother behind?"

"We're all one family."

Thunder boomed and lightning flashed. Loq could feel the

same forces inside his chest as his impatience grew and temper roiled. He sang a song to quiet them.

"If you speak the truth, then why not take me to her? Let Carrie tell me herself."

"I can't. It's for her safety and that of the people we ride with. We have many enemies now. Traitors too." The rider tilted his head. "Are you one, brother?"

"I'm Carrie's brother, not yours. You haven't earned that right."

"All Native people are brothers and sisters. Or did you forget while serving in the oppressor's army in Vietnam and now in another branch of the military that enforces the invader's tyranny over the land and water they stole from us?"

Loq sang another verse of his patience song. His pulse slowed to keep tempo with the images of sipping clear water from a pool as a doe and fawn watched from a meadow while a great bird with outstretched wings glided overhead, the sun perched on its broad shoulders.

"Telling each other who's right and wrong doesn't change a thing," he said. "Carrie's children and mother cry for her. They fear they will never see her again, that she has swallowed a lie that is poisoning her."

"White man lies are poisoning you, not me."

"They want me to find her, talk to her, hear it from her own lips, her own heart, that she has freely chosen this path that leads to her certain death, leads them to become orphans, leads our mother to swallow a grief that will choke the life out of her."

"And if Carrie tells you that, will you accept it and leave her to ride by my side?"

"Take me to her and we'll see."

A grimace pulled the corners of his lips. "In all my travels, in all the gatherings I've attended, the demonstrations, the days in court, the years in jail, I'd never met a Klamath until Carrie Horse. Now I've met two."

"And now you know I won't stop until I see her with my own eyes, hear her words with my own ears."

"Carrie doesn't want the law coming after you too. She asked me to tell you that she and I share the same vision, share the same heart. It beats in both of us as one."

"I learned your story. Everything you do, you do for yourself."

"More lies from those who try to divide our people." He looked up at the sky riven with lightning and back at Loq. "Then believe Carrie's own words in the language of your people. 'G či·s, taby´ ni. Go home, little brother.'"

"I can't," Loq said. "I won't."

"Then here's another message from your sister. 'If you harm Kills in Daylight, I'll never forgive you.' Do you want me to say it in Maklak like she taught me so you know it came from her lips?"

"No. You speak our language like your mouth is full of stones, which it will be by my hand if Carrie is harmed."

"I've grown weary of you. I could kill you right now." He started to raise his rifle.

"There'd be no honor in it. You can see I'm unarmed. If you want to try to kill me honorably, get off your horse."

They locked eyes. The rider was the first to break it off. "I won't shoot you now, but I will if you try and follow me back to our camp." He nodded at the trail behind him.

"Your camp? It's not in the hills or the mountains up there. You rode down here from a horse trailer you parked up on one of the logging roads that crisscross the mountains."

"What makes you think that?"

"Your stallion. It has no lather between his thighs. Your face has no dust on it. No sweat beads your brow."

"You think you're smart, but when I turn my horse, and if you try to reach the gun you're surely hiding beside you, the two men with rifles I positioned here before you arrived will shoot you."

"No they won't."

"You don't believe me? If I make a sign right now, they'll shoot you where you stand. You're in their crosshairs."

"Go right ahead."

"Carrie said you're brave. I say you're a fool."

"Only careful. I know your kind, Killian Daley. I was already here waiting for something like that when they arrived. A herd of mustangs doesn't raise as much dust as Willie Hawkfeather and Freddy Salish did. They're not men, they're boys. And they're certainly no warriors."

The rider's shoulders rocked backward as he failed to hold back a flinch. "Did you torture them to learn their names?"

"Ask them yourself after I turn them loose. There's no reason for me to follow you tonight. You're on horseback. You'll get to your pickup and drive away to where your camp is hidden faster than I can run up the trail. But tell Carrie this when you see her. *Ni yayna sle-a*. Go ahead, say it."

"*Ni yayna sle-a*. What does it mean?"

"She'll know."

"You're fighting on the wrong side, Loq. You should fight on ours."

"The only side I'm on right now is Carrie's and her children's."

He gave Loq a hard stare before turning his horse around, kicking his heels, and letting out a whoop. The gray stallion bolted and galloped back up the trail and into the darkness.

Loq waited a few minutes before getting in his pickup and driving back down the dirt road to a thicket of mesquite. He pulled aside cut branches to reveal a horse trailer.

Opening the rear door, he clicked his tongue. The spotted pony nickered and Loq rubbed his muzzle. He shined a flashlight inside to reveal a pair of bound and gagged teenagers. He dragged them out and cut their binds with the skinning knife he wore strapped at the back of his waist.

As they rubbed their wrists, he brandished the long blade at them. "Go home to your parents. If you keep following Killian Daley, he'll lead you to your deaths and they won't be honorable ones."

"Screw you, Uncle Tomahawk," Willie Hawkfeather spat. "Kills in Daylight has already restored our honor."

"Have it your way. He's ridden up the trail you came down. But when you climb back up it, keep your eyes open and call out your names."

"Why?"

"Because he's lying in ambush up there figuring it'll be me and intends to make sure I never see my sister again."

"What about our guns?"

"I'll hold on to them for your own good. Killian Daley sees someone coming up the trail in the dark carrying a rifle, he's sure to shoot first and check faces second. That's the kind of honor your so-called leader has."

2

The echoes of thunder retreated with each spin of the wheels as Loq drove north. The shards of dry lightning also grew duller. He was on a two-lane taking him toward Pendleton where the BIA office had been bombed. Maybe somebody there knew something that could help him get a line on where Carrie Horse might be.

The road would also take him through the Confederated Tribes of the Umatilla Indian Reservation. Loq figured Willie Hawkfeather was Umatilla. He recognized the Sahaptin word *Wawáyak* tattooed on the teen's neck. It translated to Spirit Power. The boy's family might still live on the reservation and be in contact with him. He'd find them and get them to share what they knew—either willingly or unwillingly, it didn't matter which.

Loq chewed on a piece of jerked venison as he drove. The only other vehicles on the narrow blacktop that time of night were trucks. Some were hauling fresh logs cut in the national forests that bordered both sides of his route. Others were carrying cattle from ranches to the stockyards and auction houses in Pendleton. Deer grazed on the shoulders, their eyes reflecting his headlights as he passed. Twice he saw a coyote darting across the road. He wondered if Killian Daley was a coyote too.

When two bright lights flashed in his side mirrors, he chalked them up to lightning. Then red bloomed between them. Loq checked his speedometer. While he wasn't going over the limit, the sound of a siren screeching above the whine of rubber prompted him to put on his blinker and pull over.

A patrol car followed suit. Loq kept an eye on it via the side mirror. When no one got out, he slid his sidearm out of the holster that was on the seat next to him and tucked it next to his thigh.

The driver finally exited, examined the rear of the horse trailer, and then walked toward him. Loq tapped the brakes to get a look. The pickup's taillights illuminated a woman dressed in a uniform. She wore a holster and carried a flashlight. She quickly aimed the beam at his side mirror. The bright light caused Loq to blink and turn his head.

"Both hands on the wheel! No more funny business."

Loq did as instructed.

"Use your left hand to fish out your license and registration and hold them out the window while keeping hold of the wheel with your right. Try it any other way and you're going to get hurt. Are we clear on that?"

"As a mountain stream," he said.

She closed in to take his license and registration.

Loq said, "You should know I'm armed. I'm a US Fish and Wildlife ranger."

"Then you should know better than to drive at night with broken taillights on your trailer. A speeding semi could come up behind you before the driver realized it. That's no way to treat a horse."

"Mm. Wires must've come loose. Maybe a bad fuse. I see by

your uniform, you're tribal police. There wasn't a sign saying I'd crossed into the Confederated Tribes' Reservation."

"That's because we stopped spending money on free targets for yahoos to shoot at."

"Which people are you, Umatilla, Walla Walla, or Cayuse?"

"Why do you care?"

"I like to know the person's people I'm talking with. You and I might know something or someone in common."

She glanced at his driver's license. "Your address is in Chiloquin. You're Klamath?"

"As were my ancestors, all the way back to when *Gmo'Kamc* created us."

"Just because you're Indian doesn't mean I'm not going to give you a ticket."

"Fine, but you still haven't told me who your people are."

"Umatilla. What do you know about us?"

"You're horse people. Your ancestors had herds of twenty, thirty thousand head until the US Cavalry took them. It makes sense you're concerned about the pony in my trailer."

"Since when did wildlife rangers have time to read history books instead of fish and game manuals?"

"The elders taught me the history of our people has good and bad in it, joy and sorrow too. We need to remember both, no matter how painful the bad and sorrow were, because they're part of our story and give us strength."

"What else do you know about us?"

"That the Umatilla share this reservation with the Walla Walla and Cayuse. That your people's name comes from a winter village called *imatilam*, meaning water rippling over rocks. Mind if I stretch my legs?"

"As long as you don't try anything."

Loq left his revolver on the seat and got out. She kept her

hand on the butt of her holstered sidearm and the flashlight on him as he did.

"Open the trailer. I want to check on your horse and make sure it isn't hurt."

"He'd tell me if he was, but okay." Loq unlatched the door, whispered, and stroked the spotted pony's withers. The pony turned his head and nickered softly.

"He's a mustang," the tribal cop said. "Where did you get him?"

"It's a long story."

"Then you'd better start telling it or I'll call for backup and run you in for horse stealing."

"He was wild at one time, but then forgot after Hollywood got hold of him. They were making a Western in Harney County, which is part of my territory. The head wrangler was mistreating him and so he ran off. I found him and helped him remember he's a mustang."

"They didn't arrest you for rustling?"

"I didn't steal him. I traded for him."

"What?"

"I agreed to be in the movie. The pony was my pay."

"You're an actor?" She shined the light on his face. "Wait, I've seen you before."

"It was only a small part."

"No, from years ago. In Fort Klamath at the annual powwow and all-Indian rodeo. Our tribe went down for it. You were the anchor in a horse relay. Your team's horse was running at full gallop when your teammate jumped off and you ran alongside, grabbed its mane, and jumped on to beat our best team."

"Were you racing too?"

"I went mainly to dance, but I was in one race. A Klamath girl older than me was way out front the whole time, but right before the finish line, her horse went down. She got underneath it, lifted its injured front legs up and ran the rest of the way with it. She came in first, but they disqualified her because the horse was riding her, not the other way around."

The cop was nodding as she spoke.

"The judges agreed to give her a special award and a name to go with it. Woman Who Carried the Horse." She quickly drew her gun and leveled it at Loq. "Wait, she's Carrie Horse. Now I remember. You're her brother. Hands up. Don't move."

"What's your name?" Loq said.

"Officer Mantioc."

"In police training they taught you that if you pull a gun on someone, you'd better be prepared to pull the trigger too."

"I am. Carrie Horse is with Killian Daley. They're wanted for murder. You're with them."

"Wrong. I've spent the past week looking for her."

The tribal cop hesitated. "Why?"

Loq looked down his high cheekbones. "I don't believe Carrie's with Killian Daley of her own free will. I'm trying to find her so I can talk to her, tell her that her kids and our mother miss her."

"She has children?"

"Two. Boy and a girl. Do you have kids?"

"None of your business."

"You want to take your gun off me?"

She didn't. "Are you here because you think they're on our reservation?"

"They're not. At least Daley isn't. I saw him two, three hours ago outside of John Day. Talked to him there."

"He's a fugitive. Why didn't you try to arrest him?"

"It wouldn't've gotten me any closer to finding Carrie. He has her hidden somewhere."

"What did he say to you?"

"Stop chasing him."

"And you left it like that?"

"He had a rifle. I was unarmed."

"Why did you come here?"

"There were a couple of boys with him. No older than seventeen. One of them was Umatilla. Had *Wawáyak* tattooed on his neck."

"Willie Hawkfeather," she said quickly. "He's been gone for weeks."

"You know his family? They may be in contact with him and know where the group's camp is."

"We're all family here."

"Can you take me to them?"

She hesitated. "You'll need to ask the chief of police first and tell him you saw Willie. He's asleep by now, so you'll have to wait until morning."

"Then I'll wait."

The cop holstered her weapon, pulled out a notebook and began writing in it. When she finished, she tore off a sheet of paper and handed it to Loq.

"What's this, the address where the tribal police station is?"

"The address is on it, all right, but that's a fix-it ticket. You have one week to get your trailer's taillights repaired. There's a shop in Pendleton that can do it. If you can't show they've been fixed and have a cop sign off on it, you'll have to pay a twenty-five-dollar fine."

When Loq shook his head, she said, "I remember you wore your hair long at the powwow and rodeo. How come you cut it and have a long mohawk now? That's not the Klamath way."

"I enlisted soon after the rodeo and had a difference of opinion with a barber at boot camp. I cut my hair myself and left a mohawk to show I was proud of being Indian no matter how much he tried to insult me. Men in my squad—White, Brown,

Black—ended up doing the same as a show of strength and solidarity. I keep it to honor them, both the living and the dead."

"You were a Marine and fought in Vietnam?"

He nodded. "Is there a place I can camp near your police station?"

"Stay on this road and you'll come to McKay Creek. It's on the edge of town. There'll be graze for your pony there. What's his name?"

"He hasn't told me yet. Good night, Officer Mantioc."

Loq opened the door to his pickup. Before he got in, he looked back at her.

"I remember you from Fort Klamath too. Your first name is Bina. You performed the jingle dance. You wore eagle feathers at the back of your beaded headband and held a matching fan. Your dress was green and the ribbons encircling it were strung with tin cones. You jingled louder than anyone but could silence them at will."

Loq nodded to her. "Everyone felt healed watching you dance, listening to your jingles sing a medicine song. You won the competition. It wasn't even close."

He got in, fired the ignition, and drove away. Ten miles later he saw moonlight reflecting on water. A dirt road led off the two-lane toward it. Loq parked beside the creek and let the spotted pony out to graze while he chewed another piece of jerked venison. Then he stretched out on his bedroll and stared at the night sky. He watched the stars dance, and as he drifted off to sleep, he could hear them jingle.

3

The stars melted into dawn and Loq woke to the feeling someone was watching him. Without opening his eyes or sweeping away his blanket, he felt for his gun.

"Careful you don't shoot your *íwas* by mistake," a slow-speaking voice said from somewhere nearby. "Saw a fellow do that in Korea. Something I don't want to see again. Ever."

Loq opened his eyes. A middle-aged man in a tribal police uniform was sitting on a stump watching him. His hat was hanging on his kneecap and his hair was brush cut and graying like the sky. The .45 he wore was still in its holster, but the scattergun propped next to him was within reach.

"That's right, I'm the law. Umatilla Tribal Police Chief Tahamtaham."

"Black mountain in English," Loq said.

"You speak our native language."

"A few words. I do the same for all my neighbors. Numu, Newe, Takelma."

"I wish I could speak some of yours to return the respect, but I can't. I have enough trouble with English words as it is." His smile was a little crooked, pulled by a scar on his chin that could've been made by a gun butt, knife, or knuckles. "Bina said your name is Loq. What's it mean?"

"Grizzly bear."

"From the size of you, I'd say that's about right."

"She told you I'd be here," Loq said.

"Left a message on the answering machine late last night. We got one at the house now. I'm still not sure if it helps or hurts. I know it doesn't help when a drunk calls in the middle of the night to tell me I'm a sorry excuse for an Indian, and it sure does hurt when an elder accuses me of not doing enough to keep drugs off the reservation."

"All right if I get up?"

"Only if you give me your word it's to make coffee and not test if I can grab my gun faster than you."

Loq raised his empty hands straight up while still lying on his back to show he wasn't holding anything and then sprang to his feet while keeping them raised.

The police chief whistled. "To be a young warrior again. I get out of bed, it's like a dance. My wife has to grab my arms, yank me upright, and then hold on to keep me from falling backward." He showed the smile again. "I take my sugar with a little coffee."

Loq made a fire, took a pot from his stores, filled it at the creek, put it on to boil, and threw in a handful of grounds.

"Tell me about your meeting with Killian Daley," Tahamtaham said.

"You don't call him Kills in Daylight?"

"I call him by the name that's on his wanted poster and what the judge will call him when he's standing trial for murder."

"Mm. I told him I needed to talk with my sister and he told me to get lost."

"Where was this?"

"Southeast of John Day, in the Malheur National Forest. I'd

been on his trail for a week and he sent word to meet him at the end of a road down there."

"How did he know where to deliver the message?"

"I made sure he could find me."

Loq threw in a cup of cold water to sink the grounds and then poured some into a mug, adding plenty of sugar. He handed it to the tribal police chief.

"Daley sent Willie Hawkfeather and another kid named Freddy Salish to bushwhack me when I was supposed to get there."

"But you outfoxed him and got there first."

Loq filled his own mug. "Three years in country and I learned a thing or two. I imagine it was the same for you in Korea."

"Wish I'd learned how to stay warm. I thought I knew cold growing up here on the Umatilla, but it's a beach compared to Chosin Reservoir in January. Lost a toe to frostbite."

"Better than your *íwas*."

The tribal cop chuckled. "You're all right, Loq. You can call me George. And, so everything is on the table, I've heard of you. Your law enforcement work outside of your rangering duties, I mean. You and Nick Drake have earned a reputation for yourselves." He sipped some coffee. "What did you do with Willie and the other boy?"

"Tied them up and then set them free after Daley rode off. I told them to reconsider who they idolized."

"But they didn't listen, did they?"

"They're teenagers."

"We all were once. It's a wonder any of us survived the being dumber than rocks years. Willie's dumber than most. He's had a few scrapes with the law, meaning me. The last time I arrested him for boosting a car. He was on probation but took off."

"Meaning, he's on the run."

"Yep."

"I need to talk to his family. They might be in touch with him. Help me track down Daley."

The police chief raised his mug at Loq. "About that. Willie and his family are tribal members. Meaning, if anybody is going to talk to a member, it'd be me. And even then, it probably won't amount to much. Willie's father drank himself to death a few years back and his mother got bit by the hate snake. She fancies herself a *twata át*. That's an old word for female shaman. Any medicine she has isn't used for healing. She probably encouraged Willie to run off."

"But if you're going to go tell her Willie's been spotted, I'd appreciate going with you and hearing what she says."

"You would, eh?" He drank some coffee. "That's a fine-looking pony you got there. Bina told me you traded being in a movie for him. How about you and I make a trade?"

"The pony's not for sale. I plan to set him free once he tells me where he's from."

"I don't want your horse. I got a half-dozen at my place and barely have time to ride as it is. No, I mean trade meetings. I'll take you to meet Willie's mother if you come to mine."

"Who's yours with?"

The police chief studied Loq as he swallowed more coffee. "A couple of FBI agents. They're going back over the BIA bombing in Pendleton and believe I've been holding back information. I was first on the scene. Me and Bina."

"Why do they think that?"

"The same reason the feds finally allowed us to form a tribal police force so long as all we police is ourselves. Somebody from outside the tribe commits a crime on the reservation, all we can do is detain them and call the county sheriff or feds. That might change one of these days, but today isn't that day."

"Are you holding anything back?"

"Only my temper. What do you say, do we have a deal?"

"What makes you think I'll be any help?"

"You're a fed and they're feds, for starters. You must speak some of their language like you do with your Paiute and Shoshone neighbors. Then there's the fact you're the most recent person to see Killian Daley and talk with him."

"I'm only interested in finding my sister, not helping the FBI. Daley has her and I find him, I find her."

"About that, you do know she's on the same Most Wanted list as him."

Loq knew full well. Carrie started off getting fined for holding American Indian Movement demonstrations in Klamath Falls without a permit. She moved on to participating in the takeover at Alcatraz in San Francisco. Then she marched on Washington in the Trail of Broken Treaties protest and graduated to being a ring leader in the occupation of Wounded Knee. She'd been arrested several times and placed in county lockups.

Tahamtaham sighed. "Your sister's an Indian, not Patty Hearst. The feds won't think she's been brainwashed when they take him down. They'll shoot her on sight."

"That's why I'm trying to get to her before they do. I don't want to give the FBI a head start."

The police chief sipped some coffee and took his time swallowing it. "When you were in Vietnam, you didn't learn you could get intel by offering up a few things to gain the other party's trust?"

Loq thought it over. "Good point. I'll go with you."

"A couple of things. The two agents we're meeting with? They were the ones in the shootout with Daley in Warm Springs. The senior agent is more than by the book, and I mean the chapters they don't put into print. Plus, they won't be the only ones there."

"Who else is coming?"

"An investigator with the BIA."

"What's he like?"

"A lit match next to an open can of gasoline. He was in the BIA headquarters in DC when AIM occupied it a few years back."

"He still bears a grudge from that?"

"The word is they humiliated him. This time around, he had a girlfriend working in the Pendleton office when it was bombed. The explosion blew off one of her legs and left her face disfigured. He's got an axe to grind and he doesn't care who he uses as a whetstone."

"When's the meeting?"

Tahamtaham glanced at his wristwatch. "Two hours at my office. That'll give us enough time to drive over to the Hawk-feather place. I'll wait while you pack up and then you can follow me."

"Does that mean you don't think I can get there on my own or is it because you think I'll make a run for it so I won't have to talk with the feds?"

"I don't want to test either."

"How come?"

"Because you remind me of myself when I was your age. You're a headstrong warrior who thinks he can win the battle on his own and doesn't need anyone's help."

"I know my sister has a better chance of surviving if I show up at Killian Daley's camp alone rather than in the company of an army of trigger-happy federal agents."

"But the question is, would you survive? Come on, Grizzly Bear. You need our kind of help. Indian help. Mine and Bina's."

"All right, lead the way. Let's hope we both don't get shot."

"*Áay,*" George Tahamtaham said. "Amen."

They convoyed north a mile and then turned west on a

gravel road that quickly turned to rutted dirt as it wound up and down hills of baked scrubland that grew even more baked as the sun rose higher. A shack stood atop a barren hill. Smoke curled from a stovepipe. The police chief turned onto an even more rutted track and headed toward it. Loq followed but kept a little distance between them to cut down on having to suck dust.

He parked alongside the tribal police officer's rig and got out. Dead snakes hung from the shack's eaves. A stump out front was surrounded by severed snakeheads and had a hatchet stuck in it. Both the stump and blade were darkened with blood.

"Keep your pony in the trailer and don't let her see him," the chief said. "Watch where you step. We talk to her, we do it outside. You don't want to go inside. Trust me."

They picked their way through snakeheads, rotting chicken carcasses, and piles of garbage to the front door that was a dirty blanket hanging from nails. The tribal cop knocked on the wooden doorframe, then quickly took two steps to the side and two more back. He motioned with his eyes for Loq to do the same.

"Belinda," he called. "It's George Tahamtaham. I have news about Willie."

A raspy cough sounded from the other side of the blanket followed by phlegm being hawked up and spit out. "Who's that out there with you?"

"The man who saw your son last night. He spoke to him."

"What sort of man?"

"A good man. From the Klamath Nation."

"A Maklak? Pshaw. He's here to steal horses like they always done."

"You don't have any horses, Belinda, and Loq's no thief. You want to hear about Willie or not?"

More rustling came from behind the dirty blanket and then the woman swished it aside and stepped out. Dark moles dotted her cheeks and thin whiskers curled from her chin. A corncob pipe was clenched between what few teeth she had. The moldy smell of kinnikinnick smoke coming from it was nothing compared to the stink that rolled out from inside of the shack.

"What about my boy?" she wheezed. "Did you arrest him?"

"Tell her," Tahamtaham said.

Loq did. He didn't soften it or spare any details.

"Why didn't you kill him? My boy was there to kill you."

"I had no need to. But someone else will if he keeps running with Killian Daley."

She hawked another ball of phlegm. "Kills in Daylight is a true warrior and a born war chief. He'll be talked about a hundred years from now the same as our people's greatest leaders. Yellow Bird, Five Crows. I'm honored Willie is with him. Maybe that boy will finally learn something useful."

"If he survives, the only thing he'll learn is how to bust rocks in prison," Police Chief Tahamtaham said.

She blew smoke rings that were the color of burning tires. "Because you put him there for borrowing a car."

"He didn't borrow it. He stole it. And I went easy on him. Why he was on probation and not doing time at Riverbend in La Grande. If he gets caught running with Daley, he'll end up doing hard time."

Loq said to Belinda, "My sister is with Daley too. I need to speak with her, give her a message from her children and mother. Has Willie told you where their camp is?"

"I haven't heard a word since he left. Don't got a telephone, don't get mail, don't know how to read."

"But you're a *twata át*. Your medicine is powerful. I can see that, feel it. You must see Willie when you're in dream world."

She squinted at him. "What if I do?"

"You must recognize where he is."

"Does a hawk remember each treetop when it flies? A snake

each rock when it slithers?" She grabbed the dead one hanging closest to her and gave it a squeeze. "My boy is here and there and everywhere because Kills in Daylight never stops. He's always on the move, like the wind, like the sagebrush tumbling. White men can chase him, but they'll never catch him unless he wants them to. And then—" She gave the snake another squeeze. Guts oozed out of its severed neck.

"Come on, Loq, we got to go," the police chief said. "Thanks for your time, Belinda."

They walked back to their rigs. As they neared them, a headless snake came whirling down and thumped on the ground between them. Loq started to turn back toward the shack.

"Forget it," Tahamtaham said. "If that old witch wanted to hit us, she would've."

4

<hr>

The tribal police office was a few miles east of Pendleton. The chief and Loq parked their rigs out front.

"No black sedan means no FBI," Tahamtaham said. "Yet."

Loq asked what the BIA investigator drove.

"The closest thing to a tank he could find. A Power Wagon with a full gun rack."

"I need to check my pony before going in."

"I'll be at my desk shoveling snow."

Loq opened the trailer door and filled a bucket from a canvas water bag. He also put a couple of scoopfuls of grain in a feed bag. When he stepped out, Bina Mantioc was waiting.

"You found our station," she said.

"Your chief found me first. We paid a visit to Belinda Hawkfeather's this morning."

"All those snakes. It's one of the reasons why I steered you away from going there last night."

"She chucked one at us."

"Only one?"

Her smile was as shimmering as last night's stars. Her eyes

too. She wore her hair pulled straight back into a bun held in place by a barrette decorated with colored glass beads and porcupine quills. Loq asked how long she'd been on the force.

"I joined two years ago when the Indian Self-Determination Act finally passed giving us the right to police ourselves. We're still waiting to get official authorization and the grants that go with it, but you know how long things take when it comes to Washington and us."

Loq grunted. "The director of Fish and Wildlife came out to Oregon when I signed on. He told me he'd been sent by the Great White Father."

She laughed and then said, "You're not kidding, are you?"

"What did you do before?"

"I was a nurse."

"Why the change?"

"I grew tired of patching up people. Too many women who'd been abused. Too many unemployed men who were drinking themselves to death. Too many elders with no way to pay for food and medicine."

She took a breath. "I decided the best preventive medicine I could provide was police work."

"How's that working out?"

"We'll see. Why'd you become a ranger?"

"The Service had a special program for Vietnam vets. I'm not good being inside and if someone's willing to pay me to work outside—"

"I'm the same way," Bina said quickly. "I never saw the sun when I worked in the ER. This job? I'm out here."

She waved at rolling hills covered in grass as tawny as mountain lions, the Blue Mountains in the distance that beckoned with grace and mystery, the big sky that had no end.

He asked if she was there for the FBI meeting, and when she

nodded, he said, "George told me you two were the first on the scene when the BIA office was bombed."

"We happened to be driving by. Sometimes chance is meant to be. My nursing skills came in handy."

"The BIA investigator's girlfriend who lost a leg, you saved her life."

"The training, the instincts, they kick in, you know? It's not heroics, it's—"

"What you do," he finished for her.

They stood there eying each other and not saying anything, but it wasn't awkward, and Loq felt good about that.

Bina said, "We should go in. George will want to go over ground rules before the federal agents arrive."

"Is there something I should know about the feds?"

"They have a way of reminding us they're still in charge on the reservation."

"We had a reservation when I was a kid. A million acres. Lakes, rivers, forested mountains. Home to the Klamath people since time began. But twenty years ago Congress terminated us as a recognized people. That's the official word they used, *terminated*. They took the reservation—our home, our land—away from us."

"How come?"

"Timber companies wanted our trees."

"Terminated is such an awful word to use for a people."

"My sister Carrie said it was a typo. They meant to put *ex* in front."

"All of us know loss. We were forced to give up six million acres. Now we have less than two hundred thousand. With stories like yours and mine, it's no wonder Killian Daley has attracted followers."

"But you're not one of them."

"Violence will only lead to more of our people being hurt or killed. I saw too much of that when I worked in the ER."

"And as a cop?"

"My job is to stop violence before it happens."

"The only way that worked in war was to deploy even greater violence."

"The Umatilla Reservation isn't a battleground."

"Killian Daley is trying to make it one by setting off bombs. The same with the Warm Springs Reservation by exchanging gunfire with federal agents there. He wants a war and that means waging battles. He'll strike again. It's only a question of when and where."

Bina hesitated. "Let's go hear what George has to say before the FBI gets here."

They went inside. A large red flag adorned one wall. The words Cayuse, Walla Walla, Umatilla were lettered in black above an oval with the drawing of three running horses signifying the three tribes and the importance horses played in their history and culture. A band of multicolored shapes at the bottom represented the woven blankets and beaded jewelry the tribes were known for making.

The police chief was sitting behind a desk heaped with stacks of paper. "I'm more in danger of losing blood from a papercut than a gunshot," he said.

"You sound like a county sheriff I know," Loq said.

"Who's that?"

"Pudge Warbler of Harney County."

He nodded. "Your partner's father-in-law. I've known Pudge since before his daughter Gemma married Nick Drake. I was a Umatilla County sheriff's deputy for nearly twenty years before taking this job. We worked a couple of manhunts together. Pudge is a hard man, but was always fair. How's he doing?"

Loq pictured Steens Mountain rising just south of the

Warbler ranch, curtains fluttering in an open bedroom window, eyes staring at the peak from a propped-up pillow. "He's battling cancer."

"Sorry to hear that. It's a hard enemy to beat. Never fights fair." He frowned. "What do the doctors say?"

"Nothing he wants to hear."

The police chief nodded. "Who'd he put in charge?"

"His chief deputy, Orville Nelson."

"The young man in the wheelchair?"

Loq grunted.

"I hear he packs a computing machine instead of a gun."

"Orville's handy with both."

Tahamtaham shuffled papers on his desk. "We will sing for Pudge Warbler and Orville Nelson, but now we must talk about the pair of FBI agents who are on their way here. The senior man is a special agent-in-charge. That's the top rung of the ladder when it comes to ranks for field agents. I've only met him a couple of times, but he strikes me as a hard man. I don't know if he's a fair man too."

He leaned back. "The junior man is one rung up from being a new agent trainee. I haven't been able to get a feel for him because he doesn't say anything. That's probably because he's been ordered to be seen not heard. My sense is he's Indian, or at least part, but either he doesn't know it or doesn't want to admit it."

"And the BIA investigator?"

"His name is Jack Candy, but that's the only thing sweet about him."

Tahamtaham explained how BIA policing was organized by district. Oregon was in District Eight along with Washington, Idaho, and Western Montana. Candy had special status as a district-wide criminal investigator that gave him free rein to investigate what he wanted, where he wanted, and how he wanted.

"He doesn't report to the district director, but a higher-up in a special branch at the Interior Department," he added. "Candy's hardheaded, hardhearted, and definitely not fair-minded."

"Vehicles are pulling up out front," Bina said.

"I'll make the introductions," Tahamtaham said as he got to his feet. "Once they find out you're Carrie Horse's brother, they'll play tough trying to get more details out of you. Expect them to accuse you of being part of Daley's gang and threaten to arrest you. Don't fret, there's still no law against having a sister, on or off the reservation."

The door opened. The first through it was a man in his late thirties who wore a dark suit, white shirt, and tie. He nodded at Tahamtaham and Bina, and then his blue eyes settled on Loq and stayed there. The man following him was younger by a decade or more. He wore a dark suit too, but it seemed to hang on his slender frame as if he'd bought the wrong size. He carried a black briefcase that matched his hair color.

"Welcome back to the Umatilla Reservation," the police chief said. "You know Officer Mantioc. And this is Loq, a US Fish and Wildlife ranger. Loq, meet Special Agent-in-Charge Robert Sexton and Special Agent Sal Tujunga of the Federal Bureau of Investigation."

Neither the senior agent nor Loq made a move to shake hands. Sexton said to him, "Been a long time, soldier."

"What happened, CIA wouldn't keep you on after Operation Phoenix?" Loq said.

"You two know each other?" Tahamtaham said.

"We crossed paths in Vietnam," Sexton said. "I was MI and the Marine here lent a hand on special operations once or twice."

"Military intelligence," the police chief said to Bina. "CIA."

"What was Operation Phoenix?" she asked.

"Ancient history," the FBI agent said. "Right, Loq?"

The Klamath's expression was still as stone. "Not for everyone."

Sexton's eyes narrowed. "While it's an unexpected pleasure to see you again, there's no way in hell I believe you being here is happenstance. I know who your sister is."

He made a pinching gesture with his thumb and index finger held an inch apart. "My file on Carrie Horse is this thick and you're written up in it along with everyone else in your family."

"Does it include where Killian Daley is holding her? Because that's why I'm here. I'm looking for her."

"You have reason to believe they're hiding on the Umatilla rez?"

"No. When I spoke to Daley last night, we were miles south of it."

"What!"

"So much for walking before galloping," Tahamtaham muttered.

"He asked me to meet him so he could tell me to stop tracking him."

"Wait, you let him go?"

"I don't have a warrant for him."

No one seemed to have noticed the big man who'd followed Sal Tujunga in despite being much taller and wider. He swept the young agent aside as he strode toward Loq, the heels of his cowboy boots chattering on the linoleum. His unbuttoned Western-style leather sport coat revealed a gold BIA police badge pinned to his pearl button denim shirt and a semiautomatic strapped to his hip. The butt of another was sticking out of a shoulder holster.

"Did I hear that right, you had the murdering half-breed in

your sights and didn't drop him?" His knuckles cracked as he balled his fists at his side.

Loq gave FBI Agent Robert Sexton a long look before answering. "I learned in country that nothing backfired harder than assassinating the commander of a battalion of VC. Not only did his reputation grow in death, his ability to inspire lived forever and made his followers fight even harder."

Candy snarled. "The best way to shut up a mongrel like Daley is to put him down. Last year in Montana, a Blackfoot was riling people up with talk about taking back land and waging war. It was all cover for him to go off the rez and steal stuff. Horses, pickups, money from cash registers. I cornered him while he was robbing a bank in Browning."

He clicked his cheek. "Ordered him to drop his gun—could've been before I shot him, could've been after. Don't matter. No one's mentioned him since. Dead and forgotten."

"That's because your ears are closed to what they're saying about what you did. Closed like your heart is."

Candy's eyes were hooded by a jutting cliff of a brow. "Who do you think you are, talking to a sworn federal law enforcement officer like that? I could arrest you right here."

"You could try."

The BIA cop's glare turned to Tahamtaham. "Hey, Chief Tom-Tom. He's in cahoots with his sister and murdering boyfriend. Why haven't you locked his ass up?"

The Umatilla police chief returned Candy's glare with a look of patience and pity. "Loq came in on his own accord to tell me what he knows about Killian Daley. He didn't have to, but he did. I say we use his information and go from there."

When no one objected, he said, "Loq, why don't you show us where you met Daley. The way you told it, you'd been on his trail for a week and you got word he wanted to meet. How did he do that?"

Loq broke off the staredown with Candy and faced the Umatilla cop. "Two ways to track a man. One is to walk quietly and surprise him, the other make noise to flush him. I asked about Daley wherever I went so word would get back to him. A woman dropped a note beside my plate while I was in Prineville having breakfast. It was a hand-drawn map and instructions."

Sexton said, "Did you talk to her?"

"No. She walked right out the café's door."

"You didn't follow her?"

"She wouldn't've known anything. I finished my breakfast and drove away."

"What did the note say?"

"Time and date for a meeting and to come alone and unarmed."

The police chief unfolded a map on his desk. "Show us where."

Loq traced the route from Prineville up to John Day and then southeast into the Malheur National Forest. "It was at the dead end of a logging road right about here. There's lots of forest service roads and unsigned ones made by loggers cutting trees without permits."

"Damn gyppos," Candy said and spat on the floor.

Sexton ignored him and asked Loq why he didn't follow Daley after they met. Loq explained how the fugitive was on horseback and had ridden down from a parked vehicle.

"He'd have been long gone by the time I got to where I'd left my trailer, saddled my pony, and rode after him."

Candy groaned. "You're Fish and Wildlife. They give you a rifle to keep Bambi in line. You could've shot Daley's horse and knocked him off it. If he got up and tried to run, winged him in the leg and forced him to take you to see your sister."

The senior FBI agent asked Loq if Daley had given him any

idea what he was planning to do next or where he might be going.

"Other than insisting he was being framed, not a word," Loq said.

"Framed? That's a good one," Sexton said. "Agent Tujunga and I tracked him down to the Warm Springs Reservation based on a tip from a confidential informant. When we arrived at the CI's location, we found Daley standing over his body with a gun in his hand. He raised it at us and fired. We took cover and defended ourselves. Daley escaped out the back."

Sexton turned to the younger agent. "Anything you want to add to that?"

Sal Tujunga looked down at the black briefcase he was still holding and then back up. "No, sir. It's all in our report."

The telephone on the police chief's desk rang. Tahamtaham picked it up, listened, gave a few uh-huhs, and then said, "Got it. Thanks for the information." He listened some more. "No, you stay put and don't do anything. We're on our way."

He hung up. "That was Jimmy Two Sons. Has a ranch on the east side of the reservation. Says Daley and his gang are holed up near his place. They've circled their rigs like wagons. When Jimmy went to see if they needed help, he got a round of rifle fire for his efforts."

"Is the call legit?" Sexton said.

"Jimmy's old, but not blind. He called because he's worried they're going to rustle some of his cows."

"What makes him think it's Killian Daley?"

"He's got TV and watches the news. Figured there was no one else it could be."

"What are we waiting for, goddammit? Let's go!" Jack Candy bellowed.

"For me to show you on the map where it's at in case you get yourself lost."

5

———

Tires screeched as they sped east along a narrow and curving county road that followed the Umatilla River. George Tahamtaham led the way with red lights flashing but siren silent as they crossed a mosaic of rocky creeks, brushy gulches, and wheat fields. Bina Mantioc rode shotgun and radioed the county sheriff's department for backup.

The black FBI sedan followed. Sal Tujunga hunched over the wheel while Robert Sexton radioed his field office in Portland for a helicopter gunship to be dispatched from the nearest military base.

Jack Candy was third in line and drove alone. He didn't radio a soul because he never asked for help, believing another BIA cop would either get in his line of fire or try to stop him from doing what needed to be done.

Loq brought up the rear, his speed reduced by the horse trailer swaying behind. He didn't have a radio, but his glove box was crammed with maps. He was betting they'd come in handy if Killian Daley tried to escape on horseback.

Tahamtaham cranked the wheel and skidded onto a dirt road that dipped and climbed over grassy hills. It led to a weather-beaten cabin surrounded by an equally weather-beaten barn and corral. He got out, but left the engine running. Bina hopped out too. A rail of a man with long gray hair and a face leathered by sun and wind walked over from the barn. As he spoke to the police chief, he gestured at a narrow valley down the hill from his cabin. The others joined them. Loq brought binoculars.

"This is Jimmy Two Sons," the police chief said. "He heard vehicles last night, but it wasn't until first light that he was able to get a look."

"If he saw them at dawn, why'd he take so long to call it in?" Sexton said.

"Jimmy lives alone and had to get his chores done. It's the rule of ranch life. Tending to the stock always comes first."

"Did he see Daley? Talk to him? Talk to anyone?"

"No. As soon as he heard rifle fire, he came back up here."

"Were they shooting at him or just scaring him off?"

"What's it matter?" Candy said. "They're criminals. They got guns and fired 'em. That means we shoot back."

Loq was thumbing the focus wheel on his binoculars and counted seven vehicles, all of them pretty old, and a couple of real junkers. Two were hitched to house trailers.

"If anyone's still there, they're staying low or inside," he said.

Reverb blared from the radio in the black sedan. Sexton reached through the open window for the mike. "Senior Agent Robert Sexton. Over."

The voice coming through the speaker was punctuated by clicks and buzzes, but the message was loud and clear. It was a flight officer at the Air National Guard Base in Portland. The request for a chopper had been relayed and was being run up the chain of command, but if time was of the essence, wouldn't the agent prefer a fixed-wing fighter given the distance?

"Base's requisition for an A-10 Warthog came through last

week," the man on the radio drawled. "She's a beaut. The boys are itching to see what she can do."

"How long would flight time be?" Sexton asked.

"You're two hundred thirty miles east of us so the Hog could be there in a tick over thirty minutes once it's wheels up. Chopper'd take an hour and half easy."

"I'll take the fighter. Let me know when you get the green light."

"That's a Roger."

The agent cradled the mike and turned to the police chief. "What's your ETA for the county sheriff's?"

"One hour," Bina answered for him. "Dispatch said they were short-staffed this morning because of a two-day joint training exercise with Union and Wallowa county sheriff's. They're turning around a pair of deputies who were on their way to Hermiston to serve a warrant."

Jack Candy rolled his eyes. "It takes two boys to deliver the paper around here?"

"It's for murder. The suspect is considered armed and dangerous."

"So what? You fire a couple through the door to get his attention, kick it in, fire some more, and arrest him if he's still breathing."

"There's movement," Loq said. He gave the binoculars to the tribal police chief. "The blue Chevy sedan hooked to the house trailer, the one with all the rust."

Tahamtaham zeroed in on it. "If Daley's enlisting warriors, he's getting some pretty old recruits. The man who got in the front seat is an elder."

"Check the back window of the other trailer."

The police chief panned the binoculars. "And young ones too. The faces pressed to the glass belong to a pair of seven-year-olds."

"Those are house trailers down there, not horse trailers. Daley rode a gray stallion. I don't see him or any other horses. This doesn't look right, doesn't feel right."

"Jimmy may have jumped to conclusions, but the rifle fire—"

Reverb from the FBI sedan's radio cut him off.

"You got your green light, Agent Sexton," the flight officer at the Portland base said. "Hog's being pre-flighted. Won't take 'em but five minutes to get her airborne. Pilot'll be on your radio frequency as soon as he is. Tell him what you need, but I advise you do it from a distance. You don't want to be standing too close if he starts lighting things up with his nose cannon. Got seven barrels and fires two thousand rounds a minute."

Tahamtaham wheeled around. "The only people I see down there are an old man and children. Most likely it's a small band of sheepherders moving from one camp to another or a clan of tribal members who lived off the reservation and are moving back on. You can't attack them without finding out. This is tribal land and that makes it my jurisdiction and my decision on how to handle this."

Sexton jabbed the radio's mike at him. "Wrong, and you know it. FBI has jurisdiction on investigating major crimes committed on any reservation. Killian Daley is a fugitive from justice and wanted for murder, a bombing, and two attempteds on federal officers, namely me and Tujunga. My authority supersedes yours every which way. You can either stand down, stand by, but whatever you do, don't stand in my way."

"But we have no proof Daley's even there. All we know is what our eyes can see, and that's an old man and kids."

"Oldest trick in the book," Candy said. "They're human shields and Daley's hiding behind them."

"You don't know that."

The BIA investigator snorted. "What I do know is this. I'm a federal agent same as Sexton. That makes you bottom of the totem pole, Chief Tom-Tom."

The patience in the tribal police chief's eyes disappeared behind clouds of fury. Before he could say anything, Loq spoke so only he could hear.

"The black mountain's strength comes from the hard rock outside that endures time and seasons, not the molten rock inside wanting to erupt."

"I need to do something," Tahamtaham said through gritted teeth. "Sexton's called in a fighter plane. You served, same as me. You know how it goes once the shooting starts. It won't stop until everyone down there is dead."

Loq tilted his head so the tips of his long mohawk were angled in the direction of the vehicles pulled in a circle. "I'm going to let my pony out. He needs some exercise. You might want to be in your rig when I do."

The tribal police chief started to argue, but then said, "Indian rules. Good idea." He turned to Officer Mantioc. "Come on, Bina."

She put her hands on her hips. "But we can't let the feds—"

"That's an order."

Loq opened the door to the horse trailer, whispered, and the spotted pony backed out. He didn't have a saddle on, nor a halter.

Sexton said, "What the ...?"

Candy hooted. "Middle of everything, and he's letting his nag out to take a dump."

As soon as the two tribal cops were back in their pickup, Loq gave them a nod, grabbed a handful of mane, swung up on the pony's back, and pressed his heels. The pony took off and Loq used his knees to steer him toward a cow trail that led down the hill. Tahamtaham slammed his pickup into gear and stomped the gas pedal as Sexton and Candy cursed.

The cow trail was rough, but the pony remembered he'd grown up as a mustang and didn't stumble as he raced down it. His hooves flew over the biggest ruts, sensing them before he saw them. Loq gripped the mane with both hands, leaning low to stay on, but not too far over the pony's neck to keep them both balanced.

Only when they hit the floor of the valley, did he turn to look over his shoulder. The pickup carrying the two tribal cops was bucking like a bronco as it plunged down the same trail. Ruts grabbed at its front wheels and sparks flew from beneath the axles as they scraped over rocks, but the rig didn't get stuck or roll over.

Looking forward again, Loq urged the pony on in a straight line toward the blue sedan. As he neared it, Loq let go of the pony's mane, sat up straight, and raised both arms to the sky to show he wasn't carrying a weapon. He cleared his mind of any thoughts about rifle fire. To show fear would've meant he had no trust and couldn't be trusted himself.

This time when he sang, he did so out loud for all to hear. He sang of a time when tribes shared the land, shared the waters, and shared their food, of a time when gifts were exchanged out of respect and honor, of a time when dancing and drumming were for healing, and horse races and games for bonding.

Loq wasn't sure if the old man in the front seat could hear him or if he spoke English or Maklak or Sahaptin, but the song was from his heart and he hoped it would reach his too.

The pony stopped when they were only a few feet from the Chevy. The old man was looking at Loq. His eyes were clouded by age, his face as leathery as Jimmy Two Sons. His front teeth were long gone.

"What do you want?" he said.

"To help you."

"Why do I need it?"

"Because the men up on the hill are federal agents. They think you're someone else, someone who they're trying to arrest, kill if they can't, and kill anyone who gets in their way."

"Who is this someone?"

"Killian Daley but you may know him as Kills in Daylight."

"Have you come to arrest me also? To kill me?"

"No, only to help you."

"What do you know of this man they are after?"

"That my sister's with him. Her name's Carrie Horse. We're from the Klamath Nation."

"You do not think that man is here?"

"No."

"Why not?"

"Because I can't feel my sister's spirit here. If she's not here, then he's not here."

He looked past Loq sitting on his pony. "The men on the hill are coming."

"The first one doesn't want to kill you. That's George Taham-taham, chief of the Umatilla Tribal Police. He's come to protect you because he knows Daley isn't here."

"Why do you think I am here?"

"Because Daley sent you and your family as decoys so he can slip away. Far away."

"You are a smart man."

"My name's Loq. What's yours?"

"Man Who Was Paid to Be Here." He laughed, revealing the two missing front teeth had plenty of company left on the trail where things got lost.

Tahamtaham's pickup looked worse for wear when he pulled to a stop. The windshield was cracked and the front bumper dented on the right side where it'd struck a rock.

"I wish I'd ridden a horse like you," he said as he got out.

"You were lucky you weren't shot," Bina said to Loq when she opened her door.

Loq only shrugged, but the old man said, "Luck had nothing to do with it. We were never going to shoot anyone."

"But Jimmy Two Sons told us he was fired at when he was here this morning," she said.

"Those were only to get his attention." The missing teeth showed again. "They worked also. Here you are."

"We're not the ones you need to worry about." Tahamtaham hooked a thumb over his shoulder.

All eyes turned to the Power Wagon blasting down the hillside, its oversized tires going right over the ruts and rocks. Even dust and distance couldn't hide Jack Candy's face. It was flush with rage. Rather than coming right up to them, he drove around the circle of old vehicles, honking his horn and yelling out the window.

"You're all under arrest. Every goddamn one of you. Get out here right now. Hands up and line up."

When he finally pulled up to Loq and the others, he leapt out and pointed his sidearm at the old man who was still sitting in the blue Chevy.

"Where's Daley at?" he barked.

"He's not here," Loq said.

"I'm asking him, not you."

"He'll tell you the same thing. Daley was never here. It's only this man and his clan."

"Bullshit. They're hiding him. I know they are."

"You keep saying you know things, but your things are always wrong. These people are decoys and they won't be the only ones. Daley will have created dummies and left false trails all over Oregon to keep the law chasing its own tail while he makes his escape."

"What makes you the expert?"

Loq could've said the time he'd spent as a Marine in Vietnam and the past several years as a ranger busting poachers, but said instead, "Put down your gun."

Candy blew hard. "Nobody tells me what to do with my weapon. He's with Daley whether Daley's here or not and I'm gonna question him and everyone else. We line 'em all up and put guns to their heads, we'll see how fast they tell us where Daley's at."

He waved his semiautomatic at the old man for emphasis. "I'm gonna count to three and if you're not out by two, I'll put one between your eyes."

Tahamtaham stepped toward Candy. "No you won't. Not on our land. Not ever."

Candy swung his gun at the police chief, but Loq grabbed his wrist, pushing it upward so the barrel was pointed at the sky as the BIA investigator's finger tightened on the trigger. Rounds fired and brass ejected.

Loq didn't let go, but hooked his foot behind the big man's ankle and tripped him, shoving him backward and onto the ground. He landed on top of him, keeping his grip on his wrist so the gun still pointed at the sky as it fired. He drove his knee into Candy's crotch.

Bina jumped into the fray and pressed her forearm across the big BIA cop's neck while fishing for the second gun he kept in his shoulder holster. Candy sputtered and gasped. Finally, his grip on the gun loosened. Loq yanked it away.

"Let him up," Tahamtaham said.

Loq and Bina did. As Candy struggled to his feet, he looked into the barrel of the police chief's .45 and the two black eyes smoldering behind it.

The old man got out of the Chevy. He moved slowly, his right leg unable to bend from either old age or an old injury. He gave Bina an appraising look.

"I've seen you dance at the Pendleton Round-Up before. I didn't know you could wrestle steers also."

Tahamtaham said, "I recognize you, old one. You're Cayuse and your clan lives on both sides of the reservation's northern border."

"So we do."

"How did Killian Daley talk you into doing this for him?"

"Called on the telephone. Said he would give us a new trailer for our camp and enough gasoline to drive here and back."

Candy was still wheezing, but managed to gasp, "See. He just admitted it. Aiding and abetting."

"If you want to spend your time booking small potatoes instead of going after big fish, be my guest," Tahamtaham said.

A new cloud of dust swirled. It was being kicked up by the black sedan. The two FBI agents hadn't risked driving down the cow trail but had backtracked to the county road and then found a dirt road into the valley that led to the circle of vehicles.

"They're smokescreens," Candy said to Sexton before anyone else could, making it sound like he'd been the one to figure it out.

"Tell me something I don't already know," the senior agent said. He motioned them to join him out of earshot of the old man. "I heard from HQ. Daley's on his way to Salt Lake City where a bunch of Indians are planning to hold a big demonstration. I called off air support."

"How do they know he's doing that?" Candy said. "Your informant blew his cover and Daley blew his brains out."

"The FBI has additional assets working on this."

"But why stage a protest in Salt Lake?"

"To call attention to an Indian battle that happened back in 1850."

"That was no battle," Bina said. "It was a massacre of the Timpanogos people along the Provo River. A militia armed with guns and a cannon surrounded them and killed a hundred men. The women and children were rounded up and sold as slaves."

"There's always two sides to a war," Candy said with a grin.

Sexton gave a dismissive wave. "Why they're holding a protest isn't our concern. Daley being there is. Agent Tujunga and I are making a beeline for Salt Lake City. We'll be there by nightfall."

The senior agent turned to Tahamtaham. "I'm going to write you up for disobeying a federal officer's orders. I'm also going to recommend the Justice Department put the brakes on granting final authorization for tribal policing here."

Then he turned to Loq. "If I see you in Salt Lake City or anywhere near it, I'll have you arrested. Vietnam was a long time ago. I don't owe you a thing. Not a damn thing."

He got back in the black sedan and Tujunga whipped it around and they took off in a cloud of dust.

Loq ejected all the unfired rounds in Jack Candy's gun and handed it back. Bina did the same with the second firearm. The BIA cop holstered both and rubbed his throat. It had a mark on it as red as the one around his wrist.

"I won't forget you blindsided me," he growled. "We're gonna cross paths again. Whether it's in Salt Lake or in front of your wigwam, I guarantee it. And then we'll see who's who." He shot Bina a look. "The same goes for you, princess."

The big V8 in the Power Wagon roared as Candy sped after the FBI agents.

The old man's laugh was nearly as loud. "Salt Lake City? Kills in Daylight is good."

"You heard what the federal agent said?" Tahamtaham said.

"I may be old, but I can still hear an owl's wings."

"Daley's wanted for murder and a bombing. How can you say he's *good*?"

"Good at covering his tracks. Good at throwing them off his scent."

"You don't think he's going to Salt Lake City?"

"If the federal men think he is, that means he will be anywhere but there."

The old man walked back inside the circle of vehicles where he was greeted with whoops and songs.

Tahamtaham sighed. "I'd say let the feds deal with Daley if it weren't for Willie Hawkfeather. He's a tribal member, a minor, and he broke probation. That makes bringing him back my responsibility. If Daley's not going to Salt Lake, I need to find out where."

"I've tracked him this long, I'll pick up his trail," Loq said.

"I know where to start," Bina said.

"You do?" Tahamtaham said.

"I've been studying his profile. He's been focusing public attention on battles and massacres like Wounded Knee. Although the one at Provo River fits that, I think there's a historic war that could be more along what he wants. The timing works out too. It happened exactly one hundred years ago."

"Was it here in Oregon?" Loq said.

"The reason for it started here, but it was fought elsewhere in many places."

"Where exactly?"

"I can take you, if George okays it." She faced Tahamtaham. "If you want Willie back here, whether it's to face justice or to prevent him from getting into worse trouble, I'll need to leave the reservation."

The police chief looked at her and Loq and then past them, seeing the valley and the hills and the Umatilla River and the Blue Mountains beyond. The reservation was his home and all that remained of what was once the land of his ancestors and those of the Cayuse and Walla Walla too. He'd sworn to serve and protect each and every member of the confederated tribes who lived there, even a wayward punk like Willie Hawkfeather and his hate snake-bit mother.

"So be it," he said.

Tahamtaham's eyes found Loq's before he could protest. "I have some ancient wisdom to share with you too. A warrior's true strength is when he knows he needs help and accepts it."

6

NO MOUNTAIN

Summer days are long in Harney County and the nights are short, but trouble can come at any time regardless of daylight or darkness, in spite of hope or prayer.

I'd been on the road patrolling wildlife refuges longer than usual to pick up the slack for my AWOL partner who was searching for his sister when I arrived back in No Mountain. Usually I sped across the cattleguard that marked the entrance to the Warbler ranch so I could hug my wife and kids, but this time I pulled up short before clattering across.

A cattleguard has two jobs, keep good things in and bad things out. As I sat looking at it through the windshield, I knew my world had turned upside down because it hadn't kept cancer out and I didn't know what I could do before it ruined what was good.

I crossed and pulled up in front of the house. Another pickup was already there. A horse trailer was hitched to the back. My six-year-old daughter, Hattie, and her dog, Jake, came running.

"Daddy, Daddy. Lyle brought Johnny a horse of his own. Now we can ride wherever we want."

"Since when did the rules change?"

She put her fists on her hips just like her mother did. "I meant we can ride all the trails on the ranch and go as far as we want as long as we can still see the house. That was the deal we made and I'm sticking to it."

"Good girl."

"*Mananuu*, Nick Drake," Lyle Rides Alone said.

"Greetings to you too, my friend. Do you need any help?"

"No, this horse wants to get out of the trailer and feel Mother Earth with his hooves." He backed a three-year-old dark chestnut out.

Lyle owned a ranch near the Silvies River and was a top breeder. My wife, Gemma, had worked for him during summers when she was a girl and now Hattie was following in her boot-steps by feeding and walking his horses and currying them while standing on a portable stairway he'd made for her mother all those years ago.

Getting our son Johnny to do ranch chores was a different story. It was always a push and pull with him. We let it slide in exchange for him working to improve his English and expand his vocabulary. When he first came to live with us, he alternated between Vietnamese, broken English, and curse-filled slang he'd picked up from American GIs while growing up on the streets of Saigon.

I was glad to see he'd left his bedroom to check out the new horse even though he did so with a scowl on his face and his hands shoved deep into the pockets of his jeans.

"I missed you, son," I said and put my arm around him.

The scowl grew. "Then why didn't you take me with you?"

"Because I needed you to help out here, what with your grandfather sick and Gemma having to fly from ranch to ranch giving vaccines to all the four-month-old calves."

Johnny kicked at the ground. "Nagah always go with her."

"You know the answer to that. Nagah's older and training to be a veterinarian like her. Plus, he pilots the plane most of the time now."

"She likes him better. You like him better."

I sighed and said what I'd said a hundred times. "Nagah chose to live with us after his grandfather Tuhudda died. Gemma and I chose you among all the other children at the orphanage to live with us and be our son."

Lyle was watching, his eyes filled with understanding as he looked out from beneath his flat-brimmed hat.

"Meet your new friend, Johnny," he said in his slow, quiet way. "This horse is special because he is like you."

"No, he's not."

"Look at him. His father was black and his mother cinnamon like yours. See, his coat and your skin are the same color. He was also orphaned far away and then came here where another mare and stallion raised him as their own."

"Not as far as Vietnam."

"For a horse, even across the river is far away."

Johnny drew a little closer. "His name's not like mine."

"His is *Kosse Bbo*. In Numu, it means Dusty Road, what we Paiute call the Milky Way." He waved his hand across the sky.

Johnny's head jerked. "I was called *bui doi*. Dust child. Father GI, mama Vietnamese."

"You can be proud of any name as long as you are proud of yourself." The flat-brimmed hat bobbed. "Call your new friend Kosse because it is quicker to say. Try it. He will come."

Lyle unfastened the lead.

Johnny hesitated before finally muttering, "Kosse."

The horse didn't budge.

"Kosse," he said a little louder.

The horse's ears pricked up.

"Kosse. Come, Kosse. Come, boy."

The horse whinnied and walked over, nosing him in the shoulder. Johnny obliged by stroking his muzzle.

"Thanks for bringing him," I said to Lyle.

"Thank Girl Born in Snow," he said, using the birth name of the old Paiute healer who lived with us instead of the one she'd been given at an Indian boarding school. "It was her idea to give him a horse to do what needs doing."

I glanced at the porch. November stood watching. I hadn't heard her come out of the house, but that wasn't surprising; she always walked silently.

"Do what?" I said.

"That is her story to tell, not mine."

Lyle closed the trailer's door and drove away.

"Take Kosse to the corral and introduce him to the other horses," I said to Johnny. "Hattie will help."

"He is a strong horse, my own eyes can see that," November said as the kids led him away.

"Lyle tells me this was your idea."

"Johnny needs a horse."

"To teach him responsibility by giving him something to care for, a horse he can ride while doing chores and also having fun."

"Yes, but now to take him where he needs to go."

"Where's that?"

"The path to manhood."

"Not yet. Remember when he first came to live with us? He was so scrawny. The orphanage didn't know how old he was. They guessed around eight. Now that he's no longer undernourished, the doctor believes he's closer to twelve or so. But he's still only a boy."

"Johnny is older than you think. Maybe not in years, but in life. He lived during a war. He was *in* the war. He fought to survive after his mother was killed, first on the streets and then in the green world."

"That was a long time ago for him and me."

"Not so long, Nick Drake. You still go there in dream world sometimes. Johnny too. I hear you both. You call out for your men who were killed. He calls out for a girl with yellow hair who was also a *bui doi*."

"He's not a *bui doi* anymore. Not Johnny *Da Den*—Johnny Black Skin. He's Johnny Drake. He doesn't have to live on the streets or in the jungle. He's here. He's safe. He's my son."

November tsked. "Johnny cannot be whole as long as his two halves remain apart. The Johnny here and the Johnny there. He must see who he really is so he will know what he can become and then be that person."

"And how would he do that?"

"Johnny will find out when he goes to find something else."

"What's the *else*?"

"A plant."

"A plant?"

"A very special plant. I need it to make tea."

"What kind of tea?"

"Healing tea for Gemma's father. White man medicine is not working fast enough to fight the cancer in his blood. It only makes him weaker and sicker. He needs healing tea."

"And your tea will get rid of the cancer."

"It will help him heal. Help Johnny heal. Help Gemma, Hattie, and you heal also."

I had lived with November long enough never to question her wisdom nor things that occurred in the High Lonesome that had no rational or scientific explanation, and so I asked her where the plant grew.

"Only one place. In a canyon in what White people call the Trout Creek Mountains."

"On the Oregon side of the border or Nevada?"

"That is Johnny's to find out. I will give him a drawing of the plant."

"A map would be better. If there's an airstrip close by, Gemma and I can fly Johnny down, pick the plant, and be back within a day."

"You cannot fly there. You can only go by horse."

"That's why you asked Lyle Rides Alone to bring Kosse for Johnny."

"The older you get, Nick Drake, the wiser you become."

If she had a twinkle in her eye, I didn't see it.

"I must go make healing soup for Pudge and dinner for us. Gemma and Nagah will be landing soon."

I cocked my head to listen for the plane. "I don't hear anything."

"That is because you are listening for things that might be bad instead of listening for things that are already good."

I grabbed my bag out of the pickup and carried it into the house. As I passed Pudge Warbler's office, I heard voices and poked my head in. The old sheriff was sitting at his desk talking on the phone. He looked thinner and sallower than when I left on patrol. The shadows around his eyes were as black as those cast by storm clouds on Steens Mountain. I was glad to see he wasn't so weak that he couldn't get out of bed like he was for days after a round of chemotherapy.

He glanced at me while nodding as he listened and then said, "Thanks, Orville. Appreciate you keeping me in the loop."

Pudge hung up the heavy black handset and swiveled his chair. "Good trip?"

"Long trip. Hard being away with Gemma flying all over Harney County and Johnny being Johnny and ..."

I let it drift but Pudge picked it right up. "Me having the cancer and looking at the short end of a calendar."

"You don't know that."

"Son, I watched my Henrietta die of cancer, leaving me on my own with a five-year-old. That taught me cancer doesn't play favorites."

"That was a different kind and medicine's come a long way since then."

"You and Gemma practice saying that together?" He didn't wait for an answer, but allowed a grin to pull at his jowls that weren't as big as they used to be.

"Sounds like you were on the phone with Chief Deputy Orville Nelson," I said.

"Acting Sheriff Nelson now. Orville was filling me in on the latest about Loq's sister and her no-count boyfriend, Killian Daley. Aka Kills in Daylight. Helluva moniker to hang on yourself. One that'll surely get himself hung if he did what they say he done."

"Did Orville have any news about their whereabouts?"

"Nothing specific, but the FBI thinks he's still in Oregon. And the answer to both of your questions is no. No, Orville isn't looking for Loq, and no, you don't have to pretend that you don't know he took off to find Carrie Horse and bring her home."

"For a man with cancer, it sure hasn't slowed down your thinking. Or your talking."

Pudge's chuckle got him wheezing. He coughed into a handkerchief, but kept it balled in his fist so I couldn't see if it had blood in it.

When he caught his breath, he said, "Reason for Orville's call is, a trio from the Fort McDermitt Reservation boosted a car and lit out to go join Killian Daley. Seems he's Pied Piper, Robin Hood, and Peter Pan all wrapped in one for a lot of folks."

"And since that reservation is south of here, it means they could be driving right through Harney County."

"Yep. Problem is, two in the group are juveniles—male and a female. The third is older, an ex-con with a bad temper. Tribal police down there thinks he either coerced the younger two or outright forced them. FBI doesn't disagree."

"No sign of them?"

"Nope. There's plenty of backroads and roads that aren't roads at all they could've taken. But the parents of the two young teenagers are worried sick about what the older one is doing to them or afeared the car went off a cliff, and so on and so forth, parents being parents."

"Hope for the best, plan for the worst, and forget about ever getting a full night's sleep again."

That got Pudge chuckling again, but he cut it off so he wouldn't start wheezing.

"What's Orville going to do about it?" I said.

"Have our deputies keep an eye out for the vehicle while on patrol. It's an Indian pickup. Junker white sedan with the trunk lid cut off. State troopers will do the same on the highways that come up from the town of McDermitt even though it's unlikely the three are on any kind of blacktop at all."

"Got a description to go with the ex-con?"

"His name's Hex Taggert."

"Hex?"

"Thinks it makes him sound meaner than Hector, though he's got plenty of mean in him. More Shoshone than Paiute, more White than both. He drifts from reservation to reservation, but he's not an enrolled member in any. Served a couple of years for assault and battery. Suspected of the murder of a railroad cop, but never charged. He was also able to beat a conviction for rape of an underage girl when she disappeared during the trial. Tribal cops couldn't determine if she'd run away or was buried in a ditch somewhere."

"What's he look like?"

"Check the fax machine. Orville just sent over a mug shot."

Hex Taggert's buzz cut showed off a couple of thick scars that looked like inchworms. He was pig-eyed and the left drooped. His neck was thick and his chest and biceps even thicker. The sheet listed him as six-foot-one and weighing 240.

"For what it's worth, I could be on the lookout for him and the teenagers," I said.

"At the Malheur and Hart Mountain refuges?"

"No, when Johnny and I are taking a horseback ride in the Trout Creek Mountains. If they're in a hot car trying to avoid the law, they might be tempted to cut across them since they run northwest of the reservation. Maps show a couple of old mining and ranching tracks, but nobody maintains them. They're more apt to be washed out or blocked by rockfalls."

"Why in tarnation are you and my grandson riding horses in that godforsaken hellhole in the middle of summer? You know how hot it gets there?"

I'd stepped in it and couldn't see a way out. "November. She's got this idea that Johnny needs to go on some kind of quest. Might settle him down some."

"November said that? Hm." Pudge's head cocked. "What's the real reason she's sending you two down there?"

"What makes you think there is one?"

"Don't shit a shitter, son. I've known that old medicine woman since she moved in here to take care of my wife and then stuck around to raise Gemma. She likes to think she raised me too."

He coughed into the wadded handkerchief again. That time I did see red.

After clearing his throat, Pudge said, "November was always coming up with some kind of special tea or mud bath or song for Henrietta. She's wanting to do the same for me, I know it."

"A plant for tea. She wants Johnny to find it and bring it back. Heal you and heal himself in the process."

"Well, you tell November I'll drink whatever poison she

brews so long as it helps my grandson come to terms with himself. Lord knows, he needs to."

The sheriff took a moment to catch his breath. "But when you're down there, keep your eyes open, including the ones in the back of your head. Hex Taggert might not be the only rattlesnake you run into. That's mighty lonesome country and dangerous as all get out. The only law is no law at all."

"Who's Hex Taggert and go where and how dangerous?" Gemma said, standing in the doorway.

7

Loq's windshield framed Sacajawea Peak in the Wallowa Mountains as he drove east from the Umatilla Reservation. Chief Joseph Mountain soared nearby. He gave both a nod of respect, not only because they were mountains, but because their namesakes had earned great honor for being brave and wise.

He was headed toward the town of Joseph, named after the legendary Nez Perce chief, though Loq preferred to think of him by his birth name, *Hinmatóowyalahtqit*. Thunder Rolling Down the Mountain. Tribal Police Officer Bina Mantioc was going to meet him there the following morning to start their search for Killian Daley, Carrie Horse, and Willie Hawkfeather. She believed Daley was planning to use the hundredth anniversary of the Nez Perce's twelve-hundred-mile march to freedom as a background for his next and surely largest and loudest protest yet.

As the miles of twisting blacktop that ran alongside the Wallowa River passed beneath his wheels, Loq's thoughts lingered on the Nez Perce's courageous but ultimately tragic journey. The US Cavalry chased them without relent or mercy for months. Eighteen battles were fought. Hundreds died. The tribe was ultimately stopped in Montana forty miles short of the Canadian border.

Loq pulled into Joseph. False-fronted wooden buildings lined the picture-postcard main street while surrounding fields gave way to a ring of cone-shaped peaks. He paused long enough to gas his pickup and restock supplies before driving south toward Wallowa Lake and turning up a dirt road that switchbacked up a forested mountainside. It led to a solitary log cabin with a dizzying perch high above the lake's blue water and dark canyons below.

Loq parked, checked on the spotted pony to make sure he'd made the bumpy ride up the rugged road without banging his head or shoulders against the trailer, and then climbed the steps to the front porch that ran the length of the cabin.

Two large elk hides were nailed to the wall on either side of a thick wooden front door. He brushed one with his fingertips. It was a touchstone to the millions of years the big animals had lived in North America after crossing the Bering land bridge. The Wallowas were home to one of the largest herds in all of Oregon, a bounty that had sustained the Nez Perce—the Nimi-ipuu, or the people, as they called themselves—and the ancient ones who preceded them.

"May your death have been quick and may your meat have fed many," Loq said.

"If you're selling, I'm not buying," a voice answered from the other side of the door. "If you're preaching, I'm not believing. And if you're arresting, I'm not going. You'd better be armed because I am."

"Greetings, Snaps. It's Loq."

"I don't know anyone by that name, dude."

"Mm. Must've gotten the wrong address. I'm looking for the Pulitzer Prize-winning war photographer who I knew in Vietnam. I heard he moved up here when he came home. I need information about the area and thought he could help."

A few moments later, the voice on the other side of the thick door said, "You were in 'Nam?"

"I was."

"What did you do when you came home?"

"Lived in the woods with bears the first year because after all that time in the jungle I couldn't be trusted to be inside my mother's or anyone else's house."

"Why bears, dude?"

"They're my spirit animal. What my name means in Maklak."

"Why'd you leave the woods?"

"I listened to the bears. They told me they didn't think about yesterday, only what they were going to do that day. They said if you're a bear, be a bear, and don't feel guilty about it."

"I don't know, dude. I'm not a bear." A minute or two passed. "Who sent you?"

"Myself."

"Why?"

"You remember that time we got pinned down? My squad was running out of ammo. You were running out of film."

"That happened to me lots of times with lots of GIs."

"But this time, you were with my squad of Marines. You and I swapped stories, thinking it might be the last time for us. You told me you had a little brother. Mikey you called him. He's the one who nicknamed you Snaps. I told you about my big sister, Carrie Horse. She's why I'm here."

"Hold on, dude! Your sister's not in here with me. I swear it. I never touched her, never even met her."

"I know that. But a bad man's got her and I think she may be nearby. Since you've been living here all this time, I thought you could give me the lay of the land where he might've taken her."

Another minute or two passed. Finally, the door swung open and Loq's first thought was he hoped he'd weathered the years since he rode the Freedom Bird home a lot better than Snaps had.

The photographer wore a blue kerchief tied on his head like a cap. Long, greasy tendrils of dishwater blond hair hung to his shoulders. His cheeks were gaunt, the crow's feet on either side of his hollow eyes were furrows. His grimy jeans bore patches and hung low on his hips. He looked like his diet was only elk and didn't include bread or potatoes or any starch at all.

"Outside Da Nang where we shared a foxhole, right?" Snaps said. "Or was it Hue? I remember you. Your mohawk was shorter. All your guys had 'em. I photographed you when you leapt up and charged those machine gun nests. *Time* ran it. Or was it *Newsweek*?"

"And you were right behind me every step of the way, snapping the shutter the whole time, didn't think twice about the lead flying, only getting the shot. What you called it, *the shot*."

"Yeah. The shot. Come on in, dude. You hungry? I got elk. Veggies too. Picked them myself. Dandelion. Watercress. Camas. Wild carrot." Snaps twitched with each word.

"Thanks, but I'm good for now."

The cabin was one room with a woodstove in the middle. Windows opened on the far wall and provided a view of the mountains and lake. The other walls were covered with photographs. There were blowups of the night sky taken with a time-lapse exposure that were so crystal clear Loq could name the stars in them.

The close-ups of great horned owls, bald eagles, and song-birds were so sharp, he could see the details of each feather. A series of portraits of the same mountain caught in different times of days, during all the seasons, showed its constantly changing mood, from its grace to its fury. Nowhere did he see any of the *Life* magazine covers of Snaps's heartbreaking portraits of war that some said had helped bring it to an end.

"No people pictures," Loq said.

"I don't do so good with them around," Snaps said.

"People or taking their picture?"

"Both. I tried. I'd aim my lens at a hiker passing by on the trail, a fisherman at the lake, but damned if their smile didn't turn into a look of horror and they died in my viewfinder just like in 'Nam."

Snaps stared at his feet. He was wearing thick wool socks. The toes of them showed darning. "I got coffee, dude."

"Coffee would be good."

As he set about making it, Loq asked what he did when he wasn't photographing nature.

"Fish, hunt, hike, climb. I've summited all the peaks in the Wallowas. Fly-fished every stream, river, and lake. I've walked every trail. Now I make my own."

"What about neighbors, friends, people in town?"

The long tendrils that hung from beneath his kerchief cap brushed his shoulders as his head shook. "I don't go to town much. When I do, I avoid people. I see them, it's the same as if I'm looking through a viewfinder."

"Does that mean you don't know anyone in the local Nez Perce community here?"

Again, the tendrils swished. "Not really. I mean, I've read about the tribe, what happened to them. I read a lot of books. Winter's cold, long, and dark here."

Snaps explained how the Nez Perce's homeland was once millions of acres stretching from Wallowa Lake to Montana. How bad treaties, land grabs by gold miners, loggers, and ranchers, not to mention all the wars they had to fight to survive, whittled it down to the only thing they had now, a reservation across the border in Idaho.

"Even their name isn't their own, dude. It's a mistake. French Canadian fur trappers called them that, thinking they pierced their noses. They didn't."

Snaps filled two mugs and handed one to Loq. His hands shook as he did. "You're the Indian. Why ask me?"

Loq told him about Killian Daley, how he'd been looking for Carrie Horse, and what he learned on the Umatilla Reservation.

"The tribal police officer, Bina Mantioc, makes a good case for Daley using the Nez Perce's flight since it's the hundred-year anniversary," he said. "The centennial, she calls it. Could be he's planning to make a last stand like the tribe did."

"Are you the only one looking for this guy, what did you say he calls himself, Kills in Daylight?"

"The FBI and Bureau of Indian Affairs are too."

"And the Umatilla tribal police?"

"They're still on it. Police Chief George Tahamtaham is working it from his office on the reservation and Officer Mantioc in the field."

Snaps waved his mug at Loq. "In the field meaning where? Here?"

Loq nodded. "Bina's packing her gear and getting her horse and then we're going to meet up."

"But not *here*, here, right?"

Snaps started looking around nervously. Coffee lapped over the rim of his mug.

"Why, is that a problem?" Loq said.

"No, yes, I mean, yeah. A big one. I mean, look around. I'm not set up for guests. Not women. Especially not women, dude. Kids either. No way." He started shaking hard, his face contorting with pain.

Loq put his hand on Snaps's shoulder. "It's okay, brother."

"No, it's not. It never will be. I took their pictures. Soldiers were one thing, but women and kids in hooches that were set on fire another. Piles of them executed by VC thinking they were traitors. A dead mother still holding her baby."

He shuddered. "I took those photos. I filed them. They were published. I got paid for them. Blood money. I can't ... I can't get them out of my head. The women. The kids. I stole their dignity, dude. I stole it. Lock, stock, and barrel."

"It was war. You showed people at home the true cost of it. The human one."

Snaps was still shaking. Loq kept his hand on his shoulder. Any minute, he'd have to reel him in and hug him. Tell him he was safe, that it wasn't his fault, that he was only doing his job, a job he did well. He'd made a difference.

"Easy now," Loq said, "When I said here, I meant Joseph. We arranged to meet in town tomorrow. I thought you and I could look at some maps and you could tell me what you think are the most likely spots on the Nez Perce trail where Daley could get reporters and photographers to cover what he's planning. You were in the news business. You'd know where better than me."

"Yeah, news. I was in it, wasn't I?"

"You were. You won the Pulitzer to show for it. After that, we can have dinner. Elk steaks. I'll do the grilling. And don't worry, I sleep outside. Always do."

"With the bears?"

"With the bears. That be all right?"

Snaps gave a final shudder. "Yeah, I can do that. For sure, dude."

Loq pulled his hand away and Snaps started looking at the nature photographs pinned to the walls.

"You ever think of going back?" he whispered.

"To Vietnam?" Loq said.

"Yeah. Back."

"No, never have. The war's over. At least for our side."

"I know, but to go back and see it, you know, not in war, but in peace. The people just living like they did before. Raising their families. Growing rice. Selling all that cheap shit they make on the streets in Saigon. The jungle. Rain falling on bamboo. The water buffalo in the paddies. The mountains. The rivers. You know, not see it all blown apart, but whole again. Healthy like. Beautiful. You wouldn't go back?"

Loq thought about it. The only thing that would make him even consider it was if someone asked him because they needed him to help them do something, find someone, save someone close to them. And the person asking would have to be someone close to him. Very close.

"Depends," he said, "but, yes, if asked, I'd go back."

8

Bina Mantioc was riding a blue-gray roan with a black mane and matching tail in an open field on the outskirts of Joseph. Loq parked his pickup and watched. She'd switched her uniform out for jeans and a tan buckskin jacket. He didn't see a badge, but he hoped she hadn't forgotten to bring her sidearm.

Horse and rider moved as one, but that didn't surprise him. She saw him and rode over. Loq got out and stroked the roan's muzzle.

"I would've bet you rode a cayuse," he said.

"A lot of people on the rez do out of tradition, but, no, they're too short and stocky for my legs."

"So I noticed."

"You've been looking at my legs?"

"Only how tall you are."

"Like you." Her eyes did the shimmering thing again. She leaned forward and patted the roan's shoulder. "Did you learn anything useful from your source?"

"A couple of things. Have you had breakfast?"

"No, I left before sunup."

"There's a café across the street. We can talk there. Need any help trailering your horse?"

"Why, do you always need help trailering yours?"

He cocked his head and then said, "I'll get a table."

As he walked across the street, he thought he heard the roan whinny, but couldn't be sure it wasn't Bina laughing.

The café was half full and a waitress waved her hand. "Anywhere you like. Coffee?"

"Two." He thought if Bina took exception to him ordering for her, he'd know more about her, and he needed to know everything he could if he was going to have to depend on her.

Bina didn't seem to mind at all when she joined him. She grabbed the coffee mug eagerly, added a generous dollop of cream, and took a drink. It left a white mustache. Loq kept his grin to himself.

When the waitress returned, Bina ordered bacon and eggs with wheat toast and a side of blueberry pancakes. "And not a short stack either," she said.

Loq nodded. "Same here."

He asked her what her horse's name was.

"She hasn't told me yet." Bina watched to see if he got the joke, but when he didn't react, she said, "Túxin. Our word for sky."

"It fits her. Her coat covers every color of it from dawn till dusk except sunrise and sunset. She moves like she could run from one end to the other and never tire."

"A warrior poet. I bet you're a singer too," Bina said under her breath.

"What?"

"Nothing, only something my grandmother warned me about."

He grunted. "You live with your grandmother?"

"What you're really asking is, do I live with a boyfriend or husband. And the answer to that is, no way, no how, not ever. Last thing I need is a man telling me what to do."

"I was asking about your grandmother because you said she warned you. That makes me think your mother's not around anymore. If so, may she have been welcomed by family and friends when she arrived in the spirit world."

A frown crossed Bina's face, and Loq was glad to see it, because it meant she wasn't afraid to let her feelings show. That meant she was confident and strong. Both were going to be necessary when it came time to going up against Killian Daley. He'd already decided that's what it was going to take to get to Carrie.

"You're right," Bina said. "My mother died of the flu when I was very young and my grandmother raised me."

"And your father?"

Again, the frown. "She came down with the flu and he couldn't shake the sadness. These days they'd call it depression. His disease took a little longer to kill him than hers did."

"Is your grandmother alive or did she make the journey too?"

"She's very much alive and never lets me forget it. I work too hard. I don't go out. I'm not married. Don't have children. Don't cook traditional. Truth is, I don't cook at all."

"Mm."

"What about you? Is there a Mrs. Loq?"

"My mother lives in Chiloquin where many of our people stayed even after they took our reservation away. She's raising my sister's kids right now."

"I meant if you were married."

"I know what you meant."

Bina pursed her lips. "Your mother has Carrie Horse's children. Does that mean their father's not around?"

"Dead and buried in a potter's field in LA. He was an alcoholic with a bad temper. My sister put up with him for years, but one time when he took a swing at her, he struck one of the kids. That was it. Carrie fought back."

"What did she do?"

Loq could see it the way Carrie had described to him when he came home from Vietnam. How she defended herself and the kids by hitting him upside the head with his bottle of booze. How she thought she'd killed him and so she dragged him onto the frozen lake and lit a circle of gasoline around him so the ice would melt and his body would sink. How the ice was too thick and he wasn't dead after all, only knocked out. How she dragged him to her car, drove him to the bus depot in Klamath Falls, bought a one-way ticket to LA, and put him on the Greyhound with a warning never to come back or she'd kill him for real.

"It's her story to tell, not mine," he said instead.

"She's strong-willed. I got that from seeing her win that horse race at Fort Klamath and reading her file—the FBI shared it with us. But from what you're not telling me about what she did to her husband—and that actually says a lot—I can't understand why she puts up with a man like Killian Daley. It doesn't fit."

"Carrie is the strongest woman I know. Physically, mentally, spiritually. But she has a soft spot too. She took up the Indian rights cause because she's seen the injustice and lived with it. Carrie doesn't want her kids to have to too."

"But Daley doesn't have a soft spot. If what those FBI agents say is true, he killed that informant in cold blood. Bombing a BIA office full of innocent people? That's more than cold-blooded. It's sick. One of the injured women is Walla Walla."

"Either he's holding Carrie against her will or she believes if she wasn't with him, he'd hurt even more people."

"Or else she sees something in Daley that no one else does."

"Mm."

The food came. Bina drenched her pancakes with maple syrup. Loq moved his sunny-side eggs on top of his stack and crisscrossed the bacon on top of them. He sliced the stack into columns and ate them one by one. When he finished, he pushed his plate away and unfolded a map on the table.

"The man I met with yesterday had a book that showed the Nez Perce's historic trail. I traced the first section onto this map and did the same for the sections of the trail that run through Idaho and Montana on these maps." He fanned them out. "This is us here and that's Wallowa Lake. Chief Joseph's trail began there."

"Four months ago," she said.

"What?"

"The Nez Perce left here in spring of 1877. It's now August. I think we need to look farther along the trail."

"You think Daley is trying to match the actual days?"

"Battles more likely. There were several major ones and lots of skirmishes. You know what prompted their flight, right?"

Loq nodded.

The government was trying to force the Nez Perce off their ancestral homeland in the Wallowa Valley and go live on the Lapwai Reservation in Idaho. The tribe refused because they wanted to live free like they always had. Chief Joseph decided to lead his people in search of a new home. Their journey became a chase and a running gun battle with the US Army because the government didn't want other tribes to get the same idea. The army won, but not before a lot of blood was shed on both sides.

Bina grimaced. "The history books call it the Nez Perce War, but it should be called the US War. The government instigated it."

"Nothing we can do about that now. What we can do is find Daley and stop another war from happening. Maybe he's picking the Nez Perce's final battle to make his statement."

"I don't think so. The Battle at Bear Paw Mountain didn't start until the last day of September and was over in a few days. Daley knows the FBI is chasing him. It's only a matter of time before they catch up to him. He knows he won't last until fall."

"You've been reading history books along with FBI reports."

"I think we should focus on the earlier battles."

"White Bird Canyon, Cottonwood, the Clearwater, Big Hole, and Camas Creek," Loq said.

"So, I'm not the only one who reads history."

"I studied a lot of battles after I was deployed. Vietnam had many similarities to the so-called Indian Wars. Small bands of people fighting for their homeland against a bigger, better equipped, and more modern army."

"And did your studying help?"

He looked down his high cheekbones. "Didn't convince the generals and we lost the war, but it helped keep some Marines alive."

"You mean, you kept them alive."

He didn't acknowledge that. Bina had no experience with anything close to being in a war, but her own battles of surviving on a reservation, getting an education, and landing a good job had required survival skills too.

"Let's take the battles in order," she said. "White Bird Canyon was the first big one. The Nez Perce had already made it across the Snake River, but then ran into problems with settlers along the Salmon River, which spurred the cavalry to come after them."

As she spoke, Loq used his finger to trace the route from where they were sitting. Then he moved it down south to the Malheur National Forest outside of John Day where he'd seen Daley.

"He has to get from there to Idaho. He can't risk going on the major highways if he's traveling with dozens of people and assorted vehicles. Horse trailers too. A convoy that size would draw attention."

"Then they must be doing it in onesies and twosies," she said.

"No, Daley will want to maintain control of his troops. He can't risk anyone deciding they've had enough and go AWOL or get a ticket for a broken taillight on their horse trailer and say something wrong to the cop who pulled them over."

Bina smiled. "Point taken."

"His best strategy is to stick to forest service roads."

"But Daley will still have the same obstacle everyone else does driving to Idaho from that part of Oregon."

"The Snake River."

"Right. The Nez Perce used to ford it during low water at Dug Bar. Looking at your map, that's about sixty miles northeast of here."

"A century ago was long before all the dams were built," Loq said. "The water is much higher now."

"It was pretty high when Chief Joseph and his people set out that spring," she said. "The Snake was at flood stage. They had to put the old ones and children on rafts made of horsehide pulled by swimming horses. Men and women who weren't riding horses had to swim for it. The tribe's cattle and dogs too. Many drowned."

"Daley's going to use a bridge."

"But which one?"

Loq stabbed the map eighty miles downriver from Dug Bar. "He has several to choose from, but if I'm him, it'd be this one."

Bina drew closer and hunched over the map. "The Oxbow Dam? Why?"

"It's remote, little used, and accessible by forest service roads coming out of the Wallowa-Whitman National Forest here," he said, pointing to a spot at the south end of Hells Canyon.

"Do you think he's already crossed it?"

"Probably not. It's only been two days since I saw him. They can only drive at night to keep from being spotted."

"Then let's get going."

"First, we need to answer the question neither of us has asked."

"What's that?"

"What if we're right and spot him. What then? Do we alert Sexton and the FBI or deal with it ourselves?" Loq let it sit for a while as they continued staring at the map. Finally, he looked up at her. "You know where I stand."

Bina met his gaze. After a long moment, she said, "How about we cross that bridge when we get to it."

9

———

Bina Mantioc's uniform wasn't the only thing missing. She'd swapped her tribal police patrol car for an unmarked pickup. A horse trailer for the roan mare was hooked to the back. Unlike Loq's rig, hers was outfitted with a CB radio. She radioed George Tahamtaham before leaving Joseph. He picked up and instructed her to switch to another channel, saying the number in their dialect of Sahaptin. When they reconnected, he told her it was more secure and less likely to be monitored by other law enforcement agencies as well as truckers and ham radio operators.

After Bina confirmed they were going to follow the Nez Perce historic trail into Idaho, she asked the police chief if he'd heard from the FBI.

"The feds are keeping a tight lip," Tahamtaham said. "As far as the reporters and public know, Daley's pulled a disappearing act. County sheriff's departments between John Day and Salt Lake City are doing flyovers, but it's a waste of time and fuel, you ask me. Daley will be laying low during the day and traveling at night."

"That's what we think too," she said.

"We, huh? Does that mean you two are in agreement on this plan or is Loq trying to lead you to where he wants to go so he can do what he wants to do, meaning grab his sister and throw down on anybody who tries to stop him?"

"We're like-minded so far, but I'm not about to let him forget I'm police and he's a wildlife ranger." Bina took a breath. "Anything new on the BIA bombing or the murder and shootout in Warm Springs?"

"Since Pendleton's outside the reservation, the Umatilla County sheriff isn't asking for my help even though you and me saved a couple of lives there. As far as Warm Springs goes—"

"Which is on a reservation."

"True, but not ours."

"Since when did that ever stop two tribal police chiefs from talking?"

"It hasn't. Why do you ask?"

"The way Agent Sexton described what happened made me think there's more to it than he let on. He sounded so cut and dry."

"'Just the facts, ma'am,'" Tahamtaham said.

"What?"

"It's from an old TV show. The detective Joe Friday always said it."

"My grandmother wouldn't allow a set in the house. Said I should read instead."

"She's a wise one. Quite a story talker too. When she tells legends from the old days, she puts you right there. The one about the boy who was turned into a chipmunk? Now, every time I see one, I can hear your grandmother explaining how it got its black stripes."

He chuckled. "Anyway, cut and dry is the FBI's way. They don't want to say anything that could come back and bite them in a courtroom."

"But there's something about the whole incident that doesn't feel right. Sexton and Tujunga didn't see Daley shoot the informant, did they?"

"No."

"Do we know if they did any ballistics?"

"If so, they haven't shared the results with Warm Springs tribal police. They're not required to."

"Even if the victim is Indian? He was a member of the Warm Springs tribe, wasn't he?"

"Yes, but he hadn't lived on the reservation for years. He was doing hard time for armed robbery. Daley was sent to the same prison and they were cellmates for a while. After Daley won his appeal and got sprung, the feds offered the Warm Springs inmate a way to get out early."

"By becoming an FBI informant."

"You got it."

"Why is Sexton convinced Daley discovered he was an informant?"

"A bullet in the back of the head speaks pretty loudly."

"But who's to say someone else didn't shoot him? Maybe he had a girlfriend whose husband came after him. He could've made enemies in prison. Maybe he double-crossed someone when he was committing armed robberies. He was a criminal. Live by the gun, die by it too."

Static filled the radio as Tahamtaham thought it over. "Your instincts for policing are starting to grow. One thing to keep in mind is how he was shot. Jealousy is always accompanied by rage. A man who discovers he's being two-timed would want his outrage seen face-to-face, not by the back of a head. Same with a robbery accomplice who was nursing a grudge."

"I still think it's worth finding out why Sexton is so certain Daley killed him. Jack Candy acts like he bought the FBI's story too."

"No surprise there. You saw the way Candy is. He may work for the Bureau of Indian Affairs, but he doesn't like Indians."

"I wonder how long Sexton and Candy will stick around Salt Lake."

"That's assuming Kills in Daylight will be a no-show."

"I have a good feeling we're right about this. But if we're wrong and he does go to Salt Lake, then at least I'll have had a nice drive through the mountains and a visit with our Nez Perce brothers and sisters."

"Which will be counted as vacation days, budget being what it is," Tahamtaham said.

"You're kidding, right?"

"The only thing I'm not joking about is, be safe. Daley's dangerous. That's an order."

"Will do. Let me know if you learn anything more about the Warm Springs killing and what the feds are up to, especially Jack Candy. He makes my bones turn cold. I'll radio you from Idaho."

She cradled the mike and flashed her headlights. Loq had been idling in front of her and pulled out. They'd agreed beforehand that taking both vehicles made sense in case a rig had a breakdown on the narrow dirt roads they were going to use to cut across the mountains and through the national forest. It also provided them with options if they needed to split up to track down their quarry.

Loq led them off the blacktop and onto a network of gravel and dirt roads. Some were marked with Forest Service numbered signs. Most weren't. He relied on the position of the sun and natural features for navigating, following ridgelines and creeks that ran down the east slope of the Wallowa Mountains toward the Snake River.

They passed turnoffs to forest service campgrounds as well as dirt parking lots beside trailheads that led to the range's higher peaks. Seeing them reminded Loq of his first solo climb. He was twelve years old at the time, about to turn thirteen, the age when many Klamath boys underwent instruction by their fathers and tribal elders as part of their journey into manhood.

The final rite of passage was a vision quest. Loq chose to climb to the top of what was once a great mountain and then climb down to the lake inside it. White people called it Crater Lake, his people, *Gii-was*. For them, it was sacred, having been created by an epic battle between the great spirit chief *Gmo'Kamc* and *Monadalkni*, chief of the underworld.

It was winter when young Loq set off on foot from his home in Chiloquin. Though a road to the crater's rim had been built after Teddy Roosevelt declared Crater Lake a national park, Loq was forbidden to step foot on it. He was expected to blaze his own trail. To do otherwise, would lead to a bad vision and brand him as weak and dishonest.

He followed deer trails and a frozen creek up the east side of the dormant volcano. The going was steep, tricky, and, in places, the snow so deep, he plunged up to his hips until he fashioned a pair of snowshoes out of tree branches. It took him fifteen hours of steady climbing to reach the rim of the crater. By then the stars were out and a sliver of a moon murmured among them.

Loq spent the night huddled in the lee of a boulder, shivering inside the embroidered wool jacket his mother had made for the occasion. At dawn, he scrambled over the crater's rim and began the even steeper climb down to the lake. It was more of a slip-sliding scramble. Halfway there, he lost his footing on an icy patch and fell. As he tumbled head over heels, he flailed his arms to try and grab hold of something to halt his plunge.

When he smacked into a boulder, it knocked him out. For how long, he didn't know, but the sun was overhead when he finally regained consciousness. The cold had seeped deep into his bones and his teeth chattered and body shook. He tried to sit up, but couldn't find the strength.

"Go back to sleep," a voice called to him. "Sleep and you will be warm. Sleep and you will never be cold again."

Loq closed his eyes and started to drift.

"Do not listen to *Monadalkni*," another voice said. "He is trapped beneath the top of the mountain I hurled upon him. He needs you to join him in the underworld so he can grow strong again and escape. You must get up. You must continue your vision quest."

"I can't," Loq replied.

"Have you learned nothing from your father and the elders?"

"I'm not strong enough."

"You are the one who chose to make this journey in winter. That proves you have strength."

"*Gmo'Kamc* lies," the first voice said. "You do not even believe in him. He is only a legend the old ones tell to scare children from playing up here and falling into the water. Go to sleep and you will be warm and when you awake, you will be home."

"It is he who lies," the second voice said.

"Stop! I can't tell which of you is telling the truth," Loq cried.

"It is I," the first voice said. "Only I tell the truth."

"What about you?" Loq asked the second voice. "Are you telling the truth?"

"Only you can answer that. What does your heart tell you?" the voice answered.

And that told Loq all he needed to know. He fought off the warm embrace of death, pulled himself up, and stood. His nose was bloody, his ankle sprained. He'd lost a glove. But he hadn't lost his resolve. He put one foot in front of the other and trudged to the edge of the lake.

When he reached it, he looked down at its mirrored surface and saw the face of a man staring back. It was his own reflection.

He knelt, cupped his hands, and drank the sacred water of *Gii-was* and sang his first song, a song to *Gmo'Kamc*, a song of reverence and gratitude.

As he hiked back home, he felt himself growing stronger with each step. His family was waiting at the door when he returned. "*Ni yayna sle-a*," he said. "I have seen the mountain."

The memory of his vision quest was so clear, that Loq didn't see the green pickup coming his way as he steered around a sharp curve. The pickup honked and Loq slammed on the brakes and the horse trailer fishtailed behind. The spotted pony neighed his disapproval. Loq glanced at the side mirror. Bina had left a gap between them and was able to stop with room to spare.

A steep hillside on one side and an equally steep cliff that dropped to a creek below left little room for him or the oncoming green pickup to pull over and let the other pass. The driver opened his door. When he did, it revealed a US Forest Service emblem on it. The ranger's red hair showed beneath a green ball cap that matched his uniform. He wore a service revolver on his hip. Loq knew it was a Smith & Wesson .357 magnum, the same as US Fish and Wildlife rangers were issued.

"Apologies," Loq said as he stuck his head out the window. "Yours is the first vehicle I've seen in the past two hours."

"Understandable, but, still, you need to pay attention up here. Tow trucks are scarce and ambulances even scarcer."

The ranger looked past Loq's rig. Bina was walking toward them. He touched the brim of his ball cap. "Afternoon, miss."

When Loq got out, the ranger took a step back. His eyes shifted between the pair, checking their hands and hips. "Where you coming from?"

"Pendleton," Bina said.

"The Umatilla Reservation?"

She nodded.

"What brings you out this way?"

"We're headed to Burns," Loq said quickly.

"Kinda taking the long way, aren't you? Highway 395 would've been a straight shot."

Bina put her hands on her hips. "Honey, I told you that raven pointing his left wing to the turnoff back in Joseph was wrong."

"Guess he was testing my trust in you," Loq said.

The ranger shifted uncomfortably.

Bina smiled. "Indian humor. We're taking a summer vacation. You know, do a little camping, horseback riding, fishing. Sightseeing too."

Loq noticed him studying the front license plates on both pickups, his lips moving as he committed them to memory.

"I thought you were going to Burns," the ranger said as his right hand inched toward his holster.

"I am after our vacation here," Loq said. "She's got to go straight back home for work. Why we're in two rigs."

The ranger had yet to relax. "What's in Burns?"

"Sick friend."

"Sorry to hear that. Is it serious?"

"As serious as cancer gets. Maybe you know him. Pudge Warbler. He's the county sheriff."

Mention of a lawman seemed to make the ranger relax a little. "Can't say I've had the pleasure."

"Too bad. He's a good man."

The ranger looked from Loq to Bina and back again.

Before he could ask another question, Loq said, "You know, it'd be easier if you backed up rather than we try it with the trailers."

He hesitated, but then said, "Of course. By the way, where do you plan on camping? I can recommend a spot that's next to a good trout stream."

"Lick Creek, but if you know a better one—"

"No, that's the one I was thinking of. Pretty and lots of fish. Room to tether your horses too. Okay, well, hope you catch your limit."

The ranger got in his rig and backed up to a wide spot. Loq and Bina drove forward. As they passed, the ranger touched the brim of his ball cap. Two miles on, Loq stopped and walked back to Bina's rig.

"He certainly was suspicious," she said. "He acted like he knows Killian Daley was spotted in Oregon."

"Sexton probably had the FBI issue a new order for all government personnel to be on the lookout for any Indians on the move, especially if they're heading east toward Salt Lake."

"He studied our license plates, but didn't ask for our names or demand to see our driver's licenses."

"He had no cause and didn't want to spook us. Why he wanted to know where we're spending the night."

"Does that mean you think he's going to run the plates and the information will get back to Sexton and Candy?"

"If it does, all they'll know is where the ranger tells them we're camping. They can only guess where we're headed."

"That was fast thinking saying Lick Creek. Why did you pick it?"

"Because there's a mountain between it and where we'll really be."

Bina smiled. "Then we'd better step on it if we're going to make it by nightfall."

10

———

The midsummer sun still had an hour before setting, but the sky was already a pale rose. Loq and Bina left their rigs hidden behind a copse of pines that paralleled a little-used dirt track. After saddling their horses, strapping bedrolls behind the cantles, and slipping rifles into their scabbards, they set off on a trail that climbed a ridge and ran along its spine.

Loq and the spotted pony were in the lead. They crossed an outcropping of jagged rocks where a misstep would've sent horse and rider plunging off the sharp edge of the ridgeline. He shifted in his saddle to check on Bina, but needn't have bothered. She was guiding Túxin expertly over the knife-edged boulders, the roan mare walking so nimbly her shoes didn't make a spark.

When Bina caught up, Loq wordlessly pointed at the trail ahead, which had been trod by deer hooves for thousands of years. The rock walls at the entrance to Hells Canyon held the heat of the day and had turned fiery red from the waning sun. Sheer cliffs grew steeper the farther the big gorge traveled, dwarfing the mighty river below that had sculpted them.

"It's like looking straight into the heart of Mother Earth," Bina said, her voice a mix of wonder and reverence.

"That spot up ahead will give us an eagle's view of Oxbow Dam below and the road that crosses over the river," Loq said. "We can set up there and watch for headlights."

"And if they belong to Killian Daley's convoy, we'll follow, but not confront him."

The Klamath didn't say anything.

"Remember what we agreed?" she said.

"Mm," he grunted.

"I bet they make camp in White Bird Canyon."

"Unless Daley's really Coyote and playing tricks."

"There's only one way to find out."

Urging their mounts onward, they soon reached the spot alongside the trail. Loq picketed the horses while Bina spread out a tarp. They didn't bother gathering wood—light from a campfire would give them away. Sitting on their unfurled bedrolls, Loq placed his binoculars down and offered her a strip of jerked venison.

"Ever seen Hells Canyon before?" he said.

Bina nodded. "Though not from this particular spot. I've seen the Snake River many times where the Grande Ronde joins it. The entire Grande Ronde Valley was part of our traditional homeland. What about you?"

"I've spent time on the Snake for work. The islands near Nyssa are part of the Deer Flat National Wildlife Refuge. Also, further upriver where the Bruneau River joins it."

"I've heard of Deer Flat, but I didn't know there was a refuge at the Bruneau too."

"There isn't, but Nick Drake and I got a new boss who thought Bruneau Canyon would make a good one. She wanted to scout it with us and so we rafted down it in early spring."

"During runoff? What was that like?"

He thought of miles of freezing whitewater and the Shoshone legend of *Tsa-ahu-bitts*, the evil spirit Whites called the Jarbidge Monster who dwelled there. Loq resisted touching the deep scars on his chest.

"Not without consequence," he said.

Bina swallowed a bite of jerky. "But that's the life you chose. Consequential."

"Is there another kind?"

"If there is, I haven't found it, but that's because I'm not looking for it."

"Why you went into nursing. Why you became a cop."

"I didn't feel I had a choice."

"Mm."

They ate the jerky and chased it down with cold mountain stream water from their canteens. Pink turned to red and then to purple. Loq wondered if the sky would soon bloom with chrysanthemums of summer lightning like it had the night he first encountered Killian Daley. He kept his eyes on the dam below, but could see Bina sitting next to him as if he were staring straight at her, staring into her, seeing how she was like him in the way she embraced who she was, who her people were, and what her obligations were.

It was as if she were reading his thoughts because she said, "You don't question that Killian Daley might believe the same about living a consequential life? That what he's doing by staging protests and demonstrations will help all of us?"

"His actions go against what I was taught by the elders, what I saw and learned in Vietnam. Tribe before self, squad before self. Killing people and getting your own people killed can become one and the same. Just as victory and defeat can."

"But Robert Sexton didn't learn that when he was there with military intelligence before, did he?"

Loq looked down his high cheekbones at her. "You see as well as you ride and dance."

She took the compliment without smiling or comment. "What happened when you were with him in Vietnam? What was Operation Phoenix?"

"It's not a story for tonight."

"All right, but tell me sooner rather than later because I need to know what kind of man he is when I run into him again."

"Do you think hearing the story will also tell you what kind I am?"

"I already know you're not like him." Bina paused. "What about your sister? Do you think Carrie Horse will listen to you and go home?"

Loq glanced at the mouth of Hells Canyon. The steep walls had lost their hold on the heat as well as the glow of the sun. Now they were dark and cold as was the river they contained with no less tight a grip than that of a crypt.

"I don't know," he said.

"What if she doesn't? Do you know what you'll do then?"

He nodded.

"No matter the consequence?"

He could see Carrie through the years, from childhood to teen to young woman to mother to warrior. He'd always loved her, looked up to her, admired her, respected her. But now, being with a man like Killian Daley? Joining him on what was sure to be a suicide mission? Loq swallowed the gorge rising in his throat. Carrie's children needed her love, her wisdom, her strength to guide them. Getting herself killed would deny them that and, in turn, hurt the tribe too.

"There are always consequences. It goes with being alive," he finally said. "The night will be long. The day ahead too. We should get rest when we can. I'll take first watch unless you want to."

Bina answered by standing and shaking out her bedroll and lying down on her side to look at Loq, not on her back to look at the stars. She needed to convince herself that what she was feeling was the draw of what they were doing together: coming up with a plan, tracking a fugitive, and trying to save lives and right wrongs. But as her eyes closed, she conceded it was Loq himself, and that alarmed her, because she knew vulnerability would be a liability when she went to arrest Killian Daley and take him to face justice.

As she fell asleep, her last waking thought triggered fractured dreams of past encounters with criminals. Most had been caught in the act of committing misdemeanors, but one violent confrontation provoked a nightmare.

Bina had only been on the job three months and was still on probation. She'd been assigned to partner with an older officer who would teach her the ropes. Their shifts together were routine: ticket speeders, take the occasional drunk to jail to sleep it off, keep an eye out for kids cutting class, help elders round up sheep that had wandered off their properties and onto the roads.

In the middle of one evening shift, her partner suddenly announced he was ill and had to go home. They returned to the station so he could pick up his car and tell George Tahamtaham. As he drove away, the police chief asked Bina if she thought he was faking.

"Smelling is believing," she said.

Tahamtaham chuckled. "He's always been partial to beans and squash. Leave the patrol car here to air out. We don't have the budget for hazardous duty pay. You can use my rig to finish your shift." He tossed her the keys.

Bina did as ordered. It was late fall and the nights were turning crisp and the fields sprouting hoarfrost. The reservation's main town was Mission and she made her rounds through the neighborhoods and then widened the circle to patrol the outlying tracts where houses and trailers stood on small plots of land.

She went to drive by her grandmother's place. It was something she always did on evening shifts. A block away, she saw her grandmother walking in her direction. Bina pulled over and rolled down the window.

"*Katá*, what are you doing out here? It's cold and dark."

"Taking soup to Aunty Moon. She has the winter sickness and it isn't even winter yet."

"That's too far to walk. Here, give me the pot. I'll take it to her. You go back inside where it's warm."

"Who am I to stand in the way of someone who wants to help someone? Now you are helping two someones."

Bina set the covered pot next to her and drove to a tract of prefabs built a hundred yards apart on an unlit road that fronted an open field. When she passed Aunty Moon's nearest neighbor, she noticed a Camaro with fat tires and fancy rims parked in the drive. It sported Washington plates, which wasn't unusual seeing how close the border was.

"Some relative who lives off the rez come to show off the hotshot job he got," she muttered.

The young tribal cop parked out front of Aunty Moon's and carried the pot using one hand to clutch the handle and the other to hold down the lid to keep the contents warm. No light bulb burned above the front door, but that was typical. Electricity was a luxury and elders saved money any way they could. A light glowed softly behind a drawn curtain and she hoped the old woman also had her electric heater on, but she doubted it.

Bina knocked on the door using the toe of her boot. No one answered. She knocked again. "Aunty, it's Bina. *Katá* made healing soup for you. Open the door, my hands are full."

A minute passed before the door finally opened. Bina was focusing on the pot to keep from spilling it when she stepped inside. It wasn't until she looked up that she realized the old woman was naked. Her cheeks were bright red as if slapped and blood trickled from her nose.

"Oh, Aunty. You have a fever. Where's your robe? Get back in bed. Here, let me put the soup down and help you."

And then she smelled it. Not the scent of herbs rising from the pot in her hands, but the acrid sweat of shock and pain exuding from the old woman and the feral stink of a rutting man aroused by cruelty and violence.

Bina whipped around. A fat man leered. Rotten teeth showed between his mustache and beard. His flannel shirt was unbuttoned and revealed a hairy beer belly. His belt was unbuckled as if he hadn't had time to do more than pull up his jeans.

"A two-fer," he called out. "Hey, Leroy. We got ourselves a two-fer and this one's helluva lot fresher."

A shirtless man wearing a white denim jacket with rhinestone flowers embroidered on the shoulders stepped out of the bedroom. His jeans matched the jacket. His socks were white too. "Fresher is always better." He licked his lips.

"Uh-oh, she's an Indian cop," the bearded man said.

"Which means no cop at all," Leroy said. "I'm getting hard all over again thinking she'll try and draw her gun."

When they both brayed, spit speckled the man's beard and Leroy's curling lips revealed mottled gums.

He ran his fingers through his hair, started shaking his hips and twirling his hands while singing, "I'm bad, bad Leroy Brown. Baddest man in the whole damn town. Badder than old King Kong. Meaner than a junkyard dog."

The bearded fat man joined in. "All the downtown ladies call him treetop lover, all the men just call him sir. He's got a .32 in his pocket full of fun and a razor in his shoe."

Bearded man took a step toward Bina. "Leroy may got all

that, but I got this." A revolver appeared in his meaty hand. "Now drop the holster and drop your drawers. It's party time."

She glanced at Aunty Moon. The naked woman was singing too, not a song of sadness and not a death song either. Bina recognized it as the one the elders had sung to call the great herds of wild horses to come down from the hills and carry them into battle. She looked at Leroy singing and dancing. He had no idea that songs and dances were for honoring the spirits, the earth, the sky, for healing and celebrating.

"I'm a dancer," she told herself. "And I'm also a cop."

In a move as graceful as it was fearsome, she flung the pot cover at Leroy's head like a discus while tossing the pot full of soup into the bearded man's face.

The cover spun through the air and struck Leroy in the neck. He began choking and sputtering as the bearded man screamed when the hot liquid splashed into his eyes followed by the heavy pot smashing into his rotten teeth. Blinded, he fired his gun wildly, the first slug going high, the second grazing Bina's scalp. She pulled her revolver as she tumbled backward and yanked the trigger. Once. Twice. Three times. The floor thumped like a war drum when the bearded man hit it.

Leroy shrieked as she turned the gun on him, but he ducked back into the bedroom and slammed the door. She fired anyway. Wood splintered followed by glass shattering as he hurled a chair threw the window and scrambled out.

Adrenaline, fear, and anger surged through Bina with the force of all the unused electricity the elders were too poor to buy. She leapt up, saw that the bearded man was dead, and went to Aunty Moon.

"You are so brave. Your song gave me strength." She yanked a blanket off the couch and draped it over the woman's shoulders. "Stay here."

Bina raised her gun in a two-handed grip and followed it

outside, swinging it left and then right as she'd been trained. There was no sign of Leroy, but he couldn't've gone too far too fast, not in his white socks. Where would he run? She looked up the road. What had she seen when she first arrived? What was out of place? Of course. The darkened neighbor's house. The Camaro with Washington plates in the drive. That should've tipped her off something wasn't right. The pair had broken into that house, found nothing, and then went hunting.

Bina jumped in the chief's pickup and cranked a U-turn. Red taillights flashed ahead. The Camaro came backing out of the neighbor's drive, fishtailed, and then shot forward up the road. Bina gunned it, steering with one hand and grabbing the radio's mike with the other.

What were the police codes? What was the one for shots fired, one for assailant down, one for officer in pursuit? She should've memorized them.

"Chief, Chief," she yelled. "I'm chasing a Camaro. Washington plates. White male, thirties, wearing white jeans and jacket. He raped Aunty Moon. He's trying to get over the reservation line. I shot ... I shot his partner."

The pickup's wheels caught ice and sent the rig into a spin. Bina was forced to drop the mike and grab the wheel with both hands to keep from going off the road.

Taillights flared up ahead. Leroy had turned into a dead end and was backing up again. Bina closed the gap. By the time he straightened out the Camaro, she was right behind him.

Bina didn't brake. She floored it.

The police chief's pickup plowed into the rear of the Camaro and shoved it off the road and into the field. The coupe's wide wheels gave it some traction on the frosty grass, but not for long. Soon it was sliding and spinning. It nosedived into an irrigation ditch.

The door opened and Leroy jumped out. He set off at a run

that quickly turned into a hop, skip, and a trip as his white socks clumped with ice. Leroy tried to pick himself up, but kept slipping and tripping.

Bina stopped the pickup behind the Camaro and gave chase. When she caught up to him, Leroy was trying to curl into the fetal position. She trained her gun on him and thought of all the things she was supposed to say—put your hands on your head, you're under arrest, you're entitled to a lawyer. But all she could think about was how many times outsiders had come onto the reservation to do what they pleased, knowing all they had to do was scurry back over the line before they got caught and they'd never have to pay.

She held the gun and tried to form the words. Her teeth chattered from the cold, from the bullet wound in her scalp. The sound of her teeth chattering grew louder. They were as loud as the hoofbeats of thousands of wild horses coming to help, as loud as the siren of a tribal police cruiser driving into the field right behind her, as loud as gunshots. She looked at the gun in her hand and then her eyes opened and she was awake.

Loq was crouched next to her gently touching her shoulder. "Gunfire," he said.

"In my dream," she said. "You could hear it?"

"What? No. Down there. On the dam road. Killian Daley's arrived. Vehicles are crossing. Someone started shooting. Someone shot back. Hurry, we got to saddle up and ride."

11

STAR LIZARD

The nightlong yip-howls of coyotes started to let up and signaled the coming of dawn. Gemma was lying with her head in the crook of my arm. Our whispers were no louder than the swish of bedroom curtains billowed by a gentle breeze that found the open window.

"What's the latest from Pudge's doctor?" I said.

"Steady as she goes," she said, mimicking a man's gruff voice. Gemma sighed. "He either says that or we'll run some more tests or have patience or there's another medicine we can try."

"All those old saws from that old sawbones must drive Pudge nuts. I've never met a man who's more don't-beat-around-the-bush than your dad."

"It bugged him in the beginning, but then Pudge jumped straight from the denial stage to acceptance, bypassing anger, bargaining, and depression altogether."

"You don't think he's in a hurry to die, do you? He's got so much to live for. You, the kids, sheriffing, everything."

"No, but Pudge doesn't waste time thinking about what-ifs and what-might-be's. The way he sees it, fighting cancer is the same as going after a vicious killer. What it all boils down to is who's quicker on the draw. He accepts that and doesn't let it stop him from being true to himself and everyone else."

"What about you? What stage are you in?"

"Oh, I'm definitely in the anger stage, but I'm willing to bargain too."

"Same here. Why I'm going to take Johnny to look for November's plant."

"Who knows, it might work. She's a powerful healer and I trust her. I also trust you to keep Johnny safe. Keep yourself safe too."

"I won't let you down."

"But what happens if you run into that ex-con from Fort McDermitt? I don't like the sound of Hex Taggert one bit. Charged with rape and the only reason he got off was because the girl disappeared. He's likely responsible for other missing Native women too."

"He sounds bad, all right, but the odds of running into him are as remote as the mountains we'll be riding through. That range is plenty big and Southeastern Oregon is a hundred times even bigger. There's a million other places he could be."

"I know, but there aren't a million yous."

"Or yous."

I was caressing her hip as I said it.

She cuddled up even closer. "What you and Johnny are going to do is risky. So is what Loq is doing. He could get hurt."

"It'd hurt Loq more if he didn't try."

"You haven't heard from him at all?"

"No, and I don't expect to. He doesn't want to involve anyone because the FBI will go after him for trying to rescue Carrie."

"But you wish he'd asked you to help."

"Of course. We're partners, brothers."

"We're partners too."

"Yes we are, but we're not brothers."

"We're not?"

"No, definitely not."

I kept rubbing her hip and we started kissing and it wasn't long before the swish of curtains and yip-howls of coyotes were replaced by sounds of a different sort that drowned out the worries about a father with cancer, a son with deep emotional scars, and a brother crosswise with the FBI.

Afterward, when we'd shared a shower and dressed, we went to breakfast. Nagah was already seated. As usual, he was reading. His long hair hung in a single braid and he'd taken to wearing a folded red kerchief as a headband like his grandfather Tuhudda always did. He was wise beyond his nineteen years and becoming more like his grandfather every day.

November put a basket of fry bread on the table. A covered pot of oatmeal and a lidded cast-iron pan heaped with bacon and eggs were already there.

"I hope all this food means Pudge has his appetite back," Gemma said.

"Not this morning," November said. "Your father coughed most of the night. I gave him witch hazel tea, placed an herb poultice on his chest, and sang a healing song. He's sleeping now."

I helped myself to coffee and a piece of fry bread. Its coating of powdered sugar dusted my fingertips. "Is the plant Johnny and I'll be looking for a type of witch hazel?"

"If it was, you would not have to go to the Trout Creek Mountains."

"Point taken. What's it called?"

November said a Numu word that was even longer than saying Girl Born in Snow in her native tongue.

Gemma shook her head at me even though she was fluent—November had taught her Numu when she was growing up. "I got variations of words for green and thorns and sage and star and running lizard and bad water, but I'm not even sure how they all link up."

"Do you think she's pulling my leg?"

"Does it matter?"

Nagah looked up from his book. "Our people have been treating cancer with herbal remedies since time began. Burdock root, sheep sorrel, slippery elm, and Indian rhubarb root are known for their healing powers."

I pointed a piece of fry bread at November. "Give me the drawing and tell me where to look and I'll find your star lizard plant."

She tsked. "Johnny must find it, not you. How can he find the path to manhood if you're leading him?"

November had no sooner said his name than he came out of his bedroom. That was surprising because Hattie always beat Johnny to the table, morning, noon, and night. During the school year, Gemma and I took turns yanking him out of bed. Every morning was the same. He'd put up a fight and protest about going, saying the teacher hated him and all the kids bullied him for looking and talking differently. Being put in detention and threatened with expulsion for fighting had become routine.

"I'm ready to go," he said.

"Sure, right after breakfast," I said. "Have a big one because we got a long road ahead. Could be some time before our next meal."

"I already ate. I want to find the plant."

November nodded. "Johnny was up while you two were still in bed. He ate like the man he is going to become. A bowl of oatmeal, three eggs, and four pieces of bacon. I had to refill the basket of fry bread, he ate so many. Coffee too with lots of milk and sugar."

"I didn't know you drank coffee," I said, only to get a scowl for an answer.

Hattie appeared with Jake padding close behind. She tried to talk her way into joining our trip south, but gave up when Gemma told her that she'd be too busy working with the foals at Lyle's, plus her dog would miss her. That put a smile on her face.

November disappeared while Gemma and I finished eating. When she returned, she had an oilskin bag packed with food and a piece of paper with a drawing on it. She handed it to Johnny.

"This plant only grows on the side of the deepest canyon above a creek where the sun shines longest. You will know the plant by its scent."

He asked what it smelled like.

"Desert air right before a thunderstorm, but do not stay in the canyon when it starts to rain. It will flood."

"It's not going to rain. It's summer."

"When you do not expect it, then it will happen."

"Rain?"

"Everything."

Nagah nodded. "Girl Born in Snow is wise, little brother. Remember, if you ever need help, all you have to do is ask for it. Asking takes courage and will be your true strength. Tuhudda will hear you from the spirit world for he dwells among the stars now and can guide you the same as he guides Nick."

We loaded Kosse and my buckskin stallion, Wovoka, into the horse trailer. Johnny tried to pull away when Gemma went to kiss him goodbye, but she didn't let him.

As I slid behind the wheel, she glanced at my holstered sidearm on the seat and the Winchester and shotgun cradled in the gun rack.

"I thought you said the chance of running into Hex Taggert was low?"

"Since when did I ever play the odds?"

"When you asked me to marry you."

I could still see the shine in her eyes long after Johnny and I clattered across the cattleguard.

"I need to make a quick stop at Blackpowder Smith's," I told him as we drove down the block-long main street of No Mountain.

The crusty proprietor of the combination dry goods store and watering hole was standing behind the bar with his elbows propped on it and his chin resting on his fists. He was staring at a mug that I knew had more than black coffee in it.

"Why, howdy there, young fella. You caught me in my cups."

"Over what?"

"Took one too many trips down memory lane and, well, it hit me pretty hard."

"Pudge," I said.

The black hat with the snakeskin band tipped toward the bar. "Best friend a man could have outside a horse or dog, even when we was sparring over a chess game or our own pigheadedness."

"He's not gone yet."

"I know. The white coats will drag it out as long as there's money in his bank account, but we all have a *The End* sign hanging on us the moment we first draw breath."

"You know Pudge. He's not going down without a fight."

"What all my memory trips was about. Reliving every scrap we got in together, every bad man we faced down, every bank robber we cornered." Blackpowder gave a loud sniff. "Pudge always fought like a hellcat, but for the life of me, I can't count if he's spent eight or nine lives already."

"November is sending Johnny on a quest to find a plant she says could cure him."

"What kind of plant?"

"Don't know for sure. She said the name in Numu, but I'm calling it star lizard for short."

"Well, if anyone can whip cancer, that Paiute medicine woman can. Where's it grow?"

"A canyon in the Trout Creeks."

"That's as rugged as it gits. If you're stopping off for supplies, I got your back. What d'ya need?"

"I'm all set except for a couple boxes of .30-30 cartridges and 12-gauge shells."

Blackpowder tipped his head back and stroked his white billy goat whiskers. "This star lizard plant got teeth and claws?"

"It's probably nothing, but some kids took off from the Fort McDermitt rez to join up with Killian Daley and his group. An ex-con is with them. Big mean-looking fella named Hex Taggert. The parents of the juveniles are nervous. I need to make sure if I see Taggert, he's not going to get a case of the stupids when I tell him I'll be the one taking them home."

"They wouldn't be the only ones falling under the spell of Mr. Kills in Daylight. I'm told a few grown-ups from the Burns Paiute Reservation headed out to join him. What I don't git is, if they can find him, how come the FBI can't? It's their wanted poster his face is on. Not to mention our friend's sister."

He gave me a long look. "Speaking of, I haven't seen Loq around lately. Was you two on patrol together?"

"No, and I don't know where he is. Look, I'd stay and swap stories about Pudge, but Johnny's waiting in the pickup and we'd better get a move on if we're going to make camp before dark."

"Say no more. You know where I keep the ammo. Just write a chit next to it and I'll add it to your monthly bill."

The old codger looked back at the coffee mug. "Now, where was I? Believe it was the time Pudge Warbler and yours truly got sideways with a bunch of backshooting horse thieves over in the Stinkingwaters."

We drove out of town, passing the lineman's shack that was my home when I first moved to Harney County and now served as the US Fish and Wildlife Service's field office. I didn't give a moment's thought to stopping off to check the answering machine. The last thing I needed was to hear my boss, Liz Bloom, telling me she knew I'd been avoiding her calls all week and she wasn't mad, only disappointed, that I didn't trust her enough to share what I knew about Loq's extracurricular activities.

The two-lane took Johnny and me past the turnoff to the Malheur National Wildlife Refuge. Vehicles were few and far between. The only time it wasn't like that was in spring and fall when people came from all over the country to look at the more than three hundred different species of birds that stopped by as they winged back and forth along the Pacific Flyway. I kept my eyes peeled for wild burros and free-range cattle that had a habit of wandering onto the blacktop.

Johnny had been silent since leaving the ranch, but after we passed Frenchglen and were rounding the base of Steens Mountain entering into Catlow Valley, he finally spoke up.

"If I don't find the star lizard plant, will Pudge die?"

"You know, son, all people eventually die—"

"I'm not a baby! I've seen many people die. My mama. Her pimp when the GI with the tiger tattoo like yours shot him. Other GIs. Viet Cong."

"I know that. What I was going to say was, when Pudge dies —and we don't know when—it won't be because of a plant you found or didn't find. It'll be because it's his time."

"You don't understand," he said and began to sulk.

As the miles passed by, I thought about the loggerheads my soldiering father and I had when he came home after long deployments. I'd try to get his attention the only way I knew how, and that was to make him pissed off. But after I enlisted and it came time for me to ship out, I overheard him telling my mother how hard it'd been on him having to leave me all the time. The one thing that got him through, he said, was adhering to a saying from a Japanese judo sensei: Hold on tightly but let go lightly. I wondered if I could ever do the same with Johnny.

We pulled up to historic Fields Station, a café and bar with a gas pump out front. The great white expanse of the Alvord Desert shimmered to the east. I topped off the tank and double-checked to make sure the five-gallon jerry cans strapped to the pickup's bed were full too.

"They make world-famous hamburgers in there," I said, hooking a thumb at the café that had been in business since the 1880s. "Want to get one? From here on out, it'll be my cooking over a campfire."

His head shook hard.

"All right, let's move out."

We continued south and then turned east onto the road to Whitehorse Ranch. Sagebrush stubbled the desert floor like whiskers. The road crossed over sandy washes and meadows and up and down folds that turned into hills. We turned south again on a road labeled on the topographic map as Trout Creek Mountain, but no one had bothered to plant an actual sign on it. I put the rig into four-wheel drive as the road turned from gravel to dirt to ruts, twisting and turning and growing rougher with the terrain. Rocks had tumbled onto it in places and the shoulder had slid into gulches in more places than I liked.

"I'm sick of riding in the truck," Johnny said as we bounced along. "I want to ride Kosse."

"Soon," I said. "This takes us to the east side of Red Mountain where we can pick up a trail that runs west to east and crosses creek drainages and the canyons they run through. When we see the deepest, we'll know it's the most likely place to search for the star lizard plant."

I found a good spot to park the rig. Before we got out, we studied November's drawing.

"See, it's got five points like a star and its stalk does look like a lizard," I said. "She also said something about green and sage. Maybe that's its color and it grows among sagebrush. One way to find out."

Wovoka and Kosse whinnied when we unloaded them, both shaking their heads and pawing the ground in anticipation. Once our bedrolls and saddlebags were secured, I slid my Winchester into its scabbard and put the 12-gauge pump into one affixed to Kosse's saddle.

"I get to carry a gun?" Johnny said as he scrambled onto the dark chestnut.

"Your horse and saddle does." I swung aboard the buckskin. "Keep a lookout for the star lizard plant." And to myself I said, "And I'll do the same for Hex Taggert."

12

—————

Bina Mantioc wasn't buying it when Loq said they should split up, with him riding straight down to the Oxbow Dam where Killian Daley was trying to cross the Snake River and her riding back to get one of their rigs.

"No way," she said as she tightened the cinch on Túxin. "It sounds like a war going on down there and two guns are better than one."

"But we're going to need a pickup. We can't chase Daley through Idaho on horseback."

"Who says?"

Loq swung onto the spotted pony without another word and started riding back the way they came, peering at the ground for any kind of trail that led from the ridgeline down to the dam while thanking the stars for their light.

He spotted a fork not far past the outcropping of jagged rocks. The trail to the left was fainter and narrower than the one they'd ridden up, but the echo of another gunshot and the thought of Carrie in trouble kept him from hesitating. Loq pressed his right knee and the spotted pony turned down without balking. Bina and the roan mare didn't flinch either.

"Bighorn," he said to himself as the hoof-wide trail dropped more abruptly than the one at Jimmy Two Sons. "No deer made this."

The horses were using their back legs and haunches as brakes as they navigated the steep decline. Another gunshot and a flash from a barrel prompted Loq to ease up on the reins and stop pressing down on the stirrups. The pony flared his nostrils and started crow hopping bushes and rocks. It was all about trust now, that and embracing the same focus he used to get when charging into a firefight. Movement mattered. Seconds counted. Dealing was always better than receiving.

Loq could hear the snorts and heavy breaths coming from Túxin close behind. The roan's shoes were no longer quiet, but Bina was. Loq didn't turn around to see if the cop had been thrown because engines were roaring ahead, tires squealing, and a woman screamed. More muzzle flashes spurred him to urge the pony to go faster. The trail began to level out. Loq yanked his rifle from the scabbard and levered in a round one-handed.

When he'd been watching from above, he'd counted the lights on the dam. Now he counted fewer. A lot fewer. Someone had shot them out. Someone who didn't want to be a target. That accounted for some of the gunfire, but not all. More shots banged.

The trail joined a dirt road leading to the dam. The pony didn't need a command to break into a run. Taillights and head-lights blinked on as drivers reached the other side of the river and turned onto a road leading out of the canyon. Loq could see the outlines of cars, pickups, campers, and horse trailers. There were a dozen a least. Maybe fifteen.

One darkened rig remained on his side of the river. Finally, it inched onto the dam road and started to cross. The driver didn't turn on the headlights, nor tap the brakes. With most of the lights shot out on the dam, Loq couldn't make out the exact make or color, but he could tell it was a pickup limping slowly to the other side. Sensing it could be bait, he reined the pony to a halt rather than chase after it.

Bina brought the roan right alongside him. "Why did you stop? We're right behind them."

"There's something not right about that last vehicle. Could be a trap and there're shooters riding in the bed waiting to open up on whoever follows."

"That's it, you're giving up?"

"Never, but we know where they're going. There's a story here that can tell us about the gunfight. Who was shooting at who and why."

Bina hesitated before saying, "Knowledge is power. Police work 101."

Loq swung off the pony and took a flashlight from his saddlebag. He began sweeping the beam across the ground.

Bina dismounted and took the reins of both horses. "I'll tether them so they can rest. Join you in a second."

Loq started walking a zigzag pattern while Bina looked for something to tie the horses to. She needed a moment to catch her breath. The adrenaline she'd felt the night at Aunty Moon's had come roaring back. She closed her eyes and hummed the healing song she'd danced to at Fort Klamath years ago. It calmed her. Then she got her flashlight and began searching for signs.

"Brass over here," she said, shining her light on spent cartridges at the edge of what appeared to be a dirt pullout.

"Here as well," Loq said.

He crouched, picked up a couple of shells, examined them quickly, and put them in his pocket. Broken glass also littered the ground. He rubbed a chunk between his fingers. It was safety glass from a car.

"Definitely the site of a gunfight."

"Do you think it was between dam workers and Daley's group or someone who decided they'd had enough and was turning back and he tried to stop them?"

"Wasn't dam workers. None are here at night. It's all automated. I think it was somebody waiting to ambush them or somebody chasing them and tried to stop them before they crossed the river. Maybe both kind of somebodies."

"What makes you think that?"

"What caliber of brass do you have over there?"

Bina picked up a couple. "Looks to be .357 magnum. Wait, there's more. Some .38s. Also a lot of spent rifle cartridges, but I don't recognize their caliber. What do you have?"

"Some .22s. Shotgun shells too. This side was armed for hunting rabbits and birds, not a firefight. Do you have glass or anything from a vehicle?"

She rotated in place holding the flashlight out. "There's something shiny." Bina stooped and shined her light. "Shards of a mirror. Probably from a side mirror."

Loq crouched again and let his fingers read the ground. A set of tire tracks. Multiple sets of footprints and blood splatter on the side of the tracks closest to the river. A different set of tracks coming from Bina's location. The tires were wider and farther apart. Fresh boot prints next to the driver's side, getting out, walking around, and getting back in. And then deep scrapes made by the first vehicle being pushed by the second vehicle.

He followed the tracks. They led a short distance to where the impounded Snake River backed up behind the dam and formed a large reservoir. The lake-like surface was still and black except where salted with the reflection of stars. He shined his flashlight. Something glinted ten yards out, something sticking just above the surface.

It was a car roof.

Loq put down his rifle, unbuckled his holster, and kicked off his boots. He waded into the water carrying only his flashlight. The bank sloped gradually. Silt rose between his toes. The farther he walked, the deeper the water got, the muddier the bottom grew.

He reached the vehicle. It was a station wagon teetering on a submerged boulder. The windows on the driver's side were shot out. The passenger compartment was filled with water although a few inches of air remained at the top because of the car's perch.

Loq shined his light inside. A body was floating above the front seat, its wrist tied to the steering wheel. He reached inside and grabbed the shirt collar and pulled. The face turned toward him. The last time he'd seen it, there wasn't a bullet hole in the forehead. It was Freddy Salish, the teenager who'd been with Willie Hawkfeather.

He let go and looked into the back seat. Another body was there. It wasn't floating, but held in place by a seat belt as if on a drive down a country lane. Long, dark hair swirled around the head, preventing him from seeing the face. The shirt was ripped apart by bullets to the chest. Seeing the swell of breasts, he knew it was a woman.

Loq started singing his patience song, seeing the images of a doe and fawn and cool water and blue skies marked with the white carets of tundra swans winging their way to the far north and of Carrie cantering through fields of gold. He reached in, gathered the tresses of dark, wet hair and pulled them to the side.

She was someone else's sister, someone else's daughter, maybe someone's wife and mother.

Loq let go and the station wagon shifted forward as more water poured through the broken windows, so much so that the weight dislodged it from the boulder. It slid off. He breathed deep, held it, and dove. The car plunged into a deep hole on the other side of the rock and sank even deeper into years' worth of mud. The flashlight's batteries finally gave out and all went dark.

With his breath running out too, Loq kicked for the surface and swam back to shore. Bina rushed to help him out.

"What was it?" she said.

"Two of Killian Daley's warriors. They weren't killed in daylight but tonight."

"By who?"

"Do you have the spent brass?"

Bina opened her palm.

He took a look. "The who is someone who carries both a .357 magnum, a .38 backup, and is also armed with a .30-06."

"I don't know about a rifle, but we took a .357 and .38 off Jack Candy at Jimmy Two Son's."

"Mm. He's also someone who wouldn't think twice about tying their bodies inside the car and pushing it into the water so they wouldn't float and be found."

"Candy never went to Salt Lake City."

"He's been a BIA investigator long enough that he thinks like the old Cayuse in the blue Chevy back at the Umatilla. He figured Daley spread the rumor himself that he was going to Salt Lake to cover his tracks."

"If we could figure out he'd stick to forest service roads, so could Candy."

"Looks like he did."

"Do you think he knows about Chief Joseph's trail?"

"Could be, but more likely he made a circle on a forest service map using where I saw Daley as the center and chose one of the roads leading out and followed it."

"Lucky guess or process of elimination?"

"Or he's got his own confidential informant." Loq grunted. "Candy didn't try to stop Sexton from going to Salt Lake. It's why he tied the pair he killed inside the car and sunk it. He doesn't want to file a report and have the FBI getting in the way of him killing a famous outlaw Indian."

"Jack Candy wants to be famous too, he hates us that much." Bina took a deep breath, exhaled slowly. "I have to call it in. This is a murder scene. I'm a sworn officer."

"Then we'll be stuck here waiting for the FBI to show up while Killian Daley takes Carrie and Willie farther away. It'll also allow Candy to catch up to them and kill whoever else gets in his way."

"But he tried to cover up what he did here. That's against the law. I don't know which one, but there's got to be a law and he broke it."

"It'll be hard to prove he did this. We didn't witness him shooting them or shoving their car into the river."

"But ballistics could prove it. I kept some of his brass."

"Candy probably carries multiple weapons in case he has to ditch one."

Bina's sigh rang with frustration. "I don't know who I want to stop more, Killian Daley or Jack Candy."

"If we get going, we can stop both."

She raised her chin. "I need to radio this in. Not to the local authorities or the FBI, but to George Tahamtaham. He's my chief. I owe it to him. He'll steer me right."

"Okay, let's ride back to our rigs."

"Does that mean you'll go along with whatever George says?"

"Let's hear what it is first."

"But he's not your boss."

"No, but I respect him."

"What about me?"

Loq remembered what *Gmo'Kamc* said about listening to what his heart told him. "Only you can answer that."

They rode back to where they'd left their pickups. Bina couldn't get any radio reception there and so they trailered the horses and returned to the dam. Loq parked and walked back to Bina's. She was holding the steering wheel with both hands. The look on her face was equally set.

"Can't get radio here either?" he said.

"I've had time to think. It's still hours until sunup and George will be home. There's no telephone here, so I can't call him. I don't want to radio the station and leave a message with whoever is handling dispatch."

"What do you want to do?"

"Say a blessing at the edge of the Snake River for the two people in the station wagon and then go arrest their killer."

"What about Killian Daley?"

"I'm going to arrest him too."

"I have some sage we can burn. I don't know what people Freddy Salish and the woman are, but I know a blessing song. It's a good song."

"I'll sing it with you."

And so they sang as the stars quivered overhead and their reflections did the same on the still waters of the once wild river that was born in the mountains of the Continental Divide and flowed into the Columbia and on to the Pacific. When the scent of burning sage wafted higher and higher, and the words from the blessing song became echoes, the spirits of the dead were released to join those of their ancestors. Loq slipped his arm around Bina's waist and she put hers around his, and what passed between them was the spirit of life so long as it remained unbroken.

13

———

They decided to get a jump on Kills in Daylight by leapfrogging him to White Bird Canyon.

"We don't need to stick to forest service roads like he does because no one's looking for us," Bina said. "We can loop down to Cambridge and connect to Highway 95 north. That will give us time to scout the historic battlefield before he gets there and try to figure out where he's likely to camp."

The plan would only work if Jack Candy didn't catch up to him first, but Loq thought luck might be on their side. Now that he realized it'd been the BIA investigator's pickup limping across the dam road, he guessed one of his tires had been flattened during the shootout or while pushing the station wagon into the river. Maybe a .22 round had punctured the radiator or fuel line. Anything was possible when lead was flying.

It would take Candy time to fix whatever the problem was. Although Daley's convoy moved more slowly, by the time he resumed the chase, he'd have to stop at every fork in the network of forest service roads to sort out which one they'd taken and which was a smokescreen. The ruse of leaving false tracks and sweeping away real ones hadn't died out with the Old West.

Bina took the lead as they crossed the river. It was still dark and they had the road to themselves. As Loq followed the tribal cop's taillights, he wondered if Carrie Horse had known he was at Oxbow Dam when she fled. Did she sense her brother's spirit? Did she recognize his silhouette on the spotted pony galloping toward her? Did she also shoot at Jack Candy during the gun battle? Did she really love Killian Daley?

Loq shook off the unanswerable questions and turned to what he did know about his big sister. After the powwow at Fort Klamath where he'd first seen Bina Mantioc do the jingle dance and Carrie had earned her name by lifting her horse across the finish line, Loq felt increasingly restless. School was boring and being inside confining. He started spending more and more time outdoors. His intolerance reached the breaking point shortly after his sixteenth birthday when his father died.

Loq quit going to class altogether and fell in with a gang of other Chiloquin High School dropouts. They'd drive down to Klamath Falls every Saturday night, blasting hard rock on the eight track, drinking beers, and hurling their empties out the window. By the time they rolled into town thirty miles south, they'd head straight to South Sixth Street where the sons of farmers, ranchers, and millworkers were already gathering, swigging liquid courage and itching to prove themselves. No matter the sides in the brawl, the blood was all the same color when it ran from broken noses, split lips, and cut knuckles.

On the first anniversary of his father's death, Carrie Horse insisted Loq join her for a ride. It had been a long time since they'd taken their horses out for a race. At first he refused, saying he was too old for childhood games, but Carrie wouldn't take no for an answer. She also didn't ease up when they took off from their old starting line in a lakeside field and galloped toward the finish line on the shore.

She beat him by two lengths and Loq was too proud to blame it on his horse or say he really hadn't been trying. Carrie turned hers around and rode up to him so they were facing each other.

"You have to leave home," she said without preamble. "Leave Chiloquin. Leave Klamath County. Leave Oregon. You need to go because if you don't, you'll wind up either with your brains bashed in or as a fall-down drunk lying in a gutter."

Loq didn't protest because he knew she was right.

"Remember your vision quest," Carrie said. "Remember what our father and the elders told you when you set out on it. Remember what I said to you too when I encouraged you to take the hardest route there was up to *Gii-was*. What did you learn from it? What did you promise yourself back then?"

"But where would I go?" he finally said. "I have no money."

"You don't need any. Someone will pay your way. They'll pay you to be there."

"A job?"

"Better than a job. A place to find out who you really are, who you were meant to be."

"I don't know where to find such a place."

"Yes you do. What did you see when you looked into *Gii-was*?"

"Me," he said. "Who I am."

"Then be that person. Be a real warrior, not a pretend one brawling on the street."

The next day Loq went to Klamath Falls. There was a war going on in Vietnam and the Marine recruiting officer didn't need much convincing to enlist someone with Loq's build who said he was eighteen but couldn't produce a birth certificate to prove it because kids born on the former Klamath Reservation like him were never issued one.

Dawn broke as Loq followed Bina north on the state highway. The sun was just peeking over the mountains when they entered White Bird Canyon. His first impression of the long sweep of summer-baked grassy hills was they were the color of scabs and the dark gullies running through them old scars.

Bina turned onto a dirt road that led up White Bird Creek and pulled off into a field above the babbling water. Loq parked right behind.

"An army marches on its stomach," she said when they got out.

"I didn't know you served," he said.

"I didn't, but I read. Napoleon gets the credit for saying it, but I'm sure war chiefs of every tribe going back to the beginning of time have said it too." She smiled. "Since I was able to get some sleep last night, why don't you take a rest while I feed the horses and make breakfast."

"I thought you said you didn't cook."

"I don't, but you still have some of that venison jerky, don't you? I'll get it out of the saddlebag."

As she grinned, Loq unfurled his bedroll in the lee of his pickup and was soon asleep. When the warm rays of the sun finally woke him, he'd been dreaming of herds of horses thundering up and down the treeless hills. Only now it wasn't a dream. As he opened his eyes, saddleless Appaloosas were grazing all around.

Bina was standing among them. She was not alone. A man wearing a tan flat-brimmed hat that shaded a face as brown and creased as the canyon's gullied hills stood next to her. Loq joined them.

"Hope we didn't wake you," she said. "This is Himiin and these are his horses."

Loq placed his palm on the nearest Appaloosa. "Powerful as they are beautiful."

"They are descendants of the ones my people rode into battle here," Himiin said. "They helped win it for us by standing still while our warriors fired at the enemy. The cavalry's horses were frightened by gunfire and ran off. When the soldiers chased after them, their battle was lost."

"Then your horses are smart as well as beautiful. You are Nez Perce," Loq said.

"We call ourselves the same way our ancestors did. Nimiipuu."

"Then I will too."

"My grandfather rode with Chief Joseph's younger brother, Ollokot. He did not share his brother's patience and led the young warriors. While Ollokot had a great victory here at White Bird Canyon, he was killed in the final one at Bear Paw in Montana."

"And your grandfather?"

"Wounded there, but survived. He lived out his days on the reservation in Lapwai where he was eventually sent after Chief Joseph said he would fight no more forever."

"But your grandfather's grandson returned here."

"Yes, I did. With my father and mother. The horses made us do it." He held a grin in check, but his eyes gave him away. "That is what my father always told people when we came home."

"This is sacred ground," Loq said. "When I was sleeping, I dreamed of the Appaloosas." He waved at the black, gray, and white spotted horses grazing around them. "These and those who carried your grandfather and those before him."

"Ah, you are a man who knows to listen to the before times."

Loq dipped his head. "I'm only a man who tries to listen. It's up to the others if they wish me to hear them. People, horses, stars, spirits."

Himiin's tan flat-brimmed hat bobbed. "What people are you?"

"Klamath. What is your name in English so I will know what it is in mine?"

"Wolf."

"We say *Ké-uthchish* in Maklak."

"I like the sound of that. I can see your teeth when you say it." Himiin mimed a wolf raising its muzzle and howling.

Loq asked Bina if she told him why they were there.

"Only that we're interested in knowing more about the great victory his people achieved and wanted to see more of the land," she said.

One of the Appaloosas came up to Himiin and began nuzzling the back pocket of his jeans.

"She knows I carry carrots there. My wife and I grow them in our garden. We grow everything. The soil here is good because it is fertilized with the blood of victory." He pointed up the creek. "Come meet my wife. She will not be pleased if I do not invite you."

"We'd be honored," Bina said.

"Good. I will show you the battlefield afterward. Bring your horses and we can ride to a place where we will be able to see all of it."

They drove their rigs up the dirt road. Himiin rode in Bina's while the herd of Appaloosas followed behind. The ranch house was built on the side of a hill and its covered front porch shaded chairs and a table set up to view the creek and across the mile-wide canyon. The garden was festooned with multicolored ribbons fluttering from poles stuck between rows of corn, squash, and carrots.

"We put them in to keep away the crows, but they like to watch the ribbons in the wind make rainbows as much as we do and so the crows stay," Himiin said before getting out of Bina's pickup.

She asked if crows had a special relationship with the Nimiipuu.

"Yes. When Creator was going to create human beings, he called all the animals to come forward to tell them there was going to be a great change and that he wanted all the animals to say how they would help these new beings. If an animal didn't qualify, it would be turned to stone. Crow argued that he would use his caws to warn the new beings in times of danger. Creator agreed and Crow qualified."

"What happened to the animals that weren't accepted?"

"They were turned to stone like Creator said. You can see them all along the Clearwater River near Lewiston."

Himiin glanced at the police band radio fastened beneath the dash. "When Crow qualified, another black bird came out and said to Creator that he didn't want to be that small, but bigger and have a louder voice. Creator agreed and that bird was Raven."

He turned his gaze from the radio to Bina. "Raven became a trickster like Coyote. Which are you, Crow or Raven?"

"Crow," she said without hesitation. "I should have told you at the start that I'm a tribal police officer from the Umatilla Reservation. It's why I have the radio."

"And Loq?"

"He's a Fish and Wildlife ranger."

"Are you here to arrest me and take me back to the reservation in Lapwai?"

"Of course not. No one can force you to live on a reservation if you don't want to."

"I do not want to. This is my home. It has always been home for Nimiipuu since Creator made us after he made Crow and Raven."

He looked out the windshield. His wife had stepped out to the front porch. One of the Appaloosas walked toward her. "She wants another carrot, that one. You watch."

Himiin turned back to Bina. "If you and Loq had come in one pickup not two, I would think you were on a honeymoon, the way you look at each other. But if you did not come to arrest me and you are not newly wedded, why are you here?"

"We're tracking a man wanted for murder. He's not Nimiipuu and he's not from here, but we have reason to believe he's coming to White Bird Canyon and we need to arrest him before anybody else gets hurt."

"Is he Indian?"

"He says he is, but I don't know which people. He was raised White. He calls himself Kills in Daylight."

"A warrior's name. Is he one?"

Bina hesitated this time. "I'm not sure. I've never met him, never looked into his eyes, looked into his heart."

"But you are a warrior. I can tell. A police officer willing to risk your life for your people. Come, meet my wife. Share a meal with us and then we will ride to see where this Kills in Daylight might come."

"Thank you. But you reminded me I must tend to my duties first and radio my police chief. I will join you in a few minutes."

As he got out, Loq came over. Himiin gestured at the seat he'd just vacated. "Bina is going to call her chief. You will want to be part of that, I am sure."

Loq got in and closed the door. "What did you tell him?"

"That I'm Crow, not Raven, and now I must tell George that too."

14

———

George Tahamtaham didn't interrupt as Bina told him what happened after she left Joseph.

"What should we do about the pair back at Oxbow Dam?" she said.

"Let me tell you what I know first." The tribal police chief began with Salt Lake City.

Days before Kills in Daylight was scheduled to appear at a rally at the Utah state capitol building, supporters began plastering the city with posters featuring a photograph of him astride his gray stallion while holding aloft the Winchester with its silver receiver. Printed in red letters beneath his portrait was a slogan: "I don't want to be civilized. I want to be liberated."

Press releases announcing the rally were sent to newspapers and TV and radio stations. Reporters took notice when Marlon Brando was said to be flying in for the event and Johnny Cash and Buffy Saint-Marie were rumored to perform.

FBI field agents Robert Sexton and Sal Tujunga arrived and set up shop in the agency's local office. The senior agent headed a special task force comprised of the city police chief, county sheriff, and district attorney.

"Sexton wanted to throw a net over the entire city," Tahamtaham said. "Roadblocks would go up on every road in and out of town, private airfields would be shut down, and the main airport placed on high alert for potential skyjackers. He convinced the governor to put the National Guard on standby in case there was a riot. Sexton didn't care what the political fallout would be or how it played in Hollywood, Brando and Cash be damned."

The day of the rally, picket signs bobbed above a sea of chanting people in front of a makeshift stage with a curtain painted with images of buffalos, tepees, and arrows. Members of local tribes pounding on large powwow drums set the tone. A local rock band featuring Ute musicians kicked it off followed by a succession of American Indian Movement activists; each ended their remarks with a promise that Kills in Daylight was coming. Plainclothes cops milled among the attendees. Sexton and Tujunga watched through binoculars from an office building across the street.

As tensions rose and the crowd was whipped into a feverish pitch of anticipation, the final warmup speaker gave a war whoop into the microphone: "Now, the warrior you've been waiting for, the *Heyoka* whose medicine is more powerful than all of Washington's, please welcome Kills in Daylight."

The crowd surged forward as the curtain rose. Uniformed and plainclothes cops surged too. Sexton was barking orders into a handheld radio while Tujunga scanned for possible escape routes.

Kills in Daylight appeared on stage astride the gray stallion waving his Winchester and chanting. "Sovereign nationhood now! Take back our land now!"

"Not in person, but on a big screen," Tahamtaham said. "It was a movie. Not a *movie* movie like you see at the theater or a drive-in, but one using that new video recording tape cassette machine hooked to a projector."

"VHS," Bina said. "Stores began selling it this summer."

"Whatever it was, it looked very professional. Maybe he got help from Marlon Brando to make it."

"What happened next?" Loq asked.

"A plainclothes yanked the cord on the projector, but not before Daley called everybody to take up arms to fight for what was rightfully theirs. The FBI commandeered the videotape cassette to see if their lab people could determine where it was recorded. Sexton talked the local police into arresting the rally organizers, but since they had a permit and didn't break any laws, they were all released."

"Where are Sexton and Tujunga now?" Bina said.

"Headed your way. Sexton said Idaho first and then Montana, if need be."

"How do you know that?"

"He radioed me from his car. First thing he asked was where you two were."

"How did he know I wasn't at home or at the station?"

"Sexton says he's got a CI feeding him information."

"Did he tell you who it is?"

"That's the thing, he did. I suppose he was trying to save face after the fast one Daley pulled on him in Salt Lake. He said the informant is a private investigator hired by Killian Daley's father who's very public about the cases he's solved. Newspapers have written him up. He's been on TV too."

Loq asked him what kind of cases.

"Missing children, but especially rich people's who've joined cults. You know, the Moonies, Hare Krishnas, Charles Manson Family. He has a reputation for doing whatever it takes to bring them home, and if he breaks a few rules doing it, his rich clients with all their power and connections protect him."

"But Killian Daley is no kid and he didn't join a cult. He created one," Bina said.

"My guess is the investigator will charge his father even more to bring him home."

"How did Sexton find him?"

"He said they served together in Vietnam. Both were in military intelligence."

Loq looked down his high cheekbones as he sat listening in the front seat of Bina's pickup. "What's his name?"

"CD Larchmont. Sexton didn't say what the initials stand for."

"I know him."

"Let me guess. He was part of that special operation you did with Sexton in Vietnam."

Loq grunted. "Do you have news on Jack Candy?"

"Nothing more than what Bina just told me. I figure he's somewhere between Oxbow and you two chasing after Daley. Why?"

"Now that I know Larchmont is after Daley too, I can't be sure it was Candy shooting Freddy Salish and the woman and sinking their bodies in the Snake."

"Is that something Larchmont would do?"

"He's done worse. I don't know what CD stands for on his birth certificate, but his nickname was Collateral Damage when we were in country. Everybody was a combatant to him—nuns, rice farmers, old women, children, reporters."

Tahamtaham went silent. Bina clicked the mike. "Are you still there, George? Did we lose reception?"

"No, I'm thinking, is all. Might be that my fellow tribal police chief at Warm Springs is onto something. He's been doing some legwork after I told him what you said about it could've been a jealous husband or partner in crime who killed Sexton's CI. He discovered the victim had been tortured before being shot in the back of the head. Tortured by somebody who knew what they were doing."

"A Larchmont specialty," Loq said. "He could make anybody talk."

Tahamtaham cleared his throat. "Okay, listen up. Bina, this is a direct order. You're to leave those two bodies where they are. I'll take full responsibility for reporting them. Now, paperwork being what it is, it could take me two, three days, to do that. Understood?"

"Yes, sir."

"Good. My previous order still stands. Be safe. That goes for both of you."

"Ten-four." Bina cradled the mike. "Now we have two Jack Candys to deal with in addition to Killian Daley."

"Don't forget Sexton," Loq said.

Strands of hair had come loose from the beaded hair tie and were tickling her cheek. She blew at them out of the corner of her mouth. "Your sister better be worth it."

"She is."

"I'm going to have to take your word for it. Come on, Himiin and his wife are waiting for us. Let's show our respect."

Himiin's wife was named Taamsas, which meant wild rose in English. She wore a flat-brimmed hat too, but hers had a stampede string that she tied in a bow beneath her chin. It was made with the same ribbon that fluttered in the garden. She'd set the table on the front porch. A basket of corn muffins and another of wild grapes and huckleberries sprinkled with fresh mint leaves were placed in the center next to a pitcher of water drawn from White Bird Creek.

Once they took seats and said a blessing, Taamsas lifted the lid on a cast-iron pot and used a large wooden spoon to ladle stew into bowls. "This is made with biscuit root I picked myself, the vegetables come from our garden, and the rabbit from Creator."

Loq asked Himiin if they sold or traded the Appaloosas they raised.

"They raise us more than we them," he said. "But, yes, I am a horse-trader as was my father."

"Do you have children?" Bina asked.

"Two," Taamsas said. "Our daughter and her family live not far away and our son works at the clinic in Lapwai."

"Doing what?"

"He is a healer, although the piece of paper he got from university says doctor."

"You must be proud of him. I was a nurse for my people."

"You are no longer a nurse?"

"She is a police officer," Himiin said.

"Ah, the Umatilla are wise to have a woman do that job because women ask questions first and shoot later." The corners of her eyes crinkled.

"I'm only doing what all Indian women have been doing for centuries, and that is draw upon the strength Creator gave us and fight to survive and protect our families and homes."

They finished eating and Himiin said he was going to take them for a ride. Taamsas asked if she should plan on preparing supper and making up beds for them to spend the night.

"No, we're going to camp where your husband is taking us," Bina said, "but thank you all the same."

"Then I will pack supper to take with you."

Loq and Bina saddled their horses and tied on their bedrolls. Taamsas brought out packages wrapped in cloth made from meal sacks and tied with ribbons like those in the garden and her hat.

As she handed them to Bina, she said, "May the stars shine

softly on you tonight. May the stories they tell be of peace, not war, love, not hate."

The women hugged goodbye, and then Bina and Loq mounted their horses and followed Himiin who rode the Appaloosa with a fondness for carrots.

They soon turned off the dirt road and cut across a field spangled with summer wildflowers. Mountain bluebirds and red-winged blackbirds colored the tall grass and made the cloudless sky ring with their songs. White-tailed deer looked up from grazing near a stand of cottonwoods. A ferruginous hawk perched on the uppermost limb of the tallest tree, his unblinking yellow eyes following the riders.

A trail switchbacking up a hill took them higher. The summit was flat with a pond the shape of a teardrop in the middle. Himiin turned his mare to look down on the canyon. Loq and Bina did likewise.

"See it the way it was one hundred years ago," Himiin said, waving his hand in front of him as if wiping away time. "The grass is still green and as tall as an Appaloosa's legs. Tepees line both sides of White Bird Creek. Women are gathering and making food. Children are playing. Men are hunting."

He took a deep breath. "Hear it the way my grandfather tells it," he said as his voice grew deeper, slower.

"Days before we were camped at Tepahlewam near Tolo Lake. We go there in spring to gather camas that grows on the prairie. The Wallowa band journeyed from their home across the Snake River and mountains to join us.

"Their chiefs and our chiefs from the White Bird band hold council about the US government's latest betrayal. They have broken our old treaty and made a new one that takes all our land away except for a small plot at Fort Lapwai. All Nimiipuu must go there and are forbidden to leave.

"Some chiefs agree to sign the new treaty, but Chief Joseph

and Chief White Bird will not. They call it the 'steal' treaty because it steals our land.

"While at Tepahlewam, a band of young warriors seeking to avenge the murder of one of their fathers ride to the settlements along the Salmon River and kill many settlers. When council members learn of this, they know the cavalry will come to punish all of us and so we leave Tepahlewam and go home to White Bird Canyon. The Wallowa join us.

"Our scouts see the cavalry coming. Over one hundred soldiers with guns and horses. I ride with a peace party of six braves waving a white flag to parlay with the soldiers. As we near, a White man who is not a soldier but rides with them opens fire. Without trust, without respect, without honesty, there can be no peace. We shoot back to protect ourselves. More warriors ride to our aid.

"The fighting lasts all day. When night comes, it is over. Thirty-four soldiers are dead, two by my rifle alone. Only three of our warriors are wounded. It is a great victory, but our giving of thanks to Creator for protecting us is not long. We know even more soldiers will come. We break camp and leave to find freedom. We fight many battles as we ride to Canada. We have fewer than two hundred warriors while the cavalry sends two thousand after us.

"In August, we reach Big Hole. Soldiers attack us and fire into our tepees, killing many elders, women, and children, including my wife and infant son. We fight back and kill many soldiers. I have fired my rifle in so many battles, I have lost count of the soldiers fallen by my bullets. We leave Big Hole and continue our march.

"In October, we reach the Bear Paws Mountains. The weather has turned bitter. It is cold and snowing. We have traveled twelve hundred miles, fought many battles, and many Nimiipuu have died. Of the eight hundred men, women, and children who left White Bird Canyon, only four hundred of us remain.

"The army surrounds us at Bear Paw and we fight our last battle. We kill many soldiers, while they kill many of us, including three of our leaders, among them my Wallowa brother, Ollokot. I am shot twice, but still I fight.

"It grows colder, the snow grows deeper, our blankets are thin, our food runs low. Some want to fight on, some want to break through the soldier's lines and go on to Canada. But Chief Joseph does not agree with that. He knows it would only work if we leave the women, children, and sick behind. This he will not do. Sickened and saddened by all we have endured, he chooses to surrender.

"The army accepts and agrees none of us will be killed and we will be given blankets and food and our horses returned. But the government breaks their promise as they have done with every treaty. They do not send us to Fort Lapwai as was agreed. They do not return our horses. Instead, they send us to Oklahoma. Half our people die on the way. Those who survive are forced to stay there for eight years. Finally, they send us to Fort Lapwai.

"The government believed by doing that, they would break our blood forever, but by breaking their word and promises, they broke their own blood, for how can a people who lie, cheat, and steal remain unbroken?"

A breeze began to blow. The dry grass on the hillsides rippled like waves and then galloped like buffalo as the breeze grew stronger and carried Himiin's grandfather's words across White Bird Canyon and beyond.

The three sat their horses, each lost in their own thoughts as they mulled the victory there and the battles that followed, including the ones they themselves had fought to remain unbroken by discrimination and injustice.

Loq could see the battle below. He could feel the Appaloosa between his legs as he rode toward a skirmish line of cavalry while firing his weapon as they fired theirs at him. He could smell the gun smoke and hear the thuds of bullets striking flesh and the screams of wounded soldiers and the silence of the dead. And then he flashed forward to his own real combat experiences, when he'd stood shoulder to shoulder with US Marines trading shots with Viet Cong.

He shook his head, trying to dislodge the conflicting emotions that were welling inside him. He wondered if he'd been standing there with the US Cavalry one hundred years ago, would he have fired at fellow Indians? Would've he risked his life to save soldiers like he had in Vietnam? Finally, he wondered if Killian Daley and Carrie Horse might be right, that Indian people, land, and traditions were worth fighting for, no matter the cost.

15

———————

Himiin asked why they thought Killian Daley would come to White Bird Canyon.

"We believe he's planning a demonstration at one of the Nimiipuu battlefields," Bina said. "It'll be something dramatic that he can film and broadcast on TV."

"My grandfather shot bullets from a rifle and Kills in Daylight wants to shoot with a camera. Is that the way wars are fought now?"

Loq thought of Snaps and said, "Sometimes, but Daley and his followers are armed too."

The ferruginous hawk that was perched on the cottonwood took to the air, gliding on its broad wings, its feathered legs tucked close against its pale belly.

The horse-trader's flat-brimmed hat tilted as he watched the big raptor soar overhead. "Kills in Daylight will not fight with bullets or cameras at White Bird Canyon."

"Why not?"

"Because this is a place of victory. If his war plan is to show how Indian people are mistreated, it will be more powerful to do so at Big Hole or Bear Paw where soldiers killed so many of us."

"We still need to stop him before he gets there."

"Why?"

"To prevent other people from getting hurt or killed."

"The people who ride with him chose to be warriors. If they are wounded or killed, it is their right and honor. The same for the warriors who fight against him."

"Not everyone with him is there by choice. And not all who fight against him do so with honor."

"How do you know this?"

"My sister is with him. She's either being held against her will or he's fed her lies. I fought alongside two of those hunting him when we were in Vietnam. Their methods are dishonorable. Another uses his BIA badge as a license to kill Indians."

"Then you must make a choice. Stay here or go to Montana before he does. If you stay, you will be able to see headlights on every road that leads into the canyon. I will see you tomorrow when you come for your pickups. If you do not, then I will know Kills in Daylight kills in darkness also, and the next time I see you will be in the spirit world."

He started down the trail without another word.

"I hope he's right about Daley going straight to Montana and not stopping here," Bina said.

"Because you think he'll get the jump on us and send us to the spirit world?"

"So we can spend the night at this beautiful place without thinking of war and hate."

She dismounted Túxin, set her free to graze, and went about making camp. Loq remained on the spotted pony and panned the horizon with binoculars. He memorized the locations of the roads so he could find them in the dark and noted the most likely places where a large group of vehicles could hide. Fields were too exposed. Roadless hilltops unreachable. The mouths of a couple of gullies could work, but he rejected them when he didn't see a back door. After the Oxbow Dam shootout, Daley knew he was being chased by people who had no intention of taking him alive.

Maybe Himiin was right, Loq thought. Maybe Daley would steer clear of White Bird Canyon and head straight for the Montana battlefields. It would be a long, hard drive on forest service roads, but doable. But maybe he wasn't traveling with the convoy at all. Maybe duping the FBI at Salt Lake wasn't his one and only trick. He could be driving alone or riding on a Greyhound bus or on a commercial airline. Maybe he even had celebrity sympathizers flying him around in their private planes.

The ferruginous hawk screeched overhead. It spotted something scurrying far below. Loq watched as the big bird swept back its wings and dove, plucking a tiny field mouse from the tall grass without disturbing a blade, carrying the meal back to its perch high atop the cottonwood. There was no malice in the kill, no evil intent. It was just an instinctive act between predator and prey essential to keeping Mother Earth in balance.

Loq's thoughts turned to Bina and her desire to spend the night without thinking about killers. He didn't have to ask himself if he wanted the same thing.

"I'll go fetch water from the pond," he said, sliding off the pony and setting him free to graze alongside the roan.

"Since you're going, take this," Bina said.

He caught what she tossed him. It was a bar of soap.

"You've been camping every night for a week without taking a bath, haven't you?"

"I swam in the Snake last night."

"With everything but a bar of soap."

The teardrop-shaped pond was ringed with rushes. Loq stripped and waded past them to reach clear water. It was warmed by the sun and smelled and tasted fresh. He filled the canteens, lobbed them back onto shore next to his clothes, and dove. His breaststrokes took him underwater to the middle of the pond. When he surfaced, he floated on his back, occasionally kicking and sweeping his hands to keep from sinking as he closed his eyes and felt the golden rays wash over him.

He'd always liked to swim. It was freedom. Carrie had taught him how when he was four. "We live between a river and lake," she said, leading him by the hand to a pool of gentle water in the Williamson River that ran through Chiloquin. "How can you really know your home if you don't climb its trees, swim its waters, walk its paths, talk with its creatures?"

She didn't let go while they sat on a flat rock and dipped their toes in the river. "Trust me?"

"Always," he said.

"Then get on your belly, grab hold of my ankles, and skootch into the water. Keep holding on and start kicking. You'll get the hang of it. You'll see."

When he did, he felt like he was flying.

"You forgot something," she said.

"What?" he said, but then realized it wasn't Carrie talking. Loq flipped over. The pond wasn't too deep and he could stand. Bina was gliding toward him, holding aloft the bar of soap.

"You first," he said. "I can wait."

Her eyes sparkled with more than laughter. "I doubt it."

Bina glided closer before standing too. The beaded hair tie was gone and her long hair floated around her. She started soaping her neck, shoulders, and breasts, raising her hands one by one to reach her underarms. The bar disappeared as she washed below the waterline.

Finished, she jackknifed to rinse off. Her feet sliced the water without making a splash. When she surfaced, she was standing even closer to Loq.

Bina held out the bar of soap. "Your turn."

"You haven't washed your hair yet," he said.

"That's because I want you to."

"Want or need?"

"Both," she said, her eyes searching his. "And you?"

"Both."

Bina drew even closer and began soaping his neck, his shoulders, his chest. She hesitated when she realized she was touching scars that looked like they'd been made by claws. Blue showed dully between the welts.

"Is this from Vietnam?"

"No. The Bruneau River."

"Were you attacked by a bear?"

"A legend."

Her brows arched. "Did you stitch the wounds yourself? No doctor or nurse sewed you up. They're too ragged."

"Nick Drake did with a hook and fishing line."

Bina grimaced. "What did the tattoo say?"

"Semper Fi."

"Always faithful. The Marine Corps motto."

"You said you read a lot."

"Are you? Always faithful?"

"Yes."

Loq took the bar from her and began shampooing her hair. He paused when he recognized the thin scar that most people would mistake for a part. He traced it with his fingertip.

"You were shot," he said.

"Grazed. In the line of duty."

"By who?"

"A criminal."

"Did you shoot him back?"

"Yes."

"Mm. Do you still think about it?"

"Not today."

Bina dunked to rinse her hair and then took the bar of soap and flung it like a discus. It skipped across the pond and reached the shore. She didn't see it strike Leroy in the neck. She didn't see him at all, nor the fat bearded man either. All she saw was Loq and he took her in his arms and she wrapped her legs around his hips and the water rippled around them and then roiled and the sounds that filled the sky were as loud as the hawk's and just as natural and essential to keep the earth spinning round and round.

Later, when they were lying on their bedrolls with only a blanket and the twinkling lights of the universe spread over them, Bina said, "You still owe me the signed fix-it ticket for your trailer's taillights."

"You're thinking about that right now?"

"The law's the law."

"I already fixed it. A loose wire."

"I know, but I need a copy of the ticket signed by a cop to prove you did. Without it, you'll have to pay the fine."

"Then you sign it."

"It wouldn't be ethical since I was the issuing officer."

"Okay, when we get back, I'll ask George to do it."

Bina was lying with her head on Loq's shoulder watching stars shoot overhead. The moon was close enough to touch. "We will get back, won't we?" she said, no longer teasing.

"We will."

"You sound pretty sure about that."

"I learned there's plenty of things that can kill you. Doubt tops the list."

"What else are you sure about?"

"This. Right here. You. Me. What's beneath us. Above us. All around."

She slid her hand down and found him. "You're sure, all right."

He pulled her on top and they kissed long and slow and she started rocking, and this time they didn't hurry, as if they had all the time in the world and those with malice and evil intent were no closer than the furthest star.

16

Loq drove Bina's pickup after leaving his at Himiin's. They'd agreed one rig drew less attention, plus they could split the driving and gas. That's what they told themselves, but after last night, both knew the real reason. Loq also understood what it meant if he needed to save her life in a fight: as was true with his sister, he'd have to battle impatience and hesitation first.

The two-lane led northeast from White Bird Canyon and followed the Crooked Fork of the Lochsa River. It snaked up a narrow river canyon that scarred the forested face of the Bitterroot Mountains. Idaho disappeared in the side mirrors when they crested Lolo Pass. What took them four hours to reach had required Chief Joseph and the Nimiipuu six weeks, outfighting and outfoxing the US Cavalry every step of the way.

Loq kept a sharp eye as he drove down the steep and winding eastern side of the pass. Deer bolting onto the road were always a risk. So were trigger-happy Montana state troopers. They might mistake him and Bina for Kills in Daylight and Carrie Horse whose faces were on FBI wanted posters distributed to every law enforcement agency in the country.

The two-lane leveled out as they entered the Bitterroot River Valley. Cottonwoods and aspens lined both sides of the sparkling river and towering peaks etched the sky. A fisherman wading up to his thighs near the top of a riffle cast a fly and let it float toward a lazy pool where cutthroat trout waited for insects to wash down. A bull moose stood at the far end of the pool feeding on pondweed. Neither of the two mammals seemed frightened of the other.

Bina tried radioing her police chief on the secure channel again. This time she got through.

"Where are you?" George Tahamtaham said.

"We just crossed into Montana. Daley didn't show at White Bird Canyon."

"I know. He pulled another fast one, this time in person."

"What?"

He described how a Sheridan, Wyoming TV station was in the middle of broadcasting the local news when a door at the rear of the studio opened and in walked Killian Daley. He was dressed in full warrior regalia like he'd been wearing in the video shown at Salt Lake City, right down to his trademark Winchester with the silver receiver.

The station had a single security guard whose utility belt holstered a keychain and flashlight. As he considered what to do about the armed intruder, the young news anchor waved him off and stared straight at the television camera. Envisioning a ticket to a job at a Denver station, maybe even a network spot in New York, he summoned his most serious voice.

"Folks, hold on to your TV dinner trays. We have a breaking news story and it's happening live right here in our studio."

"Was Daley alone?" Bina said.

"Two young men were with him, but they stayed back to guard the door. The camera got a shot of them."

"One was Willie Hawkfeather, wasn't it?"

"Pretty hard to miss him with that spirit power tattoo on his neck. I watched the rebroadcast on the local Pendleton channel. Every station from here to Florida was airing it."

"Have the FBI identified him yet?"

"No, but it's only a matter of time. I was about to drive over to Belinda's and tell her he's alive when you radioed. I'll do it right after. Probably get a dead snake chucked at me for my trouble."

"What did Daley say?" Loq asked.

"Wait a second, are you two traveling in the same rig now?" The police chief's surprise came across the radio loud and clear.

"I left mine at White Bird Canyon."

Tahamtaham chewed on that development, but kept his opinion to himself. He launched into a recap of Daley's interview with the TV anchor who showed an instinct for the dramatic by alternating between calling him Kills in Daylight and FBI's most wanted man in America. He also reminded his viewers that he was conducting the interview while staring down the barrels of three guns.

Daley parried every question by restating his demands: The 1975 Indian Self Determination and Education Assistance Act didn't go far enough; sovereign nation status with more favorable terms needed to be granted to all American Indian tribes, including the 250 the federal government refused to recognize; tribal homelands as agreed to in original treaties—not 'steal treaties'—must be returned; and reparations paid to tribal members for two centuries of government-sanctioned genocide, land grabs, and enslavement.

"We've been slaughtered by the millions," he said as the camera pulled in for a close-up. "Our lands were stolen and our beliefs and traditions forbidden. Why? Because of greed, ignorance, and fear."

His long braids tied off at the ends with tanned deerskin whipped across his chest as his head shook in anger.

"Osage were murdered for their oil in Oklahoma; hundreds of Shoshone men, women, and children were butchered for their land at Bear River in Idaho; and Navajo were robbed of their age-old right to water from the Colorado River.

"Our children were stolen from us and imprisoned in government-sponsored boarding schools where they were forbidden to speak their own language or wear traditional garments and hairstyles. Many were physically and sexually abused. The bodies of thousands are buried in unmarked graves behind those schools.

"Our spiritual practices, including the Ghost Dance, Sun Dance, potlatches, healers, and the sacred use of peyote, were outlawed and punishable by imprisonment or execution. All this by a government sworn to uphold the US Constitution whose very first amendment guarantees the freedom of religion."

Daley paused to gather his breath. "The list of abuses is as long as the names of the tribes who were massacred in the name of Manifest Destiny. The Delaware at Gnadenhutten, the Arapaho and Southern Cheyenne at Sand Creek, the Lakota at Wounded Knee, and the Blackfeet at Marias River."

When the anchor insisted Daley answer whether or not he'd bombed the BIA office in Pendleton, killed an informant in Warm Springs, and exchanged gunfire with FBI agents there, the fugitive swore he was innocent.

"I'm being framed by the government because it fears me. They want an excuse to assassinate me like they did the great Shawnee chief Tecumseh for attempting to unite the tribes, Crazy Horse for trying to preserve the Lakota's traditional way of life, and Sitting Bull for resisting cultural domination."

Raising the Winchester over his head, Daley whooped. "While they may succeed in killing me, a thousand warriors will take my place, and for each who is killed, another thousand will stand and fight for freedom and justice."

Chanting, "We don't want to be civilized, we want to be liberated," he marched toward the rear of the studio. Willie Hawkfeather and the other young warrior opened the door and the trio vanished as quickly as they'd appeared.

"Didn't anyone call the Sheridan police or county sheriff's during the broadcast?" Bina said.

"The alert went out, but by the time law enforcement responded, it was as if Daley had sprouted wings and flown away," Tahamtaham said.

Loq grunted. "Goes with what I think. He's not traveling with the convoy. That's a rabbit for greyhounds. He's flying from place to place."

"On spirit wings or actual ones?"

"My guess is a rich man's. Some Hollywood type who's got a plane or it could be he charters one thanks to his father's allowance."

"You're probably right," the police chief said. "Daley's certainly a showman. The Sheridan broadcast was like a poster promoting the circus is coming to town. All the rebroadcasting allowed him to reach an even bigger audience than Salt Lake. Now we have to figure out where he's going to set up the big top."

"Big Hole," Bina said. "And he won't be alone. His followers will join him there."

"Not Bear Paw?" Tahamtaham said.

"The timing works better. The hundred-year anniversary of the battle is in August, remember?"

"I haven't forgotten, but we need a plan in case we're wrong and he ends up at Bear Paw."

"What about Sexton?" Loq said. "Have you heard from him since Sheridan?"

"An hour after the news aired. For an FBI agent who's been trained to have snowmelt running through his veins, he's got a temper. Sexton told me he knows you're tailing Daley. He accused me of covering it up."

"Did he threaten to report you again like he did at Jimmy Two Sons?" Bina said.

"He did."

"You don't sound very concerned."

"Why should I be? There's no one standing in line who wants my job, outside of you, of course."

"I never said I wanted your job."

"You don't need to. It's written in the stars and I trust them more than people."

The police chief clicked his tongue. "Here's what Sexton ordered. Bina, you're to come back to the rez immediately, and Loq, you're to meet him in Butte. If you both don't do as he says, he'll issue federal arrest warrants and every state trooper in every state will consider you armed and dangerous and act accordingly."

"Why a meeting?" Loq said.

"He didn't spell it out, but when he told me CD Larchmont will be there too, I believe he's planning something along the lines of what you did for him in Vietnam."

"He wants you to kill Daley," Bina said. She'd turned from looking at the radio's mike to Loq sitting next to her. "That's what Operation Phoenix was, wasn't it?"

Loq didn't answer, but she was right. Phoenix was a CIA program designed to destroy the Viet Cong through interrogation, torture, and assassination. Sexton had been up to his aviator sunglasses in it. So had Larchmont. And grunts like him with special skills were ordered to carry out the dirty work.

"When does he want to meet?" Loq said.

"As fast as you can get to Butte," Tahamtaham said. "He's already there."

"That means he knows about the historic trail."

"He does."

"How did he find out?"

"Larchmont told him."

"How did he find out?"

"He's been tailing them."

"Did he also tell Sexton that he shot and killed two of Daley's followers and sank their bodies in the Snake River?"

"Sexton wouldn't tell me if he had, but we don't know that it wasn't Jack Candy. All he said was Larchmont captured a deserter, a guy who decided he didn't want to be a warrior anymore. In exchange for being let go, he told Larchmont everything, except for the specific location for the demonstration. He insisted Daley is keeping that a secret from everyone."

Except Carrie, Loq thought. "What about Jack Candy? Is he part of Sexton's plan too?"

"I asked him that, but Sexton says he hasn't heard from him. Neither have I. It's like Candy went up in a cloud of smoke."

"Or maybe down to the bottom of the Snake River buckled in the front seat of his Power Wagon. If that's true, then the question is, did Daley or Larchmont park him there."

Static filled the radio. Loq said, "Where in Butte is the meet?"

"You're to go to the M&M Bar and Café on Main Street. It's the oldest watering hole in town. He'll leave a message for you there."

"I don't like the sound of this," Bina said.

"That makes three of us," Tahamtaham said. "Right, Loq?"

"Like doesn't have anything to do with it. Going there does."

"If you're going, then I'm going too," Bina said.

"Sexton will issue an arrest warrant if you don't come back to the rez," Tahamtaham said.

"If you think I'm going to listen to him, then go ask my *katá* how well I listen when she tells me what I should and shouldn't do."

"I don't need to speak to your grandmother to know that. It's one of the reasons I hired you. Radio me again before you walk through the M&M's doors. I might have more information for you. Over and out."

Thirty minutes later they reached Missoula. Loq pulled into a gas station near the university to fuel up. A big white letter M blazed on a grassy hillside behind the campus's clock tower. Summer classes were still in session from the look of all the jeans-clad, long-haired students passing by, males and females alike.

Bina went to use the restroom. When she returned, she said, "Guess what's plastered on the wall in there? It's Daley's FBI wanted poster only it's been turned into a call to arms. They've printed 'Liberate Kills in Daylight' in block letters across it. Underneath is the time and date of a sit-in at the dean's office sponsored by a student Indian rights group."

"When Daley's ready, he'll send word for college kids to come to Big Hole," Loq said. "He'll draw a crowd. It's less than three hours away from campus. Same from Montana State in Bozeman."

"Along with supporters from the state's seven reservations. Blackfeet, Kootenai, Crow, Assiniboine, Lakota, Chippewa, and Northern Cheyenne could all be there too." Bina breathed in deeply. "Those are our brothers and sisters."

"Mm. More the reason we must get to Butte to keep Big Hole from becoming another battlefield."

The highway ran down a valley between the Rockies and Bitterroots. Traffic was sparse. The weather changed the farther south they drove. Towering cumulonimbus clouds veined with lightning were crashing into the highest peaks. Daylight dimmed as a particularly menacing cloud blocked the sun. Thunder boomed, startling the horses in the trailer. They whinnied and stomped their hooves.

Loq slowed as the visibility worsened. When they approached an intersection near Garrison, he slammed on the brakes and brought the pickup to a shuddering stop. A jackknifed big rig blocked both lanes. A smashed-up sedan was off to the side.

"Looks like the truck T-boned it," Bina said. "Someone could be hurt. I'll check the sedan. You see about the trucker."

Loq got out and fast-stepped toward the big rig. Steam was rising from both sides of the hood. He could see the driver slumped over the wheel. Loq grabbed the door handle and yanked it open. He stepped up on the side bar. "Can you hear me? You okay?"

The driver groaned and then sat up quickly. He was pointing a gun.

Loq jerked backward and dove, figuring he could roll under the big rig's trailer and come up on the opposite side by the time the gunman either pulled the trigger or got out of the cab to hunt him down. But before he hit the ground, something whacked him in the head, and as he fell into darkness, he wondered if he'd been shot or why he hadn't sensed someone with a club sneaking up behind him.

17

———

YELLOW LOTUS

The trail from Red Mountain started off dry, scrubby, and rocky, and stayed that way as Johnny and I rode east in search of the star lizard plant. A series of giant tilted basalt blocks spewed from ancient volcanoes and riven by creeks rose in front of us. Most of the tracks on the trail had been made by deer, pronghorn antelope, and bighorn sheep.

The first drainage we reached was Stony Creek.

"What do you think?" I said as we stopped to take a look.

"No steep cliff."

"I agree. The canyon isn't very deep, but it sure is pretty."

The trail led us to the creek's headwaters and a chain of oasis-like pools. We dismounted and filled our canteens. Black-necked stilts were hunting for frogs and water insects. Willow flycatchers perched on branches. Their songs sounded like zippers zipping up and down.

We set off again and were soon riding across a sea of big sagebrush dotted with islands of desert grasses and stands of cottonwood and alder. Jackrabbits tried to hide in the brush, but their long ears gave them away. A ferruginous hawk circled overhead, its white belly and the underside of its wings resembling mares' tails against the blue sky.

Seeing it made me think of Loq and where he might be as he tracked down Killian Daley and Carrie Horse. Like the big hawk above that ranged throughout the west, he could be anywhere from Canada to Mexico, from the Pacific to the Rockies.

The trail started climbing and switchbacked up the steep side of Mahogany Ridge. As the sun reached its zenith, the baking rocks turned the color of the ridge's name.

"Help Kosse out by leaning forward," I called over my shoulder.

"I know. I'm not a baby!"

I immediately regretted saying it. Johnny had become a good rider since we adopted him. Gemma had taught him, and there was no better teacher or rider in Harney County. She had the blue ribbons to prove it from her rodeoing days competing in barrel racing, breakaway, and team roping.

It was tough going as we headed toward the summit of the ridge. The beating sun didn't make it any easier. The sweatband of my hat was soaked and rivulets were running down both sides of my face. Sweat yoked my shirt, front and back.

No shade could be found up top, and so we started down the other side. I spotted a copse of aspens and rode toward it. The air cooled when we were beneath the welcoming canopy.

"It's getting late in the day and the horses need a rest after that climb," I said. "Let's camp here tonight and get a fresh start in the morning. The next big drainage is Trout Creek. The mountains are named after it, so maybe it's the largest and deepest."

"Trout Creek is English. What's the Indian name?" Johnny said.

I shook my head. "I should've asked November what it is in Numu since her people have lived here thousands of years. I'm sure we'll see pictographs they left behind. Bighorns. Directionals. Bows and arrows. The Shoshone also live here and there's probably a Newe name for the mountains too."

"Shoshone and Paiute. Like Hex Taggert," Johnny said.

That made me sit up straighter.

"You heard Pudge and me talking about him?"

"I'm not a baby!"

"So you keep me telling me."

"Then stop treating me like one."

We found the spring that provided life-giving water to the trees. It was in a small clearing and we set up camp beside it. After picketing and unsaddling the horses, we spread out a tarp and unfurled our bedrolls.

"Your choice," I said. "You want to gather wood for a fire or rocks to make a fire ring?"

"Wood," he said.

"Small pieces are best. Dry twigs for kindling and broken branches up to about this big around." I made a circle with my fingers. "Make sure they're branches and not snakes before you pick them up." But he'd already turned his back and stomped away in a huff.

I chided myself for treating him like a little kid again. No doubt he'd lit many cooking fires while living on the streets of Saigon and later in the jungle.

With each rock I picked up and put in a circle, I said, "Show don't tell, show don't tell."

Johnny returned with an armful of wood and dropped it. Without being asked, he went to check on the horses to make sure they had ample graze and water.

I rifled through the oilskin bag packed with foodstuffs. When Johnny came back I asked if he wanted stew, cold fried chicken, or rice and beans for supper.

"I don't care," he said.

"Let's have the stew. The others will keep longer."

He shrugged.

With the fire going, I opened a plastic container and poured the contents into a pot set on a flat rock surrounded by embers. Soon, the scent of simmering beef, potatoes, carrots, and herbs began to mix with the smoke from the crackling aspen wood.

"Tea or coffee?" I said.

Again, Johnny shrugged.

I stopped biting my tongue. "November packed dessert too. Chocolate chip cookies or *banh pia*?"

That got his attention. "She made *banh pia*?"

Mooncakes were a favorite Vietnamese dessert. I knew they were special to Johnny. It was the last thing he'd eaten with his mother before her pimp stabbed her to death behind a boom-boom club on Tu Do Street.

"No," I said. "I wanted to see if you were listening or not."

"You're so mean." He simmered like the stew cooking on the campfire.

"Only trying to show you that I listen when you talk about what you went through in Vietnam. We should be able to talk about anything. I'm your father, you're my son. The more we talk, the better we know each other, the closer we'll be."

"You never talk about Vietnam," he fired back. "What you did there. How many *gooks* you killed."

I smacked my knee. "We don't use that word. Ever!"

"Boys call me that. At the orphanage. At school in No Mountain. Dirty *gook*!"

"And I've talked to the teacher and their parents about it."

"Did more than talk," I muttered to myself, remembering an up-close-and-personal "conversation" I had with a particularly thick-skulled father who resented me telling him his bullying son was only modeling his own bigotry.

Johnny scowled. "So, if I ask you a question, will you answer it?"

"Anything you want to know, fire away. But then I get to ask you one and you answer. Deal?"

"Deal. Who goes first?"

"You go."

Johnny sat next to me. I spooned stew into a bowl and handed it to him. Then I filled one for myself.

As I took my first bite, Johnny said. "How many Viet Cong did you kill?"

"I don't know. We were also fighting NVA, the North Vietnamese Army."

"You're lying. You know how many."

"I've never lied to you and never will. A soldier who counts his kills is no soldier at all. Every life is sacred, including those you're forced to take."

I ate another spoonful of stew. "When I served in Vietnam, we believed—or were led to believe—that we were fighting to protect the people of South Vietnam against their enemy. That made the North Vietnamese our enemy too."

"Not all South Vietnamese were good. Pimp who killed my mama? Bad. Man who hurt Sen Vàng? Bad. Policeman who tried to kill me? Bad."

"Sen Vàng? Who's that? My Vietnamese is pretty rusty, but isn't *sen* the word for the lotus flower?"

Johnny nodded. "*Sen* is lotus. *Vàng* is yellow. *Sen vàng* is yellow lotus. Sen Vàng is the name of the *bui doi* girl with yellow hair."

"Wait. *The* girl with yellow hair? The older *bui doi* who taught you how to survive on the streets? Who shared the goat shed with you and two other *bui doi* boys for a couple of years?"

"Yes. The girl with yellow hair is Sen Vàng."

"You never called her that before. You always said she disappeared after she went out to buy *banh pia* from a cart with the money you earned from fetching cigarettes for GIs. When she didn't come back, you went to look for her. A crooked cop grabbed you and told you the cart vendor snatched her and took her to his place and ... well, did horrible things to her."

"That's right," Johnny said.

I'd never be able to forget what happened to Johnny next. The cop told him he was going to do those things to the girl with yellow hair too after he dealt with him. He dragged Johnny to the city dump—known as the field of dead dogs—but as the cop swung his bamboo baton at the boy's head, a VC guerrilla popped up and shot him. The guerrilla took Johnny out of Saigon and left him with a group of other runaways and villagers whose homes had been destroyed. They banded together to survive. Finding food. Stealing food. Moving from place to place to stay out of harm's way.

"Why do you call the girl with yellow hair Sen Vàng? Did you find out later that was her name or did you always know?"

Johnny only shrugged and started picking the chunks of stew meat out of the bowl and eating them first. Then he ate the potatoes and finally the carrots. He lifted the bowl to his lips and drank the broth. I tried to be patient watching him, but I needed to know more. Sen Vàng. Yellow Lotus. The girl with yellow hair. She was the key to both of Johnny's halves, the one still in Vietnam and the one in America.

We finished supper and I boiled water for tea for Johnny and cowboy coffee for myself. The sun sank behind the Pueblo Mountains, the next range over. Evening stars came out one by one and then one hundred by one hundred and then one million by one million.

I added more sticks to the fire as Johnny sipped his peppermint and sage tea sweetened with honey and I my coffee brewed with curiosity.

"Tell me more about Sen Vàng," I said. "Did you ever see her again?"

He nodded.

"Where?"

"At the camp in the jungle where the Viet Cong soldier took me. Sen Vàng was already there. Another soldier had taken her. When she escaped from the *banh pia* seller, the two Viet Cong soldiers found her. She begged them to find me because she knew I'd go looking for her and the policeman would catch me. He always took *bui doi* to the field of dead dogs, how the soldier knew where to look."

"Why didn't you ever tell us this before?"

"Because I was afraid if you and Gemma knew the truth, you'd send me back to the orphanage."

"We'd never do that."

"Not even if you knew I fought alongside the Viet Cong— your enemy?"

I started to say something, but sipped my coffee instead. The bitterness I tasted was not from using too many grounds, but the realization that I'd been deluding myself all this time into believing what Johnny had originally told us. I should've known it was a fabrication because the jungle was where my war took place during the three years I led long-range reconnaissance patrols.

My squad had been ambushed by guerrillas that included fighters who would be going to grade school if they lived in the States. We'd intercepted old men and women and their grand-children hauling Chinese weapons on bicycles and in ox carts down the Ho Chi Minh Trail. They didn't always drop their cargo when ordered. I could still see a nine-year-old firing an

AK-47 at us, a girl barely in her teens shouldering a rocket launcher made from a bamboo stalk.

It was time to rip the bandage completely off, and there was no stick to bite down on.

"The girl with yellow hair saved your life by asking the VC to go look for you," I said.

"Yes, she saved it not once, but four times."

"How did she get her name, Sen Vàng?"

Johnny looked up at the stars as if he could escape answering me there, but then returned his gaze to the campfire, the flames reflecting in his seen-too-much eyes.

"I will tell you, but please don't ever tell Gemma because I don't want her not to love me."

And so he told me.

The leader of the camp called himself Comrade Minh. He wore a black shirt with a blue and red flag pinned to the left pocket, brown wool pants, a black and white checked necker-chief, and rubber sandals. An AK-47 hung from his shoulder and a Russian-made Tokarev semiautomatic rode in a black leather holster on his hip.

He greeted Johnny with a stinging slap across the face. "I do not trust *bui doi*," he said and accused him of being a spy for the *Mëo*, using the Vietnamese word for Americans.

"I'm not a spy," Johnny cried.

"You will have to prove it," Comrade Minh said. "You and the *bui doi* girl."

He dragged them to a fenced enclosure. Inside were captured South Vietnamese soldiers and civilians who'd been labeled traitors. They were bound and tied to stakes. Comrade Minh unholstered his Tokarev and shot the closest in the head. Johnny cried out, but the girl with yellow hair didn't utter a sound.

Comrade Minh handed the pistol to Johnny. "Execute the next one. Now!"

"I can't. I won't. I ... I don't know how."

Comrade Minh snatched the gun away and aimed it at Johnny. "Then you are a spy and it is my duty to execute you."

"Wait!" the girl with yellow hair said. "Give me the gun."

The guerrilla leader handed it to her.

"How does it work?"

"Simple. Point and pull the trigger."

The gun was heavy and she had to hold it with both hands. She pointed it at a man who was dressed in street clothes. "You sell *banh pia* and rape girls!" she shouted and shot him.

Comrade Minh took the gun back. "Very good. You are not a spy, but your little friend is."

"No, he's not." She turned to Johnny. "Take the gun. I will help you. If you don't, he will kill you."

Comrade Minh handed the gun to Johnny. The weight made the boy's hand drop. The girl with yellow hair grabbed his hand in hers, raised the gun, and pointed it at a man wearing a uniform.

"He's the policeman who has killed many *bui doi*," she whispered to Johnny. "He was going to kill you."

She placed her finger over his and squeezed. The gun went off. The man slumped. Johnny cried.

From then on, Johnny and the girl with yellow hair were accepted and assigned camp chores. They also received weapons training and learned how to make booby traps. Covered pits with bamboo stakes on the bottom, trip wires across jungle trails that set off explosives.

One day, they were ordered to go to another Viet Cong camp with some others and bring back ammunition. On their return, they were intercepted by an enemy unit comprised of GIs and South Vietnamese soldiers. A firefight broke out. Outnumbered, the band of guerrillas was chased into the jungle. The girl with yellow hair saw a muddy water buffalo wallow. Dragging Johnny by the hand, she jumped in. They hid in it, breathing through the hollow stems of reeds.

When they finally emerged, it was sunrise, Comrade Minh and other guerrillas spotted them. From that moment on, he called the girl with yellow hair Sen Vàng after the lotus flower that grows out of the mud beneath the water, blooms during the day, and then retreats below the surface at night.

"You are good luck," he said. "The lotus is a symbol of rebirth and you represent the rebirth of a united Vietnam."

The name stuck and Sen Vàng's reputation grew. Though she was older than Johnny by a few years, he fell hopelessly in love with her. They were sent on more missions, each more dangerous than the last, but every time, they managed to emerge unscathed.

Months passed. Johnny and Sen Vàng fought in ambushes and full-out battles. After an especially bloody firefight, Comrade Minh told them he had a secret mission for them. Since they were *bui doi* and Johnny spoke some English, he was going to send them to a *Mëo* airbase the next day. They were to pretend they were searching for their GI fathers. Playing on the *Mëo's* reputation for being soft-hearted and generous, they would get themselves invited to the mess hall for a meal. When the camp assembled to eat, they would sneak out and let in other guerrillas who were hiding outside the perimeter. Their objective was to blow up the camp's armory.

All went according to plan, but at the last moment, Johnny and Sen Vàng were discovered when a GI recognized them from a previous firefight. The pair took off running with armed soldiers in hot pursuit. They ran past a cargo plane. The tail ramp was down.

"Run up there and hide," Sen Vàng told Johnny.

"Not without you," he said.

"That's an order," she said. "I will lead the enemy to where our comrades are hiding. They will ambush them. When the shooting stops, come back down the ramp and we'll go set off the bombs."

Johnny charged up the ramp. Once inside the plane, he heard American voices. He hid behind a large crate. Suddenly, the ramp closed and he was trapped. He waited in the dark for it to open again. Time passed and he fell asleep. When he woke, the air was cold, the plane was trembling, and the noise was deafening. He'd never flown before, but had seen plenty of American fighter jets and bombers. He realized the cargo plane was airborne like them. He fell back asleep. When he woke again, he was staring in the face of a red-faced man with a big grin.

"Looks like we got ourselves a stowaway," the airman said. "Well, kiddo, here's a candy bar. Make yourself comfortable because the next stop is the good ol' US of A."

Johnny sounded weary as he finished telling the story. "I'm tired. I'm going to sleep."

He slid into his bedroll and I finished my coffee watching the flames in the campfire die and the embers slowly fade like spent meteors. My eyelids grew heavy watching them, but I knew my exhaustion was more from finally understanding why Johnny was the way he was.

I tried to be quiet so as not to wake him when I lay down on my bedroll. I did what I always did when I slept under the stars and picked out the constellations in alphabetical order.

"I'm going back to Vietnam," Johnny said. "Soon, I hope, but one day, for sure. I must."

"To look for Sen Vàng," I said.

"You know why I have to?"

"Of course, and I understand."

"You won't try to stop me?"

"No."

"Why not?"

"Because I'm going with you. I need to go back to Vietnam too. All of us who fought there have to if we're ever to find peace."

18

R ed began to nibble at the blackness. Falling gave way to spinning and then to swaying. Water washing over rocks became murmurs. Murmuring turned into singing and the singing into jingling. The blackness was a towering storm cloud and the red was lightning coursing through it like blood in a body.

But whose body? His or someone else's? And who was his? Who was he?

The jingling stopped. The water washing over rocks was washing his face. His, but who was he?

"Loq," said the singer who'd stopped singing and the dancer who'd stopped jingling. "Loq, can you hear me? Can you open your eyes?"

He tried, but couldn't. His eyes had been stitched shut. Though he couldn't see, he remembered seeing that before. A soldier in black pajamas tied to a chair. A soldier being tortured. A soldier having his eyes stitched shut if he didn't tell his captors what he knew. Tell the man who was doing the stitching the location of a Viet Cong general.

"Loq, open your eyes. I need you to respond so I know you can hear me, understand me, understand anything."

The water washed across his forehead again. Water from a strip of cloth. Water wetted his lips when the cloth was wrung. Water dripped into his mouth. He remembered seeing that before too. A soldier in black pajamas tied to a chair. A soldier being tilted back with a towel placed over his face and a bucket of water being poured as he sputtered and choked. The water not stopping until he told the man who was pouring it what he wanted to know about the popular guerrilla leader.

"Loq, I need you to open your eyes. Come on, I need you to. It's Bina." The voice gulped air. "I need you."

He could see her. Dancing the jingle dance. Riding the roan mare. Swimming toward him in a pond on top of a hill. Shampooing her hair. Looking into her eyes as they made love between earth and sky. He breathed in, breathed out, and forced his eyes open so he could see her again.

"You were dancing the jingle dance, singing a healing song," he said.

Bina Mantioc sighed with relief. "You're back. You heard me."

"I felt you. Your medicine is strong."

"*Anitá's* medicine is. That's what our old ones called Creator."

"Where are we?"

"I'm not sure. The wreck was a setup. They jumped out from behind the sedan and tied my hands and pulled a sack over my head. They shoved us into the semi's trailer. I counted off minutes while we were inside. One hundred and sixty. When we stopped moving, they pulled us out and locked us in here."

Loq sat up but faltered as the black clouds began to swallow the bolts of red lightning. Bina got her arm around him to keep him from falling backward.

"Easy," she said. "You probably have a concussion. Easy now."

He looked around as much as the throbbing in his head would allow him to shift his eyes. The room was dimly lit. The walls were made of wooden boards, straw littered an earthen floor, the rafters were open, the ceiling was the underside of a shake roof. It was a stable or a ranch's outbuilding.

His memory started flooding back. The wreck on the road to Butte. The trucker and the gun.

"Was I shot?"

"Struck from behind."

"Who set us up, Daley, Sexton, or Candy? Who hit me?"

A door swung open.

"I did, little brother," Carrie Horse said. "I had to stop you from becoming the FBI's patsy. I knocked you out to keep you from getting yourself shot by one of our warriors who was only trying to save you."

Loq's sag against Bina's arm was momentary. He shook off the red sparks and spiraling black void as anger replaced them.

"Then you made a mistake, big sister, because I won't stop until you're back in Chiloquin."

Carrie walked toward him and tilted her head, a wry expression blooming on her face. "*A'ho*, little brother, how I've missed you. I miss your single-mindedness, your fierce loyalty. And most of all, I miss racing with you and always being a step ahead, like I am now."

Someone had followed her into the room, someone who was holding a revolver.

"I'll explain everything," Carrie said, "but first I need to ask your friend something."

Bina raised her chin. "The only thing I'm going to tell you is, you're under arrest. Killian Daley too."

Carrie's eyebrows arched. "And I'll tell you something. My

brother has had many women fall in love with him and he's broken just as many hearts."

"But he's never been with a woman who's broken as many as me."

Carrie laughed. "You have a warrior's heart like him. You're ferocious, loyal, and beautiful too. But can your blood run cold and your nerves stay steel when they need to?"

She didn't wait for an answer, but launched into a story about the time Loq showed both to his tribe and all the people who lived in Chiloquin. He was fifteen at the time and spent more days out of the schoolroom than in. Loq would head into the woods with nothing more than a bow and a quiver of arrows he'd made himself in the old way. He'd be gone for days hunting deer or whatever animals that could be turned into meals for his family and neighbors.

One day when he'd been gone for a longer than usual time, a crazy man appeared on the railroad tracks that ran through Chiloquin. Ranting and raving and armed with a semiautomatic rifle, he proceeded to fire off magazine after magazine, shooting holes through fence posts, mailboxes, and at cars and houses. Klamath County Sheriff's deputies responded and cordoned off the area while they came up with a plan for stopping him without getting shot themselves.

While they were busy weighing the options, Loq came walking down the railroad track, alternating between stepping from tie to tie and using a rail as a tightrope. The shooter spotted him and fired a couple of warning shots over his head, but Loq kept on coming.

When he drew closer, the shooter ordered him to halt. "I'll drill you if you don't."

"I bet I can outshoot you," the teenager said. "Pick a target and I'll hit it with an arrow. If I miss and you can hit it with your gun, then you win and I lose."

The shooter's laugh sounded like a coyote's yip. "You're on."

He let Loq get closer. "The railroad crossing sign over there. X marks the spot. Got to hit it dead center where the two pieces cross."

Loq nocked an arrow, pulled it back, and let fly. All who were watching drew a breath. The arrow missed. The shooter howled. "Not even close. Watch this."

He shouldered his rifle, clamped his cheek to the walnut stock, sighted, and fired. The center of the X splintered when hit with a .308 round.

"Two out of three," Loq said.

"You're on."

Loq nocked another arrow and let fly. It hit what was left of the X's center. "Your turn," he said.

"Lucky shot," the crazed shooter groused.

He shouldered his rifle again, clamped his cheek, and aimed. As he zeroed in on the target, Loq quickly nocked a third arrow, drew it back, and let fly. The arrow sang sweetly as it flew and pierced both of the shooter's cheeks, pinning his face to the rifle's wooden stock.

Everybody watching cheered and the deputies rushed in. Loq reached the shooter before them. "You lose," he said. "You took your eye off the real target."

Bina said, "I would've expected nothing less of your brother, did you?"

Carrie's eyes narrowed. "Maybe Loq finally has met his match—one even both our tribes' matchmakers couldn't have bettered."

She crouched so she and Bina were looking right at each other. "I know you from the powwow at Fort Klamath. You honored every woman with your dancing. Now you do so again as one of the first to become a police officer for your people."

"Don't think I won't uphold the law."

"Sister ... may I call you sister? You might think you know all about what criminals Kills in Daylight and I must be, but hear us out before you judge us."

"I'm not a judge, only a cop, but I'll listen." Bina looked past Carrie at the young man with the revolver standing by the door. "I see you, Willie Hawkfeather. George Tahamtaham saw you on television too. We're glad you're still alive and not dead like your friend Freddy Salish."

Willie's face tightened, but he made no move to say anything.

"Did you see who killed Freddy, put him and the woman in the station wagon and push it into the river?"

He remained silent.

"Help me find out who did it and I'll help you when you come home and face the judge for breaking probation," she said.

"I'm never going back," he said.

Loq asked Carrie how they knew where he and Bina were going so they could set up the ambush. "The steam from the truck's radiator and the wrecked sedan fooled us."

She nodded. "Remember the game we used to play as children? One of us would try and track the other. I always won because you were so focused on catching me, you became blinded. I'd double back and follow you."

"I didn't forget that when I was in Vietnam. It's why I'm alive and others aren't."

"But you've forgotten it now. Wherever we've been, we left people behind to watch for trackers. We've been following you ever since you left Chiloquin. We don't need to follow too closely. People see a man like you and remember and tell us when we ask. In Prineville, outside John Day, on the Umatilla Reservation, in Joseph, and the night you two spent in White Bird Canyon."

Carrie turned to Bina. "I'm sure you talk with your police

chief by radio. We stay in touch with our scouts too. How we always know where you are. Only we speak in the Oneida language like the Codetalkers spoke in Navajo. Kills in Daylight taught us his people's tongue."

Loq said, "I heard no one really knows who his birth parents were."

"He knows, and that's all that matters."

"Is that how you knew we were going to Butte, you overhead us on the radio?" Bina said.

"No, little sister. We knew that because we know the two FBI agents who've been chasing us are there. Robert Sexton and Sal Tujunga. The agency has a field office in Butte."

"You must have someone on the inside who told you Sexton ordered me to meet him there," Loq said.

"We have Kills in Daylight. He's a powerful shaman as well as a warrior chief. He can travel anywhere by closing his eyes. He sees all, hears all. When you clear your mind of all the lies the FBI has spread about him, you'll see for yourself and understand."

"Does he understand the FBI is laying a trap for him? Sexton was military intelligence in Vietnam, another label for CIA. He's working with a man who tortured and killed hundreds there."

When Loq said it, he could see CD Larchmont stitching eyelids closed, pouring buckets of water until a captive either confessed or drowned. Regardless of whether they talked or not, all ended up with a bullet to the head fired by Larchmont himself.

"There's also a BIA investigator after you. Jack Candy. He's a killer with a grudge. His girlfriend was in the building that was blown up in Pendleton."

Carrie made a dismissive gesture. "The BIA has a long, dark history of sanctioning Jack Candys."

"That doesn't make him any less dangerous."

"We'll see about that."

"You're playing with matches. Candy is only a flame. Sexton and Larchmont are a wildfire."

"We know what Sexton is planning, but remember what our grandfather told us when he set traps in the forest. It's not what you use for bait. It's remembering where you placed them so you don't step in them yourself."

Carrie Horse stood. "I must go. Someone will bring you food. Eat, rest. I'll return and take you to Kills in Daylight." She walked toward the door. "For your own safety, don't try to escape. Our warriors are stationed everywhere."

Willie followed her out and a padlock clicked. Loq struggled to stand. Once he was on his feet, he touched the back of his head, feeling a bump but not split skin. Bina stood too and they quickly searched the room. They found no windows.

Bina drew close and whispered, "Do you think they're listening?"

He nodded. "If I kick a board loose so we can make a run for it, they'll hear it."

"Or the guards will see your boot sticking out and shine it with a bullet." She gave a sly grin.

Loq returned it. It felt good to grin. It felt good to be alive.

"What do you want to do?" she said.

"Wait to talk to Daley. We'll let him know that if we don't show up in Butte, Sexton will call out the National Guard to search for us, if he hasn't already."

"Maybe that's what Daley wants. We're the bait for the trap he's setting."

"Carrie's right."

"About the trap?"

"About you and me. We think alike."

"About some things." Bina wanted to touch his face, but resisted. "Carrie's not going to go home no matter what you say to her. The only way she will is if and when she decides to go herself."

"She's like you too. Not always doing what your *katá* tells you."

"We're both women in a changing world, changing even for our people whose ways are as old as time. We can't ignore that changes are happening. We must draw power from them, not let them overpower us. All women—all things—must grow and change or they are dead."

"Are you changing the way you think about Killian Daley?"

"I'll decide that when I meet him."

The door opened. Willie Hawkfeather escorted a woman carrying a wicker picnic basket. She wore fashionable Western-style clothes and her blonde hair had the look of regular visits to a beauty salon. Turquoise and silver bracelets gleamed on her slender wrists. They matched a squash blossom necklace.

"Hello, I'm Martha Lance. You must be hungry."

She set the basket down, pulled out a square of gingham, and spread it on the ground. Then she knelt on it and laid out plates and cutlery along with containers of food.

Beckoning them to help themselves, she said, "There's fried chicken, biscuits, tomatoes from the garden, and cookies for desert."

Bina sat cross-legged next to her and Loq squatted across from them.

"I can see the family resemblance between you and your sister," Martha said. "Carrie is an amazing woman."

Loq asked how she knew her.

"Through my husband, Benjamin. This is our ranch. In addition to raising cattle, he's also an attorney." She smiled. "Truth is, he's a much better trial lawyer than a rancher. He never loses. He's represented Killian for years. Or should I say, Kills in Daylight. Though I'm not fond of his nom de guerre. He's a spiritual man, a poet. His words will be quoted long into the future the same as Black Elk's and Crowfoot's."

"You don't think he's done the things he's been accused of?" Bina said.

"Oh, he's certainly guilty of being a rebel with a cause. Even my husband couldn't prove his innocence when he's been arrested and charged with trespassing after occupying government buildings to stage protests or the time or two he's staged a demonstration without securing a permit. But violent crimes?"

Her turquoise bracelets clinked when she waved her hand. "People will come to see him as a man of peace. Especially if the government tries to crucify him."

"What about you and your husband? You're not concerned the FBI will charge you for harboring a fugitive?"

"If only Benjamin were here to answer you. He would cite legal precedent after legal precedent about the rights of political figures persecuted by the government and the immunity rights of the attorneys who represent them. He's argued in front of the Supreme Court a dozen times and won every case. Did I already mention that?"

"Where's he's now?" Loq asked.

"Probably in the air if not a courtroom. He has offices in Washington DC, Chicago, and Los Angeles."

"He flies his own plane?"

"Oh no, he has a pilot for that. He's too busy reading cases and writing arguments."

Loq and Bina exchanged glances.

"Where are we?" Bina said. "We couldn't see anything when we were brought here."

"You'll see soon enough, but I'll tell you. Right outside that door is the most beautiful view of the Crazy Mountains. The nearest town is Livingston, but it's miles and miles away. We're out here on a hundred thousand acres of the most precious land in Montana."

"The Valley of Flowers," Bina said. "That's what the Bannock, Crow, and Shoshone people called this part of Montana."

"You know your history," Martha said. "How silly of me. Of course you do. You're Native American. Yes, this was shared hunting ground for them. It was always neutral territory and they treated it as sacred."

"But now you and your husband own it."

"Some of the valley, but not all. We bought what we could to protect it. Benjamin is working on a strategy to create a law for protecting it for all time. It will become a legal precedent for other such places. I did tell you, he always wins, didn't I?"

Loq grunted, but didn't say laws for protecting Indian land hadn't worked out too good in the past.

"What about our horses?" Bina asked.

"They're here in a corral with ours and being very well cared for. We raise quarter horses." Martha smiled. "They're all from champion bloodlines."

Carrie returned. "Come. Kills in Daylight is ready to speak with you."

19

———

Bina gasped when they walked outside. Not in reaction to the bright sunlight, but to the jagged mountain peaks that stretched across the horizon. The view was spectacular like Martha had promised, but it was also daunting. If she and Loq managed to get away, trying to cross the Crazies would be crazy.

Carrie Horse noticed her reaction. "Beautiful, aren't they? But I think the same about the Cascades as I'm sure you do your mountains back home."

"Yes, because the Blues are the blood of my ancestors."

"Do you wish you were there now?"

"I always carry it here." Bina patted her chest. "But if I go back without Willie, home will be emptier and so will my heart."

"Why?"

"Because he's a tribal member. We've lost so many already that every time we lose another, we all feel more empty."

"You haven't lost him yet."

"I will if you do battle with the FBI. They'll kill him along with you and Daley."

Carrie paused as she gazed at the mountains beyond. "Why are you so intent on taking Willie back?"

"It's my duty. I took an oath to protect and serve all our people."

"You don't feel you have the same duty to every Indian no matter their tribe?"

"I can only do what I can where I serve. I leave the dream of helping everybody else to the dreamers."

"Sometimes dreams are better than waking. Black Elk said that."

"He did, but when two men raped my Aunty Moon and then tried to rape and kill me, dreaming wouldn't stop them, only waking bullets would."

Carrie touched Bina's shoulder and they halted. "I underestimated you, little sister. You have courage as well as heart. There will soon come a time when yours helps all Indian people."

Loq and Willie caught up to them.

"What's wrong?" Willie said.

"It's what's right, my young warrior, and that's your Umatilla big sister."

They continued walking. The ranch was set at the base of the foothills and overlooked a valley bisected by a glistening stream. Two ponds had been dug to store water. A runway sporting a windsock and a hangar had been built on one side of the valley. The sprawling ranch house and its stables and barn appeared to have been modeled after the set of a popular TV series. Loq's spotted pony and Bina's roan mare, Túxin, stood in a corral among a dozen quarter horses that included bays, sorrels, and grays.

"It takes a lot of cowboys to run a ranch this size," Loq said. "You're not worried one of them will tell the law you're here?"

Carrie shook her head. "The cowboys are with the cattle up in the high country where the summer graze is. There's only a husband and wife here and they've worked for the Lances for years. They're very loyal to them. Also very sympathetic to our cause."

A yellow Wagoneer with wood paneling came up the drive from the ranch house. It stopped in front of them. An older man was driving and Martha Lance was in the passenger seat. Another woman who looked to be about the age of the driver rode in the back seat. Martha rolled down the window.

"It was so nice to meet you. We're going to Jackson Hole to visit friends for a few days. Please make yourselves at home and enjoy your stay."

Her turquoise bracelets clinked as she gave a wave and the driver switched from brake to gas.

Loq grunted. "Convenient timing."

"What do you mean?" Carrie said.

"That they'll be across the state line in a couple of hours."

"Which gives them plausible deniability for whatever you all do next," Bina said.

"Listen to you," Carrie said. "Finishing each other's sentences."

"Prison sentences is what Daley and you'll get if they don't kill you first," Loq said.

"They can try."

Carrie led them around the barn to a meadow where three tepees stood. Killian Daley sat cross-legged in front of the entrance to the middle and largest, his Winchester cradled in his lap. Drawings of buffalo, bows and arrows, and lances decorated it. Several men and women stood on either side of him. All were armed.

"I told you not to follow us," Daley said.

"And I told you I needed to speak with my sister," Loq said.

"Now that you have, you know I spoke the truth that she and I share the same vision."

"I still haven't heard her say she's willing never to see her children and mother again. That she's willing to die for you."

Daley bristled. "Not for me. For the cause of liberation." His eyes turned to Carrie. "So hear her say it now."

Carrie didn't skip a beat. "The most important thing a mother can do is make the world a better, safer place for her children. That means a world where there's no more racial discrimination and injustice, and they can be proud of their culture and freely practice their spiritual beliefs. If giving my life achieves that, so be it."

She drew a breath. "When you saw Kills in Daylight at John Day, you told him to tell me *Ni yayna sle-a*. 'I have seen the mountain.' It's what you said when you came home from your vision quest. Well, little brother, I too have seen the mountain. *Ni yayna sle-a.* And that mountain is freedom for all Indians. But it won't be given to us. We must fight for it and be willing to die for it."

Daley whooped. The warriors standing on either side did too.

"But what happens to your children if you're killed?" Bina said.

"We're a tribal people," Carrie said. "My mother will raise them. Loq will raise them. Everyone in the tribe will. My children will be the richer for it by having so many teachers and elders. They'll learn even more of our traditions, our stories, our songs, more of everything that makes Klamath people Klamath."

Loq knew Carrie meant every word she said, but it made his heart ache, and should she be killed, it would break it.

"Sister," he said and reached for her.

As he did, he heard the whine of a bullet and the echo of the crack of it having been fired and the thud of it striking flesh and the thump of the man who was standing closest to Daley falling to the ground.

Loq yanked Carrie down as Bina's voice rang out. "Shots fired. Take cover."

Another whine. Another crack. Another thud. Another one of Daley's warriors fell, groaning and holding his leg.

"Shooter on high ground," Loq said. "Eleven o'clock."

"Got it," Bina said. "The hill directly behind the corral."

Carrie was starting to get up.

"Don't," Loq said. "He's targeting you and Daley. Get behind the tepees. Snake or crawl."

Others were running toward their location from around the ranch. The shooter turned his aim on them. A third person went down.

"Order them to take cover!" Loq yelled at Daley.

They scrambled to get behind the tepees. On his way, Loq checked the two men who'd been shot. The first was dead. He grabbed the wounded one and dragged him. Bina collected their guns.

"We're sitting ducks," Daley said as they crouched behind the middle tepee. "They'll pick us off one by one."

"It's only a single shooter," Loq said. "Same caliber of rifle. No shots overlapping."

"We need to flank him," Carrie Horse said.

"We do, but not you. Your people need you here telling them what to do. There could be assault teams behind the sniper. Bina and I'll go after the shooter."

"But he's got the high ground."

"And he's one and we're two."

Daley said, "I'm going with you. We'll be three."

Loq looked at him. If he were to save Carrie, he had to save Daley too. "Stay here and consider your options if there's a full-scale assault. Remember, there's no victory in death. Lend me your Winchester and I'll make sure it gives you honor."

They exchanged stares, but Daley finally handed over his rifle. "It shoots truth."

Bina was still holding the rifle she'd taken off the dead man. She'd also collected two revolvers. She kept one and gave Loq the other.

"You ready?" he said.

"Yes, but not to run straight up the hill. Let's head for the—"

"Corral. We'll let the horses loose and use them for cover."

"And ride ours up the draws on the flanks of the hill."

Carrie said, "We'll lay down covering fire for you. As soon as you start up the draws, we'll fire over the shooter's head to keep from hitting you."

She drew a knife strapped to her thigh and slit the back of the tepee. Two men slipped in, passed out rifles from wooden boxes full of them. Then they lay prone inside with their rifles aiming out the open doorway. Others crawled around to the back of the two smaller tepees and did the same.

"Don't forget to make sure no one doubles back on you, little brother," Carrie said.

"And you," Loq said.

"On three," Bina said.

The people inside the tepees began firing. The shooter took aim and fired back. Loq and Bina started running toward the corral. When they reached it, they slipped between the rails and huddled among the horses.

"Do you think it's CD Larchmont?" Bina said.

"If it is, he's using a different sniper rifle than we did in Vietnam."

"You mean when Sexton ordered you to assassinate that charismatic general you were talking about. He did, didn't he? And there were others too. It's why you and Sexton had a falling out."

Loq didn't say yes or no, only that the shooter's rifle was louder. "Sounds like a .30-06."

"Like what was used at Oxbow Dam."

"Let's find out."

"Túxin," Bina called. The roan mare's ears pricked up. She whinnied and came over.

Loq made his way to the spotted pony. He stroked his muzzle and whispered in his ear. The pony stood still. Loq walked between the other horses that were milling around nervously. He found the gate, unlatched it, and pushed it open.

"Heh ya! Heh ya!" He slapped the rear of the nearest horse.

It did what its breed was known for and bolted into a gallop. The other quarter horses quickly followed. Loq and Bina swung onto their mounts, grabbed fistfuls of mane, and rode low as the spotted pony and roan took off.

The herd sprinted as one, kicking up clouds of dust and clods of dirt. If the shooter spotted the two riders among them and let loose a volley of rounds, their explosions were lost to the thunder of hooves. As the herd neared the base of the hill, the quarter horses veered away while the spotted pony and roan kept running straight toward it. At the last second, the pony broke left and the mare right as their riders urged them up the two draws that flanked the hill.

Loq was banking that the shooter would be closest to him if he'd remained in his original position. Measuring the distance at a glance, he clicked his tongue when he was no more than fifty feet from the top. The pony stopped abruptly and he hopped off.

Keeping low and following the barrel of Daley's Winchester, Loq quickly closed in. The crack of the .30-06 provided a sharp counterpoint to the whizzing and whining of the incoming fire from the tepees and ranch. He reached an outcropping and crouched behind the largest rock.

As soon as he heard the nearby rifle bark again, he stood up. Jack Candy was lying prone, working the bolt to jack another round into a scoped rifle mounted on a bipod sniper stand.

"Drop it!" Loq said.

Candy didn't flinch at the sound of his voice. He slowly turned his head and stared at him. "And if I don't?"

"You won't have far to fall when I shoot you."

"You're not gonna kill a federal officer. Do that and you sign your own death warrant. If the courts don't hang you, my fellow BIA agents will. We're off limits. Can't let nobody think otherwise."

"The law will see it differently when they find out you killed people in cold blood."

"Them down there? They're fugitives. I was only doing my job trying to bring 'em in."

"From two hundred yards away with a sniper scope?"

"My word against theirs."

"No, against mine."

"Mine too," Bina said as she stood on the other side of him and pointed her rifle.

Candy gave her a glance. "Well, howdy there, princess. I knew you two would join up with them renegades. It's what your kind does."

"Hands off the rifle," she said.

Candy complied.

"Roll on your back," Loq said. "Reach for the piece on your hip or under your arm and I'll shoot elbow first, knee second."

"You're both dead," Candy hissed. "It's only a matter of time before Sexton and his hired gun shoot you themselves."

Loq jabbed the Winchester at him. Candy rolled on his back and stared at the sky.

"He makes a grab for a piece, shoot him," Loq said.

Bina covered him while he approached the BIA agent and

kicked the rifle away. Then he reached down to take the holstered pistol from his hip. "Go for it," he whispered. "Give her a reason."

Candy glared at him. "If the wind had been blowing, I woulda smelled you coming."

Loq sang his patience song while he disarmed him and then whistled for the spotted pony.

"I'm not getting on that nag," Candy said. "He don't got a saddle."

"Who said anything about riding?"

20

———

Warriors whooped and raised their rifles over their heads as Loq and Bina rode down the hill. They were both on Túxin. The spotted pony followed right behind with Jack Candy draped over his back. The BIA investigator's hands and feet were tied beneath the horse's barrel to keep him from slipping off.

Killian Daley and Carrie Horse waited in front of the largest tepee. "Did my Winchester do the honor?"

"Without firing a shot," Loq said and tossed him the rifle.

Daley swallowed his disappointment that Candy was still alive. Willie Hawkfeather strode to the spotted pony, cut the ties with a long knife, and yanked Candy off. When he belly flopped onto the ground, his lip split.

"Ya'll pay for this. Pay with your lives." He spit out a tooth.

"Was he alone?" Carrie Horse said.

"On the hill," Loq said, "but there could be others down the valley hiding out of sight."

Carrie made a circling motion with her hand. Four men and women ran to the barn and then came out driving pickups. They halted long enough for others to jump in the beds before speeding down the ranch's drive.

"Our scouts will find them," she said.

Approaching the still-prostrate BIA investigator, Carrie stepped on the back of his knee. "How many are with you?"

"Go fu—"

She cut him off by grinding her heel. "How many?"

Candy gritted his teeth. "I don't need no one else. They only get in my way."

"That's what he tells himself," Bina said. "But the truth is no one wants to work with him. He's had partners in the past and they either quit the agency or wound up dead."

That started another string of curses from Candy, but this time Carrie didn't try to stop him.

Bina asked Willie if he recognized him from Oxbow Dam, but the teen didn't reply.

"Were you even there or were you already in the air with Daley on the way to the TV station in Sheridan?" she said.

"Don't answer her. She's police and asks too many questions," Daley said before turning to Bina. "Call me by my real name."

Bina glanced at Loq. "That's the thanks we get for having kept any more of his followers from being *killed in daylight* today."

Daley started to take a step toward her, but Loq slid off the pony and stood between them. "She tells the truth. We're trying to keep you all from being massacred."

Carrie put one hand on Loq's shoulder and the other on Daley's. "Now's not the time to question who's right and who's wrong. If Jack Candy was able to find us, it's only a matter of time before the FBI does too. We need to prepare."

Daley pressed the barrel of his Winchester against Candy's

head. "And you need to prepare to pay for taking the lives of the warriors you shot here and the ones you killed at Oxbow Dam."

"I didn't kill nobody at Oxbow," Candy said. "I wasn't even there."

"Then how did you find us?"

"Maybe you got a squealer."

"Who?"

"I'll tell you if you let me go."

"Why should I trust you?"

"You have my word."

"Can I trust you weren't at Oxbow?"

"I told you I wasn't. I swear it. On my mother's grave."

Daley took a step back and ordered a couple of men to pull Candy to his feet. They pinned his arms back.

"My people are Oneida," Daley said. "One of the six nations of the great Iroquois Confederacy that included Mohawk, Cayuga, Seneca, Onondaga, and Tuscarora. Our home was the woodlands that grew alongside the great ocean.

"We were here long before the Spanish, the French, the English. When we warred and took captives, we tested their courage by making them run between two lines of our people. Men, women, elders, children too. If the captive made it all the way past us, we knew he had honor and was worthy of our trust."

He drew closer to Candy. "If you can run past us, I'll trust you to tell me the identity of who told you where we are and let you go."

"You want me to run a gauntlet? You're crazy!"

"It's our way."

"And if I don't?"

"I'll kill you where you stand."

Candy licked the split in his lip. His teeth turned red with blood. He shouted at Loq and Bina, "You gonna stand there and let this happen?"

Before either could answer, Daley fired a shot into the sky. "Brothers, sisters. Two of us died today and others were wounded by this man. He says he didn't kill Freddy Salish and Margarite the Apache when we crossed the Snake River. We will celebrate their lives and speed them onto the spirit world tonight, but right now we must test this man's courage."

Someone trilled. Another did too. Soon, trills filled the air. The two men pinning Candy frog-marched him to the end of the row of tepees. Two lines formed. Someone gathered branches and limbs that had been broken up and piled for firewood and passed them out.

Killian Daley walked to the opposite end of the two lines and faced Candy. He fired another shot into the air. The two men gave Candy a shove. The big BIA investigator swore and then ducked his head and started to run. Thick sticks rained down on him. He tried to cover his head and bull through one of the lines, but the people pushed him back and swatted him even harder. He fell to his knees after a ferocious storm of blows struck his back and shoulders. Someone kicked him in the ribs. Another used his rifle butt to club him in the hip.

When Loq made a move to shoulder through the line and drag him out, Carrie threw her arms around him. "Don't. You'll only make it worse for him."

Blood was cascading down Candy's forehead from a scalp wound. His right arm dangled listlessly from a dislocated shoulder. He stumbled. He fell. He was picked up and shoved forward. More blows rained. More blood flowed. More teeth spit out.

Finally, the end of the gauntlet was in sight where Killian Daley stood. Snorting like a bull, Candy bellowed and lurched forward. The last in the parallel lines delivered the final blows. Somehow, he remained on his feet.

Teetering, his breath coming in great gulps, he gasped, "I ... I ... made it."

"So you did," Daley said.

"Then ... then let me go."

"Once you tell me who told you where we are."

Horns honked in the distance. The pickups full of scouts were returning. They weren't the only vehicles. Candy's Power Wagon was among them.

He wiped the blood from his brow and focused on his rig. "Hallelujah. My ride outta here."

The vehicles came to a stop. A driver got out and said, "Nobody else is there. His rig was hidden in a stand of trees."

"See. I ... I told the truth," Candy said. "I came alone. You can trust me."

"Give him some water," Daley said.

A canteen was passed forward. Candy took a gulp, swished it, and spit it out. It was red with his own blood. He took another gulp, then poured the rest over his head. More blood ran.

Daley said, "I'll tell you a truth and then you'll tell me a truth."

"What?"

"I didn't kill the FBI's informant at Warm Springs. He was already dead when I got there. Your turn."

Candy bit his already split lip, but didn't call him a liar. "I wasn't at Oxbow."

"I shot back at Sexton and Tujunga after they opened fire on me, but only in self-defense. They were trying to kill me."

"I don't like the FBI neither."

"I didn't blow up the BIA office in Pendleton."

Candy's face turned even redder. "My girlfriend was in there. She got hurt bad. I'm gonna catch who did and make 'em pay."

"You work for an evil government agency. The BIA has a history of corruption, stealing from us, mistreating us, imprisoning us, killing us."

Candy's one eye that wasn't swollen shut bugged out. "There's good Indians and bad Indians. It's a tough job sorting 'em out. That's the God-honest truth."

Daley's shoulders stiffened. "Why did you shoot at us today?"

"Doing my job. I was aiming at you, hoping I could wing you. Her too." He nodded at Carrie Horse. The pain made him wince. "If I winged you bad enough, you'd have to go to the hospital. Be easier arresting you there."

"But you missed."

"Your man stepped in front of you. Good luck for you, bad for him. Same with the second one."

"But you shot others."

"Trying to keep your people pinned down so I could escape." He nodded at Loq and Bina. "Didn't figure on them two coming after me."

Daley glanced down at the ground, then up at the sky, and then returned his gaze to Candy's broken and bloodied face. "Did you kill Freddy Salish and Margarite the Apache at Oxbow?"

"No."

Willie Hawkfeather broke ranks from the gauntlet and pushed forward. "He's lying. Now that I see his Power Wagon, I recognize it from Oxbow Dam. I saw the driver shoot Margarite and my friend Freddy Salish after he questioned them. He put them in the station wagon and pushed it into the river."

"You're lying, you little punk, and you know it," Candy shouted.

"For Freddy and Margarite!" Willie shouted back and whipped out his long knife and stabbed Jack Candy in the heart.

21

"You know what I'm thinking?" Bina said.

"About how we're going to get out of here," Loq said. They'd been stripped of their guns and locked back inside the storeroom.

"That too, but mostly about the Nimiipuu who were camped beside Tolo Lake on the Camas Prairie a hundred years ago. They were living the free life they'd always known and then a group of young bloods with more testosterone than common sense rode out and killed those settlers. They got their revenge, but look what it cost the tribe."

"Like what Willie Hawkfeather just did."

"I know I'm not responsible for that, but I feel I'm to blame. I should've done more to protect him."

Despite the dim light, Loq saw the glisten of tears as she bowed her head. "Maybe you could've from Killian Daley and even the FBI, but not from himself. Willie wrote his own destiny when he stopped believing there could be another path."

"Do you really believe that?"

Loq thought about the way he'd been when he and the other dropouts would go to Klamath Falls and get in fights. "I know there's more than one way to be. I've had to make that choice before."

"What about now?"

"I choose to get out of here."

"Anything else you'd choose if you could?"

He reached over and wiped away the tears. "I already did."

"Me too," she said.

Loq pulled her close and tucked her head under his chin and saw a late November afternoon when he'd gone duck hunting in Klamath Lake's marshes aboard an old wooden skiff. The winds picked up and the snow started to fly but he kept hunting so he could bag his limit. When he finally shot his last duck and headed back to the boat ramp near the mouth of the Williamson River, the lake had started to freeze. Ice slabs were bobbing and sliding around and reminded him of the shiny backs of spawning salmon swimming up a shallow stream.

The only way out was to keep doing what he was doing even though the boat was riding lower as it filled with wet snow. Visibility was down to next to nothing. Ice forming on his eyelashes didn't help as he tried to steer through the darkening gloom and the even darker thoughts that the ice might crush the hull and leave him floundering in freezing water.

A hundred yards from the boat ramp, the bow shuddered as it hit a solid shelf of ice. Loq backed off, then twisted the throttle on the outboard as far it would go and hung on as the skiff shot forward. It rammed the ice and cracked it just enough to create a notch. He did it again and again, each time gaining a little distance, each time causing more shuddering, not knowing if the cracking he heard was ice or wood.

Thirty yards out, the water grew shallower and the ice grew thicker and the outboard quit. He yanked the starter cord, but it wouldn't catch. He tried paddling. That didn't work either. Sweating despite freezing, feeling the bite of the cold on his face, but not feeling his fingertips or toes, Loq wondered if maybe this had been his fate all along.

But then he remembered his vision quest. "I have seen the mountain," he shouted to the ice. He shouted it to the storm too.

Loq scrambled to the bow, picked up the anchor tied to a rope, and tossed it onto the ice as far as he could. He braced his feet against the thwart and pulled, dragging the anchor until one of its fluke's caught and held. He hauled in the line as if his life depended on it because it did. The boat shuddered even louder as it slid up on top of the ice shelf. He kept hauling. The boat inched forward. One boat length. Two boat lengths. When the bow neared the anchor, he reached over, loosened it, and hurled it again. One boat length. Two boat lengths. Over and over again.

Finally he reached the ramp and clambered onto shore. Looking back at the frozen lake, he realized there was always a different path, but he needed the will to see it and the courage to take it. He never forgot that. Not in Vietnam. Not on the wildlife refuges when he and Nick Drake faced danger and death. And not now with Bina Mantioc.

"We're getting out of here," he said.

"How?" she said.

"Together."

They drew up a plan.

"This is what you see in every movie or TV show," she said.

"I don't watch TV."

"But Daley's people do."

"Then they'll think nobody would be dumb enough to try it and believe it's for real."

"Why do I have to be the one who pounds on the door and cries for help and you get to jump out when they come in?"

"Because I don't know how to cry for help. I've never done it."

Bina looked at him. He didn't blink. "Why am I not surprised?"

"They come in, they'll be plenty of heads for both of us to knock," he said.

"But we'll still have to make a run for the horses."

"Stealing a pickup from the barn would be easier and get us off the ranch even quicker."

"I'm not leaving Túxin behind."

"It's not forever. The spotted pony will keep her company."

She shook her head. "I'm taking my horse no matter what."

"You're Umatilla, all right."

"What are you going to use for a weapon?"

Looking around the storage room and seeing nothing, he raised his fists and bared his teeth.

"Like your namesake," she said. "You know, we might be killed doing this."

"Carrie won't let that happen. Daley either. We may be law to them, but we're Indians first. It'd send the wrong message to his followers."

Bina sighed. "Try not to get hit in the head again. You get another concussion, you might forget who I am."

"Never," he said.

She smiled. "On three."

He stood beside the door while Bina started kicking and pounding on it. "Help! Help! Loq's unconscious. He has a brain bleed from when he was knocked out. Help!"

She kept kicking, kept pounding, kept screaming. Finally, the door opened, but only a crack.

"You dance better than you act," Carrie Horse said. "Tell my brother not to jump out and slug me. I've come to get you. We're holding a ceremony and want you both there."

It was nearing sunset and the sky was dusted with pink. The men who'd been guarding the door escorted Loq and

Bina to the big meadow. In front of the three tepees stood the tall trunk of a cottonwood that had been stripped of its branches and erected upright in the ground. Long leather thongs hung from the top and reached the grass. A pile of buffalo skulls and logs was heaped nearby. Bonfires blazed. The scent of sage burning in smudge pots filled the air. Men and women stood in a circle around the pole. Many wore wreaths of sage on their heads and wrists. A drummer pounded on a powwow drum, its rhythmic beat akin to that of a giant's heart.

Killian Daley stepped out of the largest tepee. His face bore streaks of paint. He walked toward the cottonwood trunk, raised his arms, and chanted. The pounding of the drum grew louder.

He tilted his head so he was staring at the top of the pole. "Hear me, Great Spirit. Hear me, ancient ones. I am Kills in Daylight. I ask for strength and guidance as we hold the most sacred of ceremonies." His voice took on a slow, deep tone.

"Some seek atonement for actions they took in the face of the enemy. Some seek penance for thinking of themselves first and not the good of the tribe. Some seek courage."

Daley's voice grew even more hypnotic. People were swaying and the circle began to rotate.

"Some embark on the journey to the spirit world to join their elders. Some will recommit themselves to our struggle to end injustice and return what is rightfully ours. And some will pledge their loyalty to our struggle or be punished for refusing."

He lowered his gaze and turned to face his followers. "Brothers, sisters, warriors. Tonight we dance from sunset to sunset. Tonight we dance to honor the sun. Let the Sun Dance begin!"

The powwow drum pounded louder. People chanted. The circle wheeled faster.

Willie Hawkfeather emerged from the middle tepee. He was bare-chested and wore only a loincloth. The spirit power tattoo on his neck shone as he held his head high and strode through the circle of dancers.

He halted in front of Daley and bowed. The group's self-appointed spiritual leader and war chief put his hand on Willie's forehead, chanted, and then drew a skewer made of bone from a pouch. He pinched a fold of skin on the left side of Willie's chest and pushed the skewer through it. Willie didn't scream. Daley took another skewer and did the same on the right. This time, the young Umatilla groaned.

As he started to slump backward, two men rushed to prop him up. Daley gathered leather thongs hanging from the ceremonial pole and knotted them to the skewers. The men let go, and Willie leaned back and his skewered flesh puckered as the thongs tautened and twanged.

The drumming grew even louder. The chanting did too. Four more men wearing only loincloths came forward. They turned their backs to Daley who grabbed folds of flesh between their shoulder blades, skewered them, and fastened leather thongs that were tied to buffalo skulls and logs. The four men began to drag the heavy objects around the meadow.

All eyes were on Willie Hawkfeather who began dancing around the cottonwood pole by side-stepping while keeping the thongs taut.

"He'll keep that up until his flesh rips or Daley decides he's had enough and pulls the skewers out and rips the flesh himself," Loq said to Bina. "Same with the ones dragging the skulls and logs."

"Have you been to a Sun Dance where they performed self-mortification?"

"Once when visiting a friend in Oklahoma. You?"

She shook her head. "I've seen and danced Round, Circle, Bear, Hoop, Stomp, and Jingle, but the Sun Dances I witnessed never had this part."

Carrie was standing next to them. "Kills in Daylight participated in a Blood Sun Dance with a Lakota clan in Canada. It lasted four days and so did he. His flesh didn't tear so he ripped out the skewers and thongs himself, cut off the flaps of flesh with his knife, and offered them to the sun."

Loq grunted. "He has a death wish, sister. If you do too, then you've become someone I no longer recognize."

"I don't wish to die, nor does Kills in Daylight, but we're not afraid to either."

"Can you say the same for the dancers, for everyone who's watching?"

When Carrie hesitated, Loq said, "He reminds me of a guru from India who established a cult on a ranch near No Mountain when Nick Drake first started living there. He could convince them to do anything he wanted. Maybe Daley is a shaman. Maybe he's Coyote. But unless you can say his followers' wills are their own, then they're being led to their deaths without agreeing to it."

"What makes you so sure?"

"It was the same in Vietnam."

"But the Viet Cong won the war. North and South joined to become the Socialist Republic of Vietnam."

"Not everyone was a winner. There were countless reprisal killings. Many people were sent to what they called reeducation camps, but they're no different than forced labor prisons. Most are still in them."

Carrie frowned. "What would you have me do?"

"Let Bina and me go. We'll meet with Robert Sexton in Butte and send him on a wild goose chase."

"How?"

Bina said, "By convincing him you're going to hold a big demonstration at the Bear Paw Battlefield instead of Big Hole."

"Who told you about Big Hole?"

"We figured it out."

"How?"

"It's August, the centennial of the battle. When you're there, you videotape record it. Also bring in reporters sworn to secrecy to cover it. Maybe Daley's bigshot lawyer can convince some elected officials to come. Celebrities too. You tell the world what's happening and state your demands."

"How would you trick Sexton?"

"With your help. Send a small group of your warriors to Bear Paw. Make sure they get seen and heard. He'll chase them."

"And afterward, what happens to Kills in Daylight and me and everyone else?"

"You surrender. Daley can give his version of Chief Joseph's speech," Bina said. "The feds will release everyone but him and you. You'll both be arrested and there'll be a big trial. That's more attention, more opportunity to tell the world what's going on."

"The FBI will handpick a judge and rig the jury."

"They can try, but my police chief and I'll find out who really bombed the BIA office and killed the FBI informant before you go to trial."

"And Willie Hawkfeather, what about him?"

"Honestly? I don't know. He killed Jack Candy. Everyone saw him. But I do know the tribe will do whatever they can for him."

"Kills in Daylight will never go along with it," Carrie said. "I'm not sure I can either."

"Then you'd better convince him," Loq said, "because time's running out. It won't take long for Sexton to put two and two together about Daley's lawyer owning a ranch in Montana."

Carrie's gaze shifted from her brother to Daley. He was beckoning to her.

"What's he want?" Loq said.

"You. He wants you to prove you're a true Indian by performing the Sun Dance."

Loq looked down his high cheekbones. "I don't need to prove anything to anyone. I know who I am."

"He doesn't take no for an answer."

"Neither do I, especially when it comes to preventing you from making your kids orphans."

Before she could say another word, Loq pushed through the wheel of dancers and stood in front of Daley.

"So, you want me to dance the Sun Dance." His voice rose above the drumming and chanting.

"To prove you're really one of us. I'll pierce your flesh and tie the thongs myself," Daley said.

"I don't need to prove my blood to you or anyone."

Loq ripped his shirt open, bared his chest to Daley, and then turned to show everyone the deep scars marring his Semper Fi tattoo.

"I was a warrior in Vietnam for three years and served with many brave warriors from other tribes. They are my brothers in life and in death."

His glare moved from person to person.

"I danced with *Tsa-ahu-bitts*, the man-eating Shoshone demon who dwells in the Bruneau River Canyon. The demon left his mark on me as all can see, but I left mine on him too."

He made a slashing gesture as if holding his skinning knife.

"I am Loq. I am a proud member of the Klamath Nation. Does anyone here doubt my blood? Does anyone doubt my courage?"

Loq stared them down and then turned back to Daley. "If you're really as strong and courageous as you say, you won't lead your followers to certain death at Big Hole. Ask Carrie Horse about another way you can win your war. She'll explain everything."

He pushed back through the dancers who were no longer dancing and reached his sister. "If you want to save all these people, leave this place fast and get to Big Hole two nights from now with the reporters and your lawyer. The next day you will hold your demonstration."

"Why do you think I can convince Kills in Daylight to go along?"

"You've always had the power to do so. Yours is greater than his because he sees himself first while your vision sees everyone but you."

"Can you really trick Sexton into going to Bear Paw?"

"Yes."

"But what if you don't?"

"Then we're all doomed."

Carrie put her palm on his chest. "*Tsa-ahu-bitts* may have left his mark on you, but our ancestors made an even deeper one. Go to Butte. We hid Bina's rig in the barn. Your gear, weapons, and saddles are still in it."

Loq nodded. "Before you leave, bury Candy's Power Wagon in a deep hole along with his body and those he killed. Sweep your trail from here to Big Hole of all signs like you and I used to do when we played at tracking each other. This time, it's no game."

"Will I see you at Big Hole, little brother?" Carrie said.

"If not there, then in the spirit world."

22

TROUT CREEK

Early morning light found its way through the canopy of aspens in the Trout Creek Mountains and scattered sparkles atop the spring's waters. I opened my eyes and turned to wake Johnny, but he wasn't there. I yanked my revolver from under the rolled-up jacket I used as a pillow and sprang to my feet.

Sweeping the .357 in front of me, I surveyed our campsite while picturing the mugshot of Hex Taggert. Then I looked at the horses. Wovoka and Kosse were munching on bunchgrass, but Johnny was nowhere in sight. I crept alongside them and peered into the woods.

Nothing was moving among the trees, but no birds were singing either. That was unsettling because songbirds were always active early in the morning. I slipped away from the horses and soft-stepped to the nearest aspen, careful to avoid snapping dead branches or kicking rocks.

Moving from trunk to trunk, I soon reached the other side. There! Up the hill. Movement on an escarpment. A silhouette. I focused on it and then breathed a sigh of relief. It was Johnny. He was standing at the edge. I quickly joined him.

"What are you doing?" I said.

"Looking," he said, his voice uneasy.

"At what?"

"All that!" And he pointed.

A long dark scar ran through a sea of scrubland. Beyond it rose a jagged ridgeline.

"It's only Trout Creek."

"No, not that," he said, his voice still uneasy. "All the open countryside. All the nothing. There's no place to hide."

Like there is in the jungle, I thought, where every leaf as big as an elephant's ear can shield you when the enemy is hunting you, where every tall tree with a dangling vine can provide you with an escape route.

I suddenly realized it wasn't only all the strange new people Johnny had trouble adjusting to, it was the strange landscape itself and its harsh conditions—hot and bone dry in summer, bone-chilling cold in winter, a wind that never showed mercy. The high desert at the Warbler ranch was little different than Trout Creek Mountains. No wonder he stayed in his room most of the time.

"Sorry," I said. "I should've known this side of Oregon would be a shock to you when Gemma and I brought you home from Medford. It's very different compared to all the greenery on that side of the Cascades. And it's nothing at all like Vietnam."

Johnny shivered. "Did you feel the same way when you came here?"

I hesitated before answering. "Truth is, the opposite. I liked the openness. I wanted it. No, I needed it. I needed a place so different than Vietnam it'd help me see things in a different way, a new way. It'd help me heal."

"From the gunshot you got in the war."

"Yes, but help more up here." I tapped the side of my head without mentioning my combat fatigue, addiction to heroin, and months-long stint in the rubber room at Walter Reed all those years ago. I wasn't ready to tell him about that.

We stood quietly looking out on the High Lonesome.

"Do you think it could help me too?" he said, his voice growing less uneasy. "I don't like being mad at everybody and everything all the time."

"It will if you let it. And Gemma and I'll help you if you let us. Hattie, Pudge, and November too."

"Help me, including going back to Vietnam to look for Sen Vàng like you said you would last night?"

"Of course. I'll help you find the girl with yellow hair."

We scrambled down the escarpment and returned to camp. I asked if he wanted eggs and bacon for breakfast, but he said we should get going.

"Early bird catches the star lizard," I said.

"What?"

"Dumb joke. Okay, trail mix it is and no coffee either."

We broke camp and saddled the horses.

As we mounted up, I said, "Since you were out scouting early, how about you lead the way?"

Johnny gave Kosse a nudge with his bootheels. "Follow me."

I pulled down the brim of my hat and clicked my cheek.

The trail led out of the aspens and cut a straight line across a desert scrubland tinted blue-gray by big sagebrush. A kettle of turkey vultures swirled in the distance. That many scavengers meant the carcass below was something big. Maybe a deer or a pronghorn. Even a cow that wandered away from a distant ranch. The image of an Indian teenager's body that had been dumped there flashed, but I blinked it away.

A couple of hot, dusty hours later we reached the rim and looked down on Trout Creek. It looked more like a lush river valley than the steep, sheer-walled canyon I had imagined. Aspens, willows, and mahogany grew along the creek's banks. A beaver dam had created a large pool that served as a mirror for the sun.

"I thought it would look different," Johnny said.

"Me too, but according to the topo map, this is Trout Creek." I pointed toward a high plateau upriver. "Could be the canyon gets narrower and steeper at the headwaters."

"The star lizard plant must be down there somewhere. November said it's where the sun shines longest, and it would do that more in a valley than a canyon."

"Someone's been doing more than studying English," I said.

"Nagah gives me his books. At first, I only looked at the pictures, but then I wanted to know what the words beneath them said. He's been teaching me."

"And does that book say ride on down and start looking?"

"It does. While the sun's still high."

The trail down was fairly gentle and when we reached the creek, we let the horses drink. Across the water, unblinking yellow eyes stared at us from holes dug in the side of the bank. It was a colony of burrowing owls. A juvenile started making defensive noises that sounded like a rattlesnake's warning. That startled Kosse who laid his ears back and crow-hopped. Johnny quickly brought him under control.

"Let's follow the creek upriver," I said. "Which side do you want?"

"The side with the owls. It's getting the most sunlight."

He turned Kosse and crossed the creek. The water barely reached the dark chestnut's fetlocks. Wovoka and I kept pace with them on our side as we moseyed upstream. The longer we rode, the more the wind picked up. Clouds were gathering high overhead and I knew we'd end up using the canvas lean-to I'd packed.

We stopped for lunch and ate some of November's cold fried

chicken washed down with creek water that was surprisingly icy given it was August.

Once back in the saddle, we continued following the creek. It alternated between calm flat stretches and boisterous white-water splashing down cobbled channels and rushing over boulders.

I lost sight of Johnny in a particularly brushy section that walled off the creek on both sides. I bent low, pressing my chin against Wovoka's mane as he pushed his way through.

Johnny started hollering.

"Go, boy!" I said and gave the buckskin a taste of my heels. He bolted and crashed through the last of the brush.

When we emerged on the other side, I saw Johnny waving at the hillside that rose sharply on his side of the creek.

"I see it! I see the star lizard!"

I squinted, but couldn't tell what he was waving at. Grabbing my binoculars, I panned the hillside. The sight of a five-pointed leaf attached to a stalk that resembled a lizard prompted a "Well, I'll be damned."

Up until that moment, I would've bet the ranch the plant was the equivalent of a rainbow's pot of gold that November had cooked up as a way to give everyone a shot of hope about Pudge's cancer as well as a chance for Johnny and me to reunite after having been away on patrol.

Wovoka sensed my excitement and charged across the creek before I could issue a command. Johnny was already out of his saddle and looping Kosse's reins around a branch.

"Take this," I said, and handed him an empty flour sack. "And this." I gave him my clasp knife, congratulating myself for not adding a warning about being careful not to slice off his finger.

Johnny shoved the knife into his back pocket and began scaling the hillside. There were plenty of ledges to use as steps and handholds. As I watched, it was as if I could see him climbing rungs in the ladder of life. Childhood. Teenager. Young adult. Work. Marriage. Fatherhood. It made me suck in my breath and blow it out slow. I wanted to witness him doing all those things for real. I wanted to be able to share it with him as his father, to celebrate his triumphs, to commiserate his defeats.

He reached the star lizard, deftly sliced its stalk with the blade, put the plant into the flour sack, and then moved on to another. I flashed on Vietnamese farmers working a terraced rice paddy. It was stoop labor using primitive tools, but they did it with grace, dignity, and respect for a time-honored tradition that had sustained families and villages in peacetime and war.

I kept watch as Johnny climbed higher while moving farther up the creek. As he stretched for a plant that was just beyond his reach, he glanced over his shoulder to check how high he was. He let out a cry.

"A car! I see a wrecked car. Over there."

I was still sitting on Wovoka and immediately drew my Winchester from the scabbard as I called to Johnny. "Climb on down but stay right here with Kosse. I'll go check it out. Wait for me!"

The sun was in my eyes as I rode upstream, but when the creek took a slight bend, I saw the turkey vultures circling overhead and the glint of metal at the bottom of a steep and narrow gulch that dumped into the creek. I glanced at the top and recognized the telltale signs of a fresh slide. A road of sorts must be up there and had given way, sending the vehicle over the side and crashing onto the rocky ground below.

I rode closer. The car had rolled from the look of the crushed roof and dented doors and fenders. It had ended right side up with its grill wrapped around boulders. A body was hanging halfway out of the shattered windshield, the head, shoulders, and chest sprawled on the accordioned hood. I could make out long black hair, but couldn't tell if the corpse was male or female.

"Easy," I whispered to Wovoka. "Easy now."

The closer I got, the more of the story I got. The white sedan's missing trunk lid told me it matched the description of the stolen car from the Fort McDermitt Reservation. The body's thin frame and long hair told me it wasn't Hex Taggert. Its position on the passenger side said it hadn't been the driver either. I looked around. Maybe the driver and other teen had been thrown clear when the car went over the side. Maybe they'd been able to walk away from the wreck. Maybe they were still inside.

I dismounted, shouldered my rifle, and drew closer. The dead passenger was a male teenager. The blood on the hood was dry, but the body hadn't started to bloat. That meant the accident was fairly recent. The fact that the turkey vultures hadn't landed confirmed it. I looked through the hole his head had made through the windshield, but the front seat was empty.

The dented front doors were jammed shut when I tried to open them to see into the back. The rear doors were the same and their windows too spiderwebbed to get a good look inside. I smashed one with the butt of my rifle. The glass shattered into cubes. I leaned the Winchester against the rear fender and peered in.

Another body was lying on its right side on the floor, pinned between the back of the front seat and the bottom of the rear seat. I couldn't see a face, but the long black hair told me it was the teenage girl from the reservation, not Hex Taggert. I gritted my teeth at the thought of her parents. Their sorrow was only beginning, and I knew if that was Hattie lying there, a piece of me and Gemma would've died with her and we'd never be whole again.

Then I heard it. A burble. And it wasn't coming from the

creek. I cleared away the rest of the glass and stuck my head inside.

"Can you hear me?"

I got a burble for an answer.

"Can you move? Even a finger."

Another burble is all I got, but it was proof of life. I backed out and tried yanking on all four doors again, but couldn't get any to budge. I went back to the now glassless window frame and stuck my right arm in, stretching to reach the girl. My fingers brushed the top of her head and then her neck. I felt for a pulse.

"Be there," I said. "Be there!"

I felt it. Barely, it beat so slow. I moved my hand up and put it in front of her nose and mouth. I held my breath and waited to feel hers. There. I felt it.

Sticking my left arm through the open frame too, I tried climbing in headfirst, but my holster caught and stopped me. I backed out, unbuckled it, and let it drop. Then I started squeezing through the opening again.

I was halfway in when powerful hands grabbed my ankles and yanked me back out and swung me around before letting go, sending me flying into the side of the car. It knocked the wind out of me, but didn't knock me out.

Hex Taggert snarled. He was battered and bloodied from the car wreck, but as dangerous as a wounded bear. When he bent down to pick my holstered gun off the ground, I tossed a handful of dirt in his eyes and kicked his hand away. Then I threw my arms around his tree trunk-like legs and tried to pull him down. He roared and hammered my shoulders with both fists as he fought to stay upright. I headbutted him in the side of his knee and jammed my bootheels into the ground like a bulldogger.

Sledgehammer fists started pounding my shoulders and

then began smacking both sides of my head. Stars burst and flames leapt off the surface of the sun, but I wouldn't let go. I couldn't. I knew what would happen if I did. I lowered my grip on his legs and threw my weight against his ankles. Hex started to waver, then staggered, then toppled.

When he hit the ground, the oomph coming out of his mouth smelled like roadkill. I scrambled on top of him and punched his kidneys over and over. He threw his arms around me and squeezed, pressing my arms hard against my ribs to halt my fists. If he kept it up much longer, he'd break more bones in me than the girl in the sedan might have.

I drove my knee hard into his crotch and sunk my teeth into his chest. He bellowed and arched his hips to try and buck me off. I drove my knee into him again and took another bite. His arms loosened, but he was only relaxing his shoulders to roll himself onto his side and then onto me.

That's when the 12 gauge boomed.

23

———

The high peaks of the Crazies reflected the sparkle of the galaxy and made Loq think about the months he'd spent in LA finishing up work on the Western movie and living with Dani Reyna, the tempestuous actress who played the film's femme fatale. Like shooting stars, their romance blazed bright and hot, but eventually burned out. He glanced at Bina sitting beside him as they drove toward Butte and realized this felt different. They were more like planets orbiting the sun than meteors streaking across the night sky—unafraid of the pull of gravity, excited by moving in sync.

Bina brought him back to the moment. "It's too late to radio George at the station, but I need to talk to him tonight and let him know we're still alive and what we're planning to do."

He leaned forward to look up through the windshield. "Don't see an owl. You know they're messengers for our people. We'll have to find a pay phone instead."

"Is that what you think passes as humor?"

"You must. I heard the smile in your voice."

"I know a joke when I hear it."

"But can you tell one?"

"Of course. My people are known for humor as well as horsemanship."

"First time I met Nick Drake, he didn't know how. Always screwed up the punch line."

"Were you able to teach him?"

Loq pictured him, knowing he was going through it, what with his father-in-law having cancer and his adopted son having a worse case of combat fatigue than Nick had himself.

"Mostly, but sometimes he forgets."

"Are you two close?"

"As brothers."

"Now that I've met your sister, I'll have to meet him. Your mother too. The whole family."

"Why?"

"When I see you through their eyes, I'll see you more clearly."

"Mm."

Lights appeared ahead. "Looks like a gas station," Bina said. "They might have a phone."

"Hope you got change. I don't carry any. Not even a buffalo nickel for luck."

Bina laughed. "Another attempt at joking, right?"

"The truth. Habit from Vietnam. I don't want anything jingling in my pocket when I'm sneaking up on people or wildlife."

"I'm surprised by that."

"How so?"

"You sure seem to like it when I jingle."

"Mm."

"Bet you can't name the three men who modeled for the nickel's Indian head," she said.

"Is that a trick? There's only two. The Oglala chief Iron Tail who toured with Buffalo Bill, and Two Moons, the Cheyenne chief who fought at Little Big Horn."

"There's actually a third. Chief John Big Tree. I thought you would've known that since you were in a Hollywood movie. He starred in fifty."

Loq wondered if she was a mind reader, knowing he'd been thinking about Dani.

When he didn't reply, she said, "You know what we're doing right now."

"Making a phone call," he said, turning into the gas station.

She touched his knee. "Making small talk to make it seem like what we're about to do in Butte is normal."

"There's nothing normal about CD Larchmont. I haven't forgotten that."

He pulled in front of a pump to fill up and check on the horses while she walked over to the pay phone and called George Tahamtaham's house.

"What happened to contacting me every day?" the tribal police chief said.

"Carrie Horse and Killian Daley is what happened." She quickly gave a recap and explained the plan to send Sexton to Bear Paw so Daley and his followers could stage their demonstration at Big Hole without interference.

"I don't have to tell you how many ways that can go sideways. Sexton issued an APB for you two when Loq didn't show in Butte. He called me to see if you'd come home. I had to tell him the truth, I didn't know where you were."

"We figured on the APB. We swapped my Oregon plates for Montana ones before we left the ranch."

"That might buy you from getting a second look from a state trooper, but they still got the make and model of your rig."

"It's late, it's dark, and we only have an hour to go," she said.

"You'll need more than wishful thinking for your plan to work. Sexton convinced the Montana governor to put the National Guard on standby and there's still the problem of CD Larchmont and Jack Candy operating on their own. Both have gone dark."

As Bina debated whether or not to tell him about the BIA investigator, Tahamtaham said, "You're holding something back."

She took a breath. "Candy killed the pair at Oxbow after they told him about the ranch. He sneaked in with a sniper rifle and tried to shoot Daley and Carrie Horse. He missed them, but killed two and wounded others."

"Did he get away?"

"No. Loq and I captured him."

Tahamtaham sucked in his breath. "He's law, they're fugitives. Interfering with him put you in a bad way legally speaking. Do they still have him?"

"His body. Willie Hawkfeather killed him when he learned Candy had murdered his friend Freddy Salish and a woman called Margarite the Apache."

The police chief started muttering in Sahaptin.

"Are you cursing or praying?" Bina said.

"Both," he said.

"What should we do about it?"

"Nothing right now. What's done is done. We'll have to sort it out later. The most important thing is to save lives and that comes down to how things work out at Big Hole. Meaning, your plan better work. Anything else I should know?"

"No, I've told you everything. Loq and I'll meet with Sexton, Carrie's going to send a decoy group to Bear Paw, and Daley will work with his lawyer and sneak in some friendly reporters. What about you?"

"What about me?"

"Come on, George, I know you. You're not about to sit this one out. You're planning something. What is it?"

"Wait and see, Officer Mantioc. Wait and see."

A click followed by a dial tone buzzed in her ear. She got back in the pickup.

"What did George say?" Loq said.

"That we'd better pull this off, but he wouldn't tell me what he's going to do. I know he's planning something because he called me Officer Mantioc."

"Good."

"What do you mean by good?"

"Good that he didn't tell you. Surprise is a powerful weapon. Battles often turn on them."

"The whole point of this is to avoid a battle."

"That would be an even bigger surprise."

Loq put the pickup in gear and drove to Butte, parking several blocks from the M&M Bar and Café. He went the rest of the way on foot. The joint was impossible to miss. A vertical neon sign that occupied most of the front of a two-story brick building pointed a bright green curving arrow toward an Art Deco ground-floor facade.

Despite the late hour, the place was jammed. It had been open twenty-four hours a day, seven days a week since it first opened in 1890 as a saloon, eatery, and gambling house. The cloud of cigar and cigarette smoke was thick, the country-and-western music loud, and the people drinking, eating, and talking even louder.

Loq registered faces without staring as he walked past counters lined with stools and tables whose tops were laminated with dollar bills. Making his way to the bar drew him a few looks, but no one challenged him. The bartender took his time coming over.

"What'll it be?"

"The message you got for me."

"Huh?"

"A message. Someone gave it to you to give to me."

"Do I look like a mailman?"

Loq took in the bartender's face. His expression was fixed in place by having spent years in a boxing ring and years breaking up brawls. He had scarred brows, a flattened nose, and cauliflower ears.

"I was told you'd have a message for me."

"Who's this supposed message from?"

"Robert Sexton."

"Don't know nobody by that name."

"Maybe he didn't tell it to you."

"Why wouldn't he?"

"Because he's an FBI agent and thought you wouldn't want your customers to know you're working for him."

The barflies on either side of Loq hushed.

The bartender put his fists on the bar and stuck his ugly face in Loq's. "I'm gonna drag you out back and beat the shit out of you."

"Or you could do it here."

They stared each other down and then the bartender looked left, then right, then leaned even closer. "If I did have some kind of message, how am I supposed to know I'm giving it to the right guy?"

"You think anybody else in here wants to get a note from the FBI?"

The bartender had to think about that for a good minute, but then lumbered over to the cash register, took an envelope from beneath the bill drawer, and lumbered back. He slid it across the bar.

Loq tore it open and read it while the bartender watched. "Tell him I'll be there at eight in the morning."

He pushed through the crowd and back out the door without turning around. Loq didn't return to the pickup but cut down an alley, took a side street, walked half a block and stepped into another alley, backing up against the brick wall, careful to stay out of the glow of the streetlight. Drawing his gun and holding it at his side, he sang his patience song. A couple of minutes later a man appeared at the alley's entrance, his elongated shadow cast by the streetlight reaching Loq's feet.

"You still got it," the man said. "Saw me sitting at the bar and didn't even register surprise."

"I've seen plenty of ghosts before, Larchmont."

"Difference is, ghosts are dead."

"Thanks to you."

Larchmont stepped closer. He didn't look as if he'd aged. His hair was cut like a Marine's, his steely blue eyes neither blinked nor shifted, and his jaw might as well have been made of stone.

"Don't give me the high and mighty, Loq. Your hands have blood on them. But I'm not here to debate how we took care of business in country. I'm only interested in present business."

"Your client's son, Killian Daley."

"I don't keep it a secret. Advertising's good for business. Sexton knows all about where my allegiance lies." The barest of grins crossed his lips. "My bank account."

"But you don't tell him everything."

"What makes you say that?"

"If you did, you wouldn't be talking but drawing a gun and marching me down to the FBI field office."

"I see you're holding one. Some way to welcome an old partner."

"We were never partners. My CO assigned me to support Sexton's special ops group. I was carrying out orders. You were carrying out a blood lust."

"Don't tell me you're wetting the bed for having pulled the

trigger on General Nguyen Tran. That was a shot in a million from that distance, especially after having hacked our way through the jungle for ten klicks with a horde of Charlie on our ass."

Despite the gloom of the alley, Larchmont's eyes sparkled. "I was proud to be your spotter mathing out the wind and drop for you. Kept your ass alive too when we were running back to the dustoff."

"But you couldn't get enough blood," Loq said. "Telling the chopper pilot after he picked us up to take a pass at that village and fire his rockets, ordering the gunner to sweep the hooches with his fifty cal. Only kids and women there. No combatants."

"Bullshit. Everyone was a combatant. Every last one of them."

Loq sang another verse of his patience song. "I was supposed to be in Butte a couple of days ago. Did Sexton order you to maintain surveillance on the M&M this whole time?"

"Sexton doesn't order me to do squat. I'm no longer government-issued. I feed him info when it works out for me. I knew the only way you wouldn't've shown up is if Daley had buried you. But I've seen you in action. If Ho Chi Minh's hordes couldn't kill you, some wannabe Geronimo can't either. He won't as long as he's screwing your sister."

"Am I supposed to get angry and come after you so you can draw the semi on your hip and drop me? I've seen you do that to others before."

"Tell me where Daley is and no one's got to get shot. I'll swoop in tonight, grab him, and nobody will know, not even your sister until she wakes up in the morning and realizes she's the only thing keeping the bed warm."

"Only person I'm going to tell anything to is Sexton. He's FBI and can do something about it. Only thing you can do is get a lot of people killed."

Larchmont's jaw stabbed the air. "Daley's daddy is so rich, he can't even count it all. He gave me a blank check to spend whatever I need to bring his son home. I'll pay you five grand cash to tell me where he's at. No one else needs to know."

Loq stayed mum.

"Okay, make it ten grand." Larchmont waited. "Fifteen, but that's it. Word of advice? Take it because the alternative doesn't pencil out for you."

"How's that?"

"I fill you full of lead. Right here and now. You know I'm faster than you even with yours already out of the holster. That time we went into Cambodia? Those two gooks jumped out and I dropped them both before you could blink."

"Because I could see one was our guy and the other the prisoner he was bringing in."

"What does that matter? I was faster then and still am."

"Keep your money. I'm only talking to Sexton."

"I'm not bullshitting. I warned you."

"Then I'll warn you. Reach for your gun and you're dead."

"You'll never raise yours."

"I don't have to. My partner will shoot you."

Larchmont laughed. "I take it back. You trying that means you really don't have it anymore."

"Yes he does," Bina said standing behind him.

Loq finally saw Larchmont blink. He walked up to him, yanked the semiautomatic out of its holster, and ejected the round in the chamber and the magazine.

"Looks like you don't have it anymore," he said.

Larchmont seethed. "What I promised you about your sister? That's null and void. So's she."

Loq shouldered past him, knowing to say nothing bit more than any threat he could've made.

They quickly made their way back to the pickup and drove away from downtown.

"No coins in your pockets," Loq said. "He never heard you following him from the M&M."

"Because I'm a dancer," Bina said. "I'm light on my feet."

"So I noticed."

They drove in silence for a few blocks. "Isn't the FBI office downtown?" she said.

"It is, but I left Sexton a message that we'll meet him in the morning. This way we can buy Carrie and Daley tonight to pack up and leave the ranch and tomorrow night to sneak into Big Hole under cover of darkness."

"Sexton will know you're here when the bartender calls him. He'll search the town."

"But he won't be able to find us."

Loq made a left onto a road that started climbing. Pavement turned into gravel and then dirt. The lights of the city fell behind. The stars above grew closer.

"Where are we?" Bina said.

"On top of a mountain of copper ore. Or what's left of it. Most of it's been mined. Shafts here run a mile deep or more. Over there is the largest open pit in the state."

They found a place to park behind a pile of tailings. Loq fed and watered the spotted pony and Túxin. He shut them inside the trailer and joined Bina who'd spread out their bedrolls. The moon hung right over them. It was the color of bone.

"Day after tomorrow we'll either be watching your sister and Killian Daley hauled away in handcuffs, or we'll be in jail, on the run, or dead," she said.

"Or doing something else," he said.

"What?"

He pulled her close and kissed her. "This."

"*This* is better," she murmured and kissed him back.

"And this is too," he said and began unbuttoning her shirt.

They quickly began pulling each other's clothes off and fell onto the bedrolls. Their lovemaking was more comet than orbit as they tried to erase the memory of Willie stabbing Candy and the bodies of the fallen Indians at the ranch and the thoughts that those portended more to fall at Big Hole.

When the heat and the bright lights began to subside and they were clinging to each other, feeling the other's heartbeat finally slow and their breathing slowing too, they told each other the words said between couples since time began by using the ancient language of their own people.

"*Átawisamas*," she said.

"*Moo ams ni stinta*," he said.

Neither needed a translation.

24

———

The FBI field office in Butte was located in a five-story brick building. It was nicknamed Siberia because many of the agents had been exiled there after a falling out with J. Edgar Hoover. Loq and Bina got the opposite of a frosty reception. Robert Sexton was boiling mad as he gave them the third degree.

"I'm locking you both up for disobeying my orders and violating federal laws," he yelled. "Your jobs? They're over, do you understand? The closest you'll ever get to a wildlife refuge again is picking up litter, and that's after you spend a few years behind bars for obstructing justice.

"You call yourself a cop, Officer Mantioc? You're a disgrace to the uniform. I don't care how hard George Tahamtaham tries to fight it, your career is over. And if he knew what you've been up to, I'm going after his badge too."

Loq looked down his high cheekbones. "Are you going to keep shouting or do you want to start listening to where you can find Killian Daley?"

Sal Tujunga looked up from a report he'd purposely been keeping his eyes glued to while Sexton had been ranting.

The senior agent took a deep breath. "What game are you playing now?"

"Not a game. I know where he's going to be. The reason I'm late getting here is because we spent the last couple of days locked in a room where he's hiding out."

"I don't believe you."

"Why would I lie?"

"To protect your sister."

"I'm telling you *to* protect Carrie. We were coming here right after we got off the radio with Tahamtaham who told us you wanted me in Butte and Bina to go home. Since we were in her rig, she's here too."

Bina nodded. "We were on the way when we happened on a traffic accident in Garrison. We stopped to help—I'm a trained nurse. Turned out it'd been staged by Daley. They knocked Loq out, tied us up, and threw us in a semi's trailer. When we got to where they'd been hiding, they locked us in a room."

"Bullshit," Sexton said.

"You want to feel the lump on my head?" Loq said.

"If you were locked up, how'd you escape?"

"We didn't. Daley let us go."

"Why'd he do that?"

"To tell you what he's going to do next."

"Wait a second. Where were they holding you?"

"Doesn't matter. They've already left."

"Indulge me. Where?"

"They took us in and out in a big rig. They dropped us back at Bina's rig."

"Back last night, you mean."

Loq nodded. "The M&M bartender told you I was here, not CD Larchmont."

"Why do you say that?"

"Because Larchmont tailed me out of the bar and into a back

alley. When he couldn't buy me to tell him where Daley is, he threatened to kill me."

"Well, he didn't because here you are."

"You haven't heard from him, have you? That's because he's on his own mission. Unless you stop him, the blowback will be on you."

"No, it won't. Larchmont's not on my payroll. He's an independent operator. Same as it was when we were in country. You know how it worked there. Operatives were given wide latitude as long as they got the job done."

"Keep telling yourself that."

"You know who else I haven't heard from? Jack Candy. How about you?"

Loq shook his head.

"Just what I don't need. Someone besides you two running around with their own agenda. Larchmont may be in it for the money, but Candy? He's in it for revenge." Sexton rubbed his jaw. "Okay, tell me why Daley snatched you in the first place."

"To get to us before we met with you."

"How'd he know I was here?"

"Didn't say, but he knew. Could've been he was listening in when we were talking to George on the radio."

"Did you speak to anybody else besides Daley?"

"My sister."

"Where?"

"In the locked room."

Sexton gave an exaggerated groan. "Okay, what's Daley going to do next?"

"Tell the world they're right and the FBI's wrong. They're going to hold a big demonstration where he makes a big speech. Afterward, Daley shows he's a man of peace and surrenders. My sister will too. You arrest them and let the others go because they'll get off anyway. Daley and Carrie are willing to take their chances in court."

"With the help of a money lawyer paid for by his rich father." Sexton threw up his hands. "Daley and Carrie are fugitives. They're wanted for murder. What part of they're the ones who are wrong don't they get?"

"You'll have plenty of time to ask after you arrest them."

"What makes you think they won't go down without a fight."

"That'll be up to you."

"I'm not about to give them what they want or meet them on their terms. I go in, it's with the Montana National Guard. They're already locked and loaded in Helena and waiting for my call. We'll see who wins that fight."

"And you'll be playing right into Daley's hands," Bina said. "You saw what he did in Salt Lake City and the way he got national attention by commandeering a TV station in Sheridan. His demands were aired everywhere. How do you think it'll go over with the American people when uniformed soldiers start shooting at him and a hundred men, women, and children."

"That's how many followers he has with him?"

"You're missing the point. It'll be like what happened when the Ohio National Guard was sent to Kent State a few years ago, only bigger. Much bigger. Do you want that many deaths on your conscience?"

"You'll be the FBI's newest fall guy," Loq said. "They won't even reassign you here to Siberia. You'll be the one in prison, not us."

Sexton engaged in another stare-down, only this time he wasn't focusing on Loq or Bina, but the back of his own eyeballs as the scene they painted played out.

"Okay, Montana's a big state. Where's he going to give his speech?"

"At the Nez Perce historic battlefield at Bear Paw. It's east of Havre, near Chinook."

"When?"

"Sometime tomorrow."

"Why there?"

Bina said, "Because Chief Joseph laid down his arms and ended a long-running war to keep the last of his people from being killed. He said he'd fight no more forever and surrendered."

Sexton turned to Tujunga. "You've been working up several theories and pouring over maps and talking to locals. What have you come up with?"

The junior agent held up a page from the report in front of him. It was a state map. A bright red star was on it. He tapped it with his finger. "I narrowed it down to the same place. Bear Paw. It's also the most logical given its historical significance."

"Why there and not anywhere else where Indians fought the cavalry?"

"Timing, sir. The Nez Perce War took place exactly one hundred years ago. This is the centennial anniversary. It's a news hook and will get more play in the media because reporters will be able to file background stories on the nation's last Indian war. They'll also be able to profile Chief Joseph. He's a legend because his words became a popular slogan during the anti-Vietnam War demonstrations."

Sexton blew air. "I'll probably see the same damn reporters at Bear Paw as I did in Saigon. They were more of a pain in the ass than Charlie ever was."

He stewed on what he'd heard and then slapped the table. "Okay, I need more clarity on this. I'm going upstairs to talk to the station chief about how many assets he can deploy and then call Quantico and the governor. While I'm doing that, keep an eye on these two. Cuff them to their chairs if you have to. Shoot them if you must."

He stormed out. When the door slammed behind him, Bina smiled at the young field agent. "You have very good investigative skills. How long have you been with the Bureau?"

"Nearly three years, ma'am."

"Call me Bina. What were you doing before then?"

"I was in college."

"Where?"

"Cal State San Bernadino."

"Oh, you're from California. Which part?"

"Near where I went to school."

"Has your family always lived there?"

He nodded.

"What did you study?"

"Criminal justice."

"That makes sense. Tujunga. Is that Spanish?"

"Lots of names in California are."

"What's it mean in English?"

He hesitated. "Old woman's place."

"I took some Spanish classes when I was at Blue Mountain College studying nursing. If I remember right, old is *viejo*, woman is *mujer*, place is, uh, *lugar*, I think. I don't understand how your last name translates to old woman's place."

The young agent didn't respond.

Bina cocked her head. Her beaded hair tie sparkled under the overhead fluorescent light. "You know what I think? It's not Spanish at all, but an Indian word. Lots of different tribes live in Southern California. Which one is yours?"

"I know what you're trying to do and it won't work," Tujunga said. "I'm FBI. I'm not going to let you go."

"I'm not asking you to. I'm only saying don't be ashamed of who you are, especially if your ancestors are Native. Most of the

Indians living in California right after the gold rush had to pretend to be Mexican so they wouldn't be killed because the governor put a bounty on them. Even so, thousands were murdered. Think of your ancestors, how proud they'd be to know their tribe—their family—still exists and you have an important job."

The agent's head dipped for a moment, but rose right back. "Tujunga is a Gabrieliño-Tongva word. My ancestors descended from them. I'm San Gabriel Band of Mission Indians on my father's side."

"*A'ho*," she said. "Pleased to meet you, my brother."

"You chose a warrior's path going into law enforcement," Loq said. "Your father must be proud of you."

"Cancer took him two years ago, but, yes, he was."

"Mission Indians, Mission Indians," Bina muttered. "Wait, only one band is federally recognized and that's the San Manuel Band. They're Serrano, not Gabrieliño-Tongva, aren't they?"

Tujunga nodded. "Our history is different than theirs. We're one of California's eighteen lost treaties tribes. The US Army forced us to give up our traditional lands in exchange for a reservation. We had no choice but to agree, but then the US Senate ordered all the treaties concealed. We lost everything."

Bina reached out to touch his hand. "I'm sorry, and I wouldn't blame you one bit if you supported what Killian Daley is trying to do to get all tribes recognized."

Tujunga snatched his hand back. "Do you think I'd still have this job if I supported Kills in Daylight?"

Bina and Loq exchanged a quick glance at his use of Daley's nom de guerre. She drew closer to the young agent. "Carrie Horse told us," she said.

"Told you what?"

"That they have someone on the inside. How they've been able to stay a step ahead of the FBI."

"I don't know what you're talking about," Tujunga said.

As he did, Sexton returned. "Don't know what about what?"

Bina turned around and smiled. "Where the ladies' room is and if it has a sanitary napkin dispenser. That's what I was asking him."

Sexton coughed. "There's nothing to be embarrassed about, Tujunga. If you had a girlfriend, you'd know what she was talking about. Go ask one of the secretaries for her. Go on, they'll know."

The young agent hurried out.

"What did you find out?" Loq said.

"It appears you're telling it straight. A state trooper spotted a convoy of Indians heading east of Big Sandy. That's on the way to the Bear Paw Battlefield. He's tailing them now. National Guard is mustering. Some will go by land. Others by air. They'll have the place surrounded by nightfall. Indians will be able to get in, but they won't get out until we want them to. And that means when we have Daley and your sister in chains tomorrow."

"How are we going to get there?"

"There is no we, Loq. There's me, my agents, and my army. You? Her? There's a nice holding cell down in the basement with your names on it where you're going to cool your moccasins until it's all over and I decide whether or not I'm going to press charges against you both."

"That's not fair," Bina said.

"Don't be mad at me, Officer Mantioc. I'm the one who's making sure you get one of those feminine products you so obviously need."

25

Two agents marched Loq and Bina down to the windowless basement. Both wore dark suits. One smelled of aftershave, the other of breath mints that did little to mask the sweet odor of bourbon.

Aftershave ordered Loq and Bina to empty their pockets and remove their belts and boots. Bourbon put the belongings in one of the lockers opposite the cell.

"Frisk them to make sure," Aftershave said.

Bourbon took a longer time running his hands up and down Bina's legs and patting down her chest and sides than he had Loq. She stared straight ahead while Loq saw an eagle plucking a fish from Klamath Lake with sharp talons and biting its head off.

Aftershave unlocked the door to the cell and swung it open. "In you go."

He slammed the door behind them, turned the key, and pocketed it.

Bourbon pressed his face against the bars. "Everyone's riding off to Indian Country. Make yourself comfortable 'cause it's gonna be a long night."

Once the two agents were gone, Loq quickly examined the cell. A metal-framed bunk bed was bolted to the wall. No springs were beneath the thin mattresses that could be fashioned into a lockpick or shiv. The sink had one faucet. He gave it a turn. The water was the color of old pennies. The tankless, seatless toilet didn't provide anything that could be fashioned into a weapon or tool. Though he knew it was a waste of time, Loq grabbed the bars on the door and gave it a hard shake. It didn't budge.

Bina sat on the bottom bunk. "I've frisked and locked up offenders before, but never had it done to me. Now I know why the toughest resist so much. They're not only the maddest, they're also the scaredest."

"We'll get out of here," he said.

"I know, but probably too late to do anything. Once Sexton gets to Bear Paw and questions the people Daley sent there, he'll realize they're decoys. He'll force one to talk, and when he finds out they're at Big Hole, he'll attack with a vengeance."

"That'll only happen if we let it."

She looked up at him. "I didn't know you were an optimist."

"I'm not. I'm a Klamath."

She looked at him quizzically and then grinned. "Okay, you do know how to tell a joke."

He sat beside her. "I've been locked up before."

"Where?"

"In Vietnam. The hardest part was not trying to keep track of time. If you count every hour, every day, it makes it seem longer. But if you don't think about when it began and when it will end, it becomes flat time."

"I don't understand."

"Round time is clock time. Flat time is like when you're riding Túxin toward the horizon. You're thinking about being with your horse, not about getting to where you're going."

Bina could see herself loping across the reservation, her long hair flying behind her the same as the roan's tail, the sound of their breath in her ears, the warmth of the sun on her face, the sight of their shadows on the ground moving as one, not a care in the world, never wanting it to end.

"Did you escape or did someone come and free you?" she said.

"They let me go."

"Why?"

"They needed me."

"What?"

"It was Sexton and Larchmont who put me in the hole. They were interrogating a prisoner and I tried to stop the way they were doing it." Loq blinked away the memory of eyelids being stitched closed, of water being poured. "Sexton received another assignment and needed me to carry it out."

"And you agreed despite what he did to you?"

"I was a soldier. I was duty bound."

"To carry out another assassination?"

"This was a rescue mission."

"Of American soldiers?"

"Only one had been taken prisoner."

"And you freed him?"

"Yes."

"He owes you his life. He must be very grateful. Have you seen him since?"

"Yes."

"When?"

"Last night."

Bina jumped. "It was CD Larchmont?"

Loq nodded, flashing on the scene of sneaking into a guerrilla camp in the jungle, taking out the guards, freeing Larchmont from a bamboo cage, leading their pursuers down a trail he'd strewn with Claymores, hearing his grandfather's words about always remembering where you set your traps.

"But he was going to kill you in the alley."

"He was going to try."

"Doesn't he think he owes you anything?"

"No."

"What kind of man thinks that way?"

"A man who believes as long as he's in someone's debt, he can never be free."

"That's crazy."

"Larchmont is."

"Do you think you're responsible for his life because you saved it?"

"No, and I'll take it back even quicker than I saved it if forced to."

"Would that trouble you?"

"Everything about Larchmont troubles me, but that? It'll end all the trouble."

Footsteps echoed on the stairway. Loq and Bina looked over to see if it was Aftershave or Bourbon coming back. It was neither.

"I brought you what you asked for," Sal Tujunga said. He was carrying a brown lunch bag with a folded top. "One of the secretaries went into the ladies' room and got it. She put it in this bag because she said the men in the office would ... well."

Bina was about to tell him she'd made it up as cover, but only said thanks.

Tujunga stopped a couple of feet short of the cell. "You should know it could be some time before anyone is free to bring you something to eat. We're all being deployed to Bear Paw except for two agents who are going to Big Hole. Agent Sexton wants to cover all the bases."

He paused, letting it sink in. "The office staff upstairs is too busy to see to you too. They're chained to their desks preparing requisitions to transmit to Quantico."

"What about our horses?" Bina said. "They're in a trailer hooked to my pickup parked in the lot. They'll need food and water. If it's hot out, the trailer will need to be pulled into the shade."

"There's nothing I can do about it. Agent Sexton is waiting out front for me. We're taking a helicopter to Bear Paw. We're going to do a flyover to see how close the mountains are to the battlefield named after them."

He switched his gaze from Bina to Loq and held it. "Then I'll be able to say, I have seen the mountain."

The phrase all but rang the steel bars. Loq nodded to him. "You really have taken a warrior's path. May it lead to much honor."

"And may yours as well." Tujunga pushed the brown paper bag through the bars toward Bina. When she took it, he spun and left.

"I was right about him," she said.

"You've been right about a lot of things," Loq said.

She opened the bag. A key lay on top of a thin blue and white box. "He's taking a big risk giving us this."

"He's been taking them the whole time being Daley and Carrie's eyes and ears. He needed to tell us about the agents going to Big Hole so we can go warn them."

"Then let's do Tujunga the honor of not getting caught."

"We'll give the agents ten minutes to clear out and then—"

"Is that flat time or round time?"

Loq returned her grin. "Neither. It's go time."

They counted off the seconds. Loq took the key, reached through the bars and inserted it into the lock. He gave a twist. The click sounded as loud as a grenade going off. The squeaking of the hinges sounded even louder. They moved quickly, gathering their belongings from the locker. Leaving their boots off, they climbed the stairs to the landing and a door marked Fire Exit. Loq pushed down the handle, gritting his teeth, expecting an alarm to scream. Nothing sounded, not even the sunshine flooding in and sweeping them back out.

Pausing only long enough to pull on their boots, they strolled hand in hand to the parking lot, taking their time unlocking the pickup, starting the ignition, and pulling out of the lot, careful to look both ways before turning onto North Main Street and then slowly driving away.

26

Loq checked the side mirrors for tails as they cut south to the Big Hole River. They followed it west on a two-lane state highway through a canyon carved between forested mountains and then into a lush valley of sagebrush scrub, fields, and pastureland.

"This was always a major trade route used by the Nimiipuu and other tribes," Bina said. "I can feel their presence. Can you?"

"Mm."

"I'm not sure what to expect when we get there."

"The two FBI agents ahead of us will have closed the battle-field and cleared any visitors out by now."

"I meant, what I'll feel being where so many people were slaughtered. What about you?"

"Sorrow, anger, and hope. Hope that we can keep more people from being killed."

"You realize we've crossed the Rubicon."

"What's that?"

"The point of no return. It's the river Julius Caesar crossed in defiance of the Roman Senate and triggered a civil war."

"We're defying the FBI all right, but we're trying to stop a war, not start one."

"I know, but we're taking Killian Daley's side against them."

"I'm taking the side of my sister and all the others who are following him without knowing the hellfire they'll face if they try and battle the FBI and Montana National Guard."

"But only one side can win."

"And both sides will lose if there's gunfire. It's a simple truth about war."

Bina sighed. "When we started out, I was sure which side was in the right, but now I don't know anymore. Especially after what George said about the CI in Warm Springs having been tortured and executed. I'm sworn to uphold the law, but Daley's followers feel like family to me. In many respects, they are. How can I side against them?"

"You're on the side of keeping them alive."

"You make it sound so easy."

"It's not going to be."

The sound of the pickup's wheels spinning on the pavement filled the silence for a few miles.

Bina finally broke it while looking at a map. "According to this, there's only one entrance to the battlefield. The road goes to a visitor's center and on to a parking lot where footpaths lead to various sites and memorials. There's sure to be a gate and the FBI agents Sexton sent there could be guarding it. Maybe Beaverhead County sheriff's deputies."

"If anybody is, they'll be National Park Service rangers who work there. The agents are probably getting a tour so they can get the lay of the land even though they're assuming Daley's on his way to Bear Paw."

"What's your plan for getting through the entrance?"

"Not go that way."

Loq slowed as they reached the outskirts of the tiny town of

Wisdom. They passed through without spotting a state trooper or sheriff's deputy. He started looking for a road leading off to the right.

Bina tapped the map. "I see what you're doing. You're going to take the Upper North Fork Road that cuts over to the northern part of the battlefield."

His long mohawk brushed the headliner as he nodded. "There's no entrance up there, at least not an official one, but the road will take us right alongside the boundary. We'll find a place to stash the rig and ride the rest of the way."

"Túxin and the spotted pony will like that. So will I."

"It won't be a flat time ride. We've got to get in fast without getting spotted and then find where Carrie and the others are likely to set up camp when they sneak in tonight. They'll probably get in the same way we are."

They made the turn and crossed a bridge over the river. The water below was as blue as the sky. Loq knew it was also a blue ribbon trout stream and was surprised no one was casting flies. The air was warm and a hatch of insects was surely on. He decided that'd be their cover if anyone stopped them, just as it had been when they were crossing the Wallowa Mountains: a happy couple on a fishing vacation. Oregon seemed like a long time ago even though it wasn't.

"Look!" Bina said, pointing toward a field where a herd of elk was grazing, a big-antlered bull standing guard against wolves and all comers.

"Wapiti. The Shawnee and Cree call them that for their white rump."

"Uh-oh. A pickup heading our way."

"Nod and wave," Loq muttered, feeling his Smith & Wesson pressed against his hip. "Nod and wave."

The oncoming vehicle slowed. So did Loq. He raised two fingers from his grip at the top of the steering wheel and nodded as they drew alongside each other. The other rig didn't have a star on the door or lightbar on the roof. The driver was White and looked to be a rancher. He nodded to Loq and returned the two-finger greeting.

"Do you think he'll report us?" Bina said.

"Don't know why he would unless there's some kind of alert on the radio. Even if he's inclined to, he'll have to wait till he gets to Wisdom. I didn't see a CB antenna on his cab."

"All the same, let's speed up round time so we can hide the rig and light out across open ground where no one on four wheels can follow us."

Another bridge took them back across the river. They found a dirt track that led off the pavement and dropped into the riverbed. It was rutted and bumpy and had been made by fishermen. The track entered a thick stand of willows and aspens. Loq pulled in as far as he could, parked, and got out. He walked back to where they'd turned in and tried to spot the pickup and trailer. They were well hidden.

He rejoined Bina. "This'll work."

They unloaded the spotted pony and roan mare, saddled them, and tied on bedrolls and gear. Loq slipped his rifle into the scabbard.

Bina frowned as she watched him. "I hope it doesn't come to that."

"Me too, but if we encounter FBI agents or rangers, we'll need to tie them up, and that'll take persuasion."

"We're way past the Rubicon now," she said as she scabbarded her rifle.

"And now we have to cross the Big Hole too and without a bridge."

Loq swung onto the pony and led the way. It felt good to be on horseback again and he knew Bina felt the same. He didn't even question that anymore—knowing what she liked, what she didn't. And though he hadn't come right out and told her, he was aware of how his allegiance between Daley and the FBI had shifted too. It was an unsettling position to be in, because feeling conflicted could lead to the same deadly risks when it came time to make a split-second decision to save a loved one: hesitation and impatience.

The spotted pony didn't balk when Loq reined him toward the water. He stepped right in and didn't spook when his hooves slipped on mossy rocks. Loq started singing and the pony's ears didn't lay back, not even when the water came up to his chest and the strong current threatened to bowl him over.

Túxin appeared to enjoy the feel of water after all the hours spent bumping around in the hot trailer. She whinnied her approval and Bina reached forward to pat her neck and say attagirl.

Climbing out of the river was harder than getting in. An eddy swirled in front of the far bank and the water grew deeper and the bottom softer. Loq clicked his tongue and tapped his heels against the pony's sides to encourage him to make a bolt for dry land. With a snort and a splash, he scrambled up the bank. Loq turned to watch Bina and the mare, but the pair got out with a lot more grace and a lot less splashing.

Riding and dancing, he thought, they're one and the same for her.

Their route took them on the backside of hills that were covered with Douglas fir trees and lodgepole pines. To their right rose the knife-edged ridges and ten-thousand-foot-high peaks of the Anaconda Range. Even in August, permanent snowfields glistened in the cirques and crowned the highest summits.

"The battlefield is on the left side of these hills," Loq said. "Let's ride to the top and take a look."

After picketing the horses between two pines, they walked

through the forest until it gave way to tall grass and sagebrush. Kneeling to remain out of sight from anyone who might be looking up from the valley, Loq started searching with his binoculars. He traced the trails that led from the parking lot. When he reached a long, flat spot along the river, he handed them to Bina.

"Down there," he said. "That's where the Nimiipuu's main camp was and next to it where they pastured their horses."

She focused on it. "Eighty-nine tepees. That's how many there were when the cavalry attacked them early on the first morning. Most were filled with sleeping women, children, and elders. One was a maternity tepee with mothers and newborns inside."

Loq closed his eyes and sang a prayer for the ninety Indians who were killed during the day and a half of fighting. Thirty-one soldiers also died.

"All of this is hallowed ground," he said. "For Daley and the National Guard to wage another war here would bring dishonor to it and all those who died. We can't let that happen."

Bina swept the binoculars. "I see the entrance. The gate's closed. A green pickup is parked on this side of it. It's a National Park Service vehicle."

"Can you see anyone standing next to it?"

"No, but somebody could be sitting inside it waiting to answer any questions from visitors who drive up and wonder why the park's closed."

She swung the binoculars toward the visitor's center. "Two more vehicles are parked in front of the building. One's another green Park Service pickup, the other a black sedan. Same make and model as what Robert Sexton was driving when we saw him in Oregon."

"Standard issue for FBI field agents."

"Maybe they're inside talking with a ranger."

"Or they're getting a tour on foot. They could even be coming our way. Keep a sharp lookout."

They watched in silence for a while. Bina said, "What are you thinking?"

"Thinking like my sister and Daley would. Where's the best place to set up camp? The best place to hold a demonstration. The best way to videotape a speech. The easiest way to get the lawyer, reporters, and celebrities and politicians here."

"We're looking at it. Not up here in the hills, but right down there. They can set up along the river. The road from the highway can bring people right to it. The valley, the river, the hills, the mountains behind, they make the perfect backdrop for cameras."

Loq studied the scene. "But if I think like a warrior who wants to stage a battle, that's a killing field like it was a hundred years ago. Daley's people would be trapped between the river and the hills. It cedes the high ground to the enemy."

He pointed. "See the trail that leads to the hill over there? During the Big Hole battle, the cavalry hauled a howitzer up there to rain hell down on the camp."

"The families in the tepees were sitting ducks," she said.

"Except the gun crew was inexperienced. They fired two rounds without hitting anyone. Nimiipuu warriors counterattacked and wiped it out. But if the Montana National Guard sets up mortars there, the shells won't miss and anyone in the valley below won't stand a chance."

"We have to convince Daley to put away his guns. It's the only way."

"Something's happening in the parking lot. Can you see it?"

Bina trained the binoculars on it. A man wearing a suit and tie came out of the visitor's center building and hurried toward the black sedan.

"He's one of the agents who put us in the cell," she said. "The one who smells of aftershave, not alcohol. He's opening the door and reaching for something inside. It's the radio mike. He's talking. Now he's listening. Okay, he hung up the mike."

Bina watched as he ran back to the building. "Maybe it was a call from Butte telling him we escaped. Or maybe it was from Sexton telling him Killian Daley was spotted heading here and not Bear Paw."

She lowered the binoculars. "What do you think?"

"Not what I think, but what I know. In battle, there are no maybes, no what-ifs. There's only action and reaction, and both result in death."

27

The FBI agents sprinted out of the Big Hole Battlefield visitor's center, jumped into the black sedan, and sped out of the parking lot. The green pickup's driver opened the gate and got out of the way as the sedan barreled past and turned onto the two-lane highway, its tires squealing.

"Looks like they're heading back to Butte," Bina said.

"Someone must've noticed we're gone and they're on the hook since they locked us up," Loq said.

"I hope they can't pin it on Sal Tujunga."

"He must be clever at covering his tracks having gotten away with it this long."

"But he trusted us not to give him up."

"Carrie told him he could. How he knew to tell me he'd seen the mountain."

The park ranger closed the gate and drove back to the visitor's center. Loq and Bina remained at their hilltop post as the afternoon shadows grew long. Dusky flycatchers began springing off branch tips, twisting in midair to snatch insects with their beaks. Yellow warblers whistled their *sweet sweet sweet, I'm so sweet* songs from perches on bushes.

At six o'clock, the park rangers exited the visitor's center and drove away, closing and locking the gate behind them.

"Do you think there's a night watchman?" Bina said.

"No need for one," Loq said. "Nimiipuu spirits guard this battlefield."

"Then there's no need for Daley and his followers to sneak in like we did. They can drive right up the main entrance."

"Let's get the horses."

They rode down the hill and into the valley. Clouds of insects roiled over the river's surface and the water dimpled as trout rose to sip them. A great blue heron stalked the shallows for frogs and fish. The iridescent head of a mallard drake gleamed like an emerald. Loq and Bina dismounted when they reached the outskirts of the historic camp and walked their horses along the edge.

"I close my eyes and can see it the night before the attack," she said softly. "Elders telling stories around the fires. Mothers putting their children to bed inside the tepees. Men talking about where they'll go hunting in the morning. But everyone knowing that after traveling this long from Wallowa Lake, and fighting so many battles, their journey for freedom is far from over and death is always close at hand."

Loq crouched and passed his palm over the blades of tall grass. "Their roots are long and deep so they can survive the heat of summer and the snow of winter to grow again each spring. The same is true of the Nimiipuu who camped here. They live again in their descendants."

"I want to dance for them," Bina said.

"The Ghost Dance?"

"The Grass Dance. It honors the departed by paying them respect and also asks Mother Earth for strength. Both are needed now. Only men danced it in the old days, but now women do too. Will you dance it with me?"

"Of course."

Both plucked handfuls of tall grass and clutched them. Bina began to hum. Loq joined in. The humming became words. They sang for the Nimiipuu who were killed there, for the ones who later perished at the Bear Paw Battlefield, and for those who would die on the long, hard trail to imprisonment in Oklahoma. They sang for their own ancestors and for all the tribes. They sang a song of thanks for the gifts Mother Earth had bestowed and they sang to ask her to give them strength to endure what was to come.

As they sang, they swayed like tall grass in a gentle breeze, grass that grew where buffalo once thundered across the Great Plains, grass on the hills where the Umatilla's horses ran free, and grass in the fields that grew beside the blue waters of Klamath Lake. They danced until the sun reddened the sky and turned the valley to gold and the shadows of the trees on the hilltops grew so long they grew into darkness.

Afterward, Loq and Bina rode down to the locked gate. A padlock shone in the moonlight. Loq pried off the hasp with his skinning knife. He left the unlocked gate closed, but draped his blanket over it so Carrie would know it was safe to enter.

Returning to the valley, they made a campfire and sat beside it while their horses grazed and great gray owls filled the night air with booming *whoos*. Two hours after midnight a pair of headlights scissored the darkness as a truck turned up the entrance road. More headlights followed, some low to the ground, some high, some close together, some wide apart. Pickups, big rigs, bobtail trucks, vans, station wagons, and old sedans formed the convoy carrying Killian Daley and his followers.

The lead vehicle stopped close to where Loq and Bina were sitting. Carrie slid out from behind the wheel. She was holding his blanket.

"Grandmother wove this for you. I helped her spin the yarn

and she taught me how to use a loom. The center design symbolizes *Gii-was* and the border the Klamath Forest. When I saw it covering you as a newborn, I was the happiest girl in the world because I finally had a brother who would always be my best friend."

Carrie touched his shoulder as she walked past and stopped where the first of the eighty-nine tepees once stood. Loq could hear her breathing, hear her murmuring. He recognized the Maklak words to a prayer for the dead.

Killian Daley came up to him. His eyes reflected the flames of the campfire. They also burned with something Loq had seen before—the look in General Nguyen Tran's eyes when he exhorted his guerrilla fighters to attack, convincing them they were invincible, that death in battle was glorious and they'd live forever as heroes. The magnetic leader's hold over his cultish followers was so strong, the CIA considered him to be the Viet Cong's most powerful weapon and targeted him for elimination by any means.

"You persuaded the FBI we'll be at Bear Paw," Daley said.

It was a statement, not a question, but Loq answered anyway. "After Bina and I told Sexton, he made some calls. He got a report from the state troopers that a convoy of Indians was headed there."

"But the honor for him going is yours."

"I didn't do it for honor. I did it to save lives. Agent Sexton will track down your decoys at first light. He'll be ruthless questioning them. It won't take him long to learn the truth. Once he does, he'll send his forces here."

"It will still take him half a day to get here."

"By road, but not by helicopter. He choppered to Bear Paw from Butte as did some of the National Guard troops from Helena. They can be here in a couple of hours."

"Then we'll prepare and greet him in kind."

"Don't bring dishonor to this sacred place by turning it into another killing field. Don't make innocent people shed their blood for you."

Daley glared. "And don't you tell me what's right and just."

"Then I'll tell you what Sexton will do. You brandish your silver Winchester even when giving your speech, and he'll convince the National Guard commander to fire. Not only will you die, but all your followers will too."

"You don't know that."

"I've seen him and the operative he employs do it before."

"Your vision is blinded because you think the worst rather than the just. Go home to Chiloquin. I have no use for you here."

Daley turned his back to Loq and began barking orders. People formed a human chain and began unloading the trucks. The camp quickly became a village. The three tepees that had been at the ranch outside of Livingston were erected. Generators were brought from a truck and electrical cords laid.

"He's setting up a stage," Bina said. "They need power to run the lights, the projector, the video recorders."

"No, he's setting up a target," Loq snapped. "Can't you see that?"

"I'm not the one you should be angry with," she snapped right back. "Go talk to your sister."

Loq stomped off and searched the site. He found Carrie unloading supplies from a van. Her hair was tied in a long braid that whipped the back of her shoulders as she took a basket from one person and handed it to the next.

"I need to talk to you," he said. "It's important."

"And so is this," Carrie said. "We've been driving for hours on ranch roads, forest service roads, back roads, and every kind of road there is. People are hungry. They need to eat before they rest. The morning is going to be even busier."

Loq saw a young man walking by. He grabbed his shoulder.

"Take Carrie Horse's spot. She needs to see something before sunup."

Carrie wiped the sweat from her brow with the back of her hand. "What's so important that it can't wait?"

"Life," he said. "Everyone's."

He led her around the battlefield with his flashlight, showing her where Sexton and the National Guard would land. Where they'd launch their wedges to drive everyone into a kill box. Where they'd set up their cordons to block escape routes. And where they'd position their heavy weapons to silence anyone and everyone with or without a gun who disobeyed or challenged them.

28

DUSTY ROAD

The echo of the shotgun blast rolled down Trout Creek Canyon as Hex Taggert locked his arms around me and squeezed while we wrestled on the ground next to the wrecked car. The click-clack of another shell being pumped into the 12 gauge's chamber quickly followed.

"Let him go or I'll shoot!" Johnny yelled.

Hex looked over my shoulder.

"Why, you're just a kid." He brayed.

"I'm not kidding."

Hex brayed again. "I said, you're a kid, you dumbass. Don't you understand English?"

I drove my knee into Hex's crotch again while jabbing my fingers into his ribs that I bet were bruised if not broken from the car wreck.

He roared in pain.

Johnny yelled again. "Let my father go!"

"Your daddy? Then you ain't gonna shoot. That scattergun'll pepper us both. Go on home."

Johnny scurried forward and jammed the tip of the barrel against Hex's forehead. "You're going home."

"Ow! You little shit. You ain't gonna shoot me. Takes a man to do that."

"I've done it before. I'm Viet Cong."

Hex hooted. "Yeah, how many men you kill?"

"Soldier who counts is no soldier at all. But I'll count you if you don't let him go."

Hex's rotten breath filled my ear. "What kinda kid are you?"

I was running out of air and so I started jabbing my elbows as hard as I could to try and break his bear hug. I elbowed his arms again and again while I kept kneeing him. It finally worked and I squirmed out. The shotgun pressing against Hex's forehead kept him pinned to the ground.

I jumped up, found my holster and drew the .357. "I got him now, son. You can back away."

"*Không!*" Johnny shouted at me. "*Tôi sẽ làm nó.*"

I recognized the words for "No! I will do it." His sudden switch to Vietnamese hit me in the gut like one of Hex Taggert's punches. It was as if Johnny was suddenly back in country and assuring Comrade Minh he'd do whatever he ordered. Execute a prisoner. Charge the enemy in a firefight. Carry a bomb onto a GI base.

I thought I'd finally gotten over Vietnam, but faced with the stark reminder of how the war kept kids from being kids threatened to pull me right back down the black hole I'd worked so hard to climb out of.

"Johnny, listen to me. It's okay. You're safe. I got you. I got this. Back away."

"No. I will do it. *Tôi sẽ làm nó.*" His finger was tightening on the trigger.

"But you don't have to. I don't want you to. Gemma wouldn't either. Pudge too. We all love you."

Johnny started to tremble. Hex started to sweat. His pig's eyes grew wide, even the one that drooped.

"Call him off! Call him off!"

"If you kill him, there's no going back," I said to Johnny. "You can't undo it. It'll be murder. You can't go back to the ranch. The law won't let you. You can't go back to Vietnam and look for Sen Vàng."

"Sen Vàng. I must find her."

"And we will. Together. But not if you shoot him. You don't want to live with that."

"But he's my enemy."

"Your war's over, Johnny. It's been over for a while."

"It has?"

"Yes. The Viet Cong won. You won."

Johnny started trembling and then screamed. He raised the gun to the sky and pulled the trigger. The explosion broke the spell. He ran to Kosse and buried his face in the horse's breast and sobbed.

Hex let out a groan. "And they call me crazy."

He started to get up, but I waggled my revolver at him. "Uh-uh. Stay right where you are."

I called to Johnny. "Get the lasso from my saddle and check the right saddlebag. Should be a pair of handcuffs in it."

"You're law?" Hex said.

"Ranger. US Fish and Wildlife."

"A deer cop? You gotta be shitting me."

Johnny brought the lasso and handcuffs. I tossed the bracelets to Hex. "Cuff your right wrist and then roll over and put both hands behind your back. Do anything else and I'll shoot you. Not dead, but you'll wish you were."

I knelt on his back and clicked the other bracelet around his left wrist and then looped the noose end of the lasso around his neck and pulled it tight.

"Ow, you're lynching me," he wheezed.

"I'll leave that to the authorities. Right now I'm going to hogtie you to the car you stole and used to kidnap those kids."

"They begged me to take 'em."

"Going to be hard to prove. One's dead and the other's close to it. I don't think their parents will be in a listening mood when they find out."

He started swearing and, although I'd heard worse, I didn't want Johnny to. I jerked the lasso tighter and cut off his air and cursing. I sat him down by the back bumper and tied him to it. Before loosening the noose, I tore a strip off his dirty shirt and gagged him with it. The anger flashing in his eyes was hot enough to light a fire and so I tore another strip and blindfolded him.

Johnny was watching me the whole time, but I didn't have time to worry about modeling good behavior. Hex Taggert was a killer. I only had to look at the dead teenager draped over the car's hood to know that. I also knew it'd be a double murder if I didn't try to do something fast about saving the girl in the back seat.

"Help me with the horses," I said to Johnny.

I tied a rope to Wovoka's saddle horn and the other end to the stuck left rear door. Johnny did the same to the right rear door with Kosse. We took our horses by the reins and led them. They dug their hooves in and heaved. Both horses pulling in opposite direction kept the car from sliding. The ropes twanged when they grew taut and metal screeched and jams buckled and hinges popped. The crumpled doors came off.

"I'll check the girl while you set up the lean-to with a bedroll under it," I said. "There's a first-aid kit in Wovoka's saddlebag."

"And I'll get one of the star lizard plants from Kosse's."

"Good idea."

I felt for a pulse in the girl's neck again. It was still beating.

"My name's Nick," I said in a calm and reassuring way that I did when Hattie had been stricken with chicken pox. "You've been in a wreck and my son and I are here to help you. I need to check to see if you have any injuries. Will that be okay?"

I didn't expect an answer and didn't get one. Still, I kept talking to her. It was what battlefield docs did. It was what Gemma did with injured livestock. It's not the words, she always said, it's the tone.

I ran my hands down the girl's left shoulder, arm, side, hip, and leg. I couldn't see any lacerations or feel any compound fractures, but there was no way of knowing what might have happened on her right side without lifting her. I ran my palm along the floor mat. When I felt wetness, I checked my fingers. Blood. Fresh blood.

Moving her risked paralysis if she had a spinal injury. Leaving her risked death from bleeding out. I didn't like the odds, but I had to play them.

"Johnny, bring a blanket."

We spread it on the back seat. Johnny took her feet and I slid one hand under her shoulder while holding her head still.

"Lift," I said.

We raised her out of the well and placed her on the blanket.

"I'm going to slide her toward me. Come around to my side and be ready to grab your end of the blanket. We'll carry her to the lean-to. Got to do it slow to keep from jostling her."

"She must be dreaming," Johnny said as we ducked into the lean-to and lowered her to the bedroll. "Her eyelashes are moving."

I didn't answer. I was too busy focusing on the jagged edge of the tibia sticking out of her right leg. Moving her had caused even more bleeding. I pulled a gauze pad from the first aid kit, placed it on the wound, and asked Johnny to apply pressure.

If he was sickened by the sight of blood and bone, he didn't show it. I assumed he'd seen worse in combat. When he placed one hand on the other and used his palm to press on the wound, I knew he'd done more than just seen it.

I continued the examination and saw that her right arm was bent at an impossible angle and the elbow was horribly swollen. It was surely broken, but no bone was sticking out. I lifted her blouse to check her ribs. Her right side was covered in bruises, but they were still reddish, not purple, confirming they were probably less than twenty-four hours old. But the bruising also meant she might have broken ribs. One or more could be threatening to puncture her lung or chest wall. Worse, cut an artery.

I'd been running on hope, but there was no denying reality right then and there. She needed a surgeon, a hospital team, emergency evacuation, and I had no way of doing any of that. Putting her on a horse or making a travois and dragging her to the nearest town would kill her as sure as a bullet to the head. I had to ride out and get help.

Thumping and growling and banging came from the wrecked car. Despite the handcuffs and being hogtied, Hex Taggert was thrashing around something fierce trying to free himself. He managed to spit out the gag and started cursing even louder and cruder than before.

"Let me go or I'll hunt you down and slit you gizzard to chin. Your snot-nosed kid too. Anybody else in your family gets the same. I'll kill 'em all, I swear it."

"Keep the pressure on her wound, Johnny. I'll be right back."

Hex kept spewing filthy threats up to the moment I cold-cocked him with the butt of my gun. That shut him up for a while, but it didn't silence the voice in my head shouting that I couldn't ride off for help and leave Johnny behind to deal with a severely injured girl and a killer who'd start trying to get loose the moment he woke up. And we both couldn't go or both stay either, because that would be signing her death warrant too.

As I walked back to the lean-to mulling over what to do, Johnny said, "I'll go get help."

"What?"

"I'll ride Kosse to the nearest town and bring back a doctor. A sheriff too."

"Uh-uh. It's too long of a ride to make by yourself and it'll be dark soon. You don't know the way."

"You have a map. Mark the trail. Kosse will take me. You'll see."

"It's too dangerous. You could get lost. Fall off the horse. Get hurt."

"You said I couldn't live with myself if I killed Hex. How's that any different than if I let this girl die?"

"Because I'll go," I said.

"You can't. You must stay here and take care of her and watch out for him. If I stay and you go, I'll have to shoot him so he doesn't find a way to kill me and her."

November had been right. Johnny was already on the path to manhood. I just didn't want to admit it because it meant he was that many steps closer to leaving home.

"It's going to be dark soon," I said. "It looks like it's going to rain."

"Then I'll take a flashlight and my slicker."

I took a deep breath and silently asked for mercy as I blew it out. "The cold chicken. There's still some left. Take that too. You'll get hungry."

"Okay."

"Remember what November said. Stay out of the canyons when it rains. Find a way to go around them."

"Okay."

"One other thing."

"What?"

"The shotgun. Take it. If you lose your way, fire it. I'll hear it and come find you. I'll always find you."

"I can do this. Don't worry about me."

"I won't," I lied.

Johnny mounted up and I watched as he and Kosse made their own trail up the side of the gulch to reach the road the sedan had tumbled from. He didn't look back at me as he rode and I knew that was good, but it didn't feel like it.

I took another blanket and draped it over the dead boy on the hood of the car. I placed a handful of sage on it and said, "While your journey to the spirit world started rough, you're safe now because you're with your ancestors."

I walked down to the creek and topped off my canteen and brought it back to the lean-to. I wet a cloth and dabbed the girl's lips, squeezing drops of water into her mouth, but not so many that she might choke. The compress on her broken bone and skin had done its job and stopped the bleeding. I cleaned the wound, dried it, placed a leaf from the star lizard plant over it, and wrapped it in gauze.

Sitting cross-legged next to her, I held her hand and listened to her breathing as night fell and the stars came out. It wasn't long before storm clouds blocked the starlight and the rain started falling. I tried not to think if the gulch the girl and I were in would flood. I tried not to picture what Johnny was doing. I tried not to blame myself for letting him go. And I tried not to think if Gemma would ever forgive me if something happened to him.

It wasn't until later that I learned what did.

When Johnny reached the top of the gulch, he saw that the road Hex Taggert and the teenagers had been driving on was little more than two ruts cut by horse-drawn wagons. He could make out the sedan's tire tracks on the other side of the slide and began following them.

Dusk settled in as the sun set. Johnny didn't stop. Nor did he when the sky turned inky and the stars began to shine. He looked up at the Milky Way.

"*Kosse Bbo*," he said, mimicking Lyle Rides Alone. "It will take me where I need to go because it has before."

It was the night after a firefight and he and Sen Vàng got separated from the rest of the guerrillas. They were hacking their way through the jungle trying to find their camp, not knowing if they were walking east, west, north, or south. The canopy of trees was so thick, they couldn't see any stars to use to navigate. They were scared they might stumble right into the enemy.

Exhausted and ready to give up, they finally reached a clearing and looked up. "*Ngân hà*," Sen Vàng said. "The Silver River. It will carry us home."

Johnny kept riding. The track led around a mountain, but then the stars grew dark and rain fell, softly at first, and then hard. Then even harder. It drummed against his slicker. It turned the track into mud and Kosse's hooves into clumps of it.

"Can't stop," he told the dark chestnut. "The girl depends on us. We have to keep going."

The track started downhill. Every so often, Johnny would turn on the flashlight to make sure they were still on it. The way grew steeper. Something was rumbling ahead. He shined his flashlight, but the blackness swallowed the beam. He kept riding. The mud turned to rocks and the track leveled off. And then he knew why.

He'd ridden into a canyon and the rocky edges of a creek quickly gave way to a torrent. Kosse whinnied and was swept off his hooves. Johnny grabbed the saddle horn to stay on. He remembered what November had told him about canyons and rain. And then he remembered what Nagah had said about true courage.

"Help!" he shouted into the storm. "Help. Anybody. I need help."

Above the din, he heard Nagah's voice. "Johnny Drake. I knew you were coming before you left. This is so."

It sounded like Nagah, only older.

"Are you ... Are you Nagah's grandfather? He said you would help me. Please. I need help."

"If you believe you need it, then you will have it, because you have all the help you need already inside you."

"I don't understand."

"How do you think you have traveled this far in this world already if you did not believe you could?"

"I ... I wanted to live."

"So, want it some more and you will. This is so."

Thunder cracked and lightning flashed and it spooked Kosse who struggled even harder to get out of the river. Johnny held on. "Go, boy. Go."

Hooves finally found bottom and then rocks and horse and rider climbed out and up the bank and then the side of the canyon and reached the top.

Kosse's flanks rose and fell like bellows as he sucked in air. Johnny was breathing hard too. He shined the flashlight around to see if there was any sort of trail or road, but with no stars, all was darkness. He pulled out the map to take a look, but it quickly became too soggy to read. He shoved it back inside his slicker.

"Help! I need help again. I need the stars to see where I'm going."

Johnny heard Tuhudda's voice once more. "If you can see one star, then you will see all the stars because they are the same as blades of grass, as birds in the sky. One is everything and everything is one. This is so."

"I don't understand."

"Look closer and you will."

"Wait!"

But all he heard was Kosse lowering his head and start grazing on grass. Then Johnny understood. The grass. The horse. Everything was connected.

The wind howled and he looked up and saw a single star and then another and another as the storm clouds blew away. Grass, horse, wind, cloud, star. One was everything and everything was one. All were joined together.

"There it is, boy, the Milky Way. The Dusty Road. The Silver River. Let's go!"

They started off again and aimed at the stars that shone closest to the ground. It wasn't long before Johnny realized they weren't stars at all, but the lights of a town.

The gray blanket of dawn lifted from the gulch and the lean-to warmed with the first rays of the sun. I was still holding the girl's hand, occasionally sliding my thumb to her wrist to check her pulse. It remained steady, more steady than the rain that had poured during the night and then had let up suddenly.

I let go of her hand and ducked out of the lean-to. Hex Taggert was slumped against the back bumper of the wrecked sedan. He was a soggy, muddy mess, but he hadn't drowned in the night.

After no sleep, and as much as I craved a cup of coffee, I didn't want to waste any hope on looking for dry kindling to start a fire because I needed all I had for hoping Johnny was okay. I rolled my neck, closed my eyes, and let the warmth of the sun hit my face.

Something rumbled in the distance, and I was about to spend a little bit of that hope on it not being a thundercloud as the noise grew closer. But then brakes squealed and doors slammed.

"Nick, uh, Dad. Up here. I made it. I brought a doctor. The sheriff. Tribal police. Everyone."

I opened my eyes and saw my son who was becoming a man standing above me and it made me proud.

One of the vehicles was hauling a horse trailer, and Johnny led Kosse out and rode down while a doctor and nurse tended to the girl. I told the doctor about the star lizard plant I'd put on her leg, and he said it must've helped because the wound didn't show any signs of infection.

Once the girl was stabilized, they rigged up a litter and we helped haul her up and put her in a Travelall set up like an ambulance. Then we brought up the boy's body. The sheriff and tribal cop debated whether to drag Hex Taggert up by his heels or march him up at the point of a gun. Johnny and I didn't stick around to see what they decided. We had a long ride to get back to the rig and a long drive home after that, and so we mounted up and rode out.

When we finally drove through No Mountain and reached the Warbler ranch, I braked before crossing the cattleguard.

"Why are you stopping?" Johnny said.

I patted the flour sack full of star lizard plants sitting between us and then his knee.

"To let the bad come out because the good's going back in."

29

The official sunrise at Big Hole Battlefield was 6:29 a.m., but by then the sky had already turned from charcoal to silver to strawberry to salmon to butter to lemon. The site's official opening for visitors wasn't for another two and a half hours, but a park ranger arrived at 7 a.m. the same as he did every workday. He found a delivery truck blocking the gate. Getting out of his pickup to investigate earned him a gunny sack yanked over his head and his hands cuffed behind his back.

His two coworkers arrived several minutes later and received the same treatment. The trio were taken to the visitor's center and locked in a storeroom while their pickups were parked in the lot. The gate was shut and the delivery truck moved back to block it.

Loq hadn't slept all night, nor had most of Killian Daley's followers as they continued to work through the early morning hours preparing for what was going to be either a day of triumph or tragedy.

He walked past the three tepees to a field kitchen that reminded him of the mobile ones used during maneuvers. A woman who looked to be the age of his mother beckoned him with an empty mug and asked if he wanted coffee. Loq thanked her and tried not to picture her aiming a gun at a guardsmen or falling in a crossfire of automatic weapons fire.

Bina waved at him with a piece of fry bread she'd plucked from a Hopi coil basket.

"Hungry?" she said.

"No."

She handed it to him anyway. "Did you get a chance to speak to Daley again?"

"Didn't try. He's going to do what he's been planning all along." He pointed at a nearby picnic table.

Daley was seated in the middle with warriors sitting on his left and right. The table was heaped with plates of food and jugs of water. His hair was unbraided and cascaded over his shoulders. He was wearing a white buckskin tunic with a red folded blanket draped over his left shoulder.

The intake of Bina's breath was sharp. "DaVinci's *The Last Supper*. That's not a coincidence, is it?"

"Mm. I see Willie Hawkfeather is seated closest to him. Killing Jack Candy appears to have earned him a promotion."

"Maybe it's because he danced the Sun Dance."

"Either way, I don't like the feel of this."

"What about Carrie? Did she give you a sense of what she'll do?"

"She said she'd think about it. I haven't seen her since."

"It's daylight in Bear Paw too. The battlefield there is twice the size of this, and while it's not as forested or hilly, there's still lots of places for people to hide. Sexton will have to chase one down and force them to talk."

"Yes, but he's got helicopters to search for them."

Bina lost her taste for the fry bread. "How much longer do you think we have?"

"Three, four hours. A lot shorter if the Park Service is

expecting the rangers here to report in and send someone to find out why they haven't."

Loq and Bina had gone down to the visitor's center after Daley arrived, planning to use the radio to try and contact George Tahamtaham. When they got there, the building was occupied by armed men who told them they'd cut the telephone line and destroyed the radio. The radios in the two Park Service pickups had also been destroyed after the rangers were locked up.

"Visitors could start showing up at nine expecting to get in," Bina said to Loq.

"Daley will station someone down there wearing a ranger uniform with a made-up explanation."

"I guess that leaves only one thing."

"What?"

"We saddle up, gallop in, and grab Daley. You throw him over the spotted pony and we ride off. Without him, I doubt the rest will stay and fight. Demonstrate and make speeches maybe, but not start a war with the National Guard."

"One problem with that."

"Which is?"

"Willie Hawkfeather and the men sitting with Daley. They're all armed and haven't left his side since they got here. We'd have to shoot a few and they'd shoot back."

"Then you come up with a plan."

"We get to Sexton the moment he arrives. We tell him everything's the same, that only the location is different. Let Daley give his speech and then he and Carrie will surrender."

"What makes you think he'll believe us?"

"We'll have to convince him because I don't have anything else."

They were facing each other, oblivious to the people around

them, and then Bina looked past Loq. "Let's hope we can because we're about to find out."

Loq spun around and followed her gaze. A black bug that became a black bird that became a black helicopter came whirring in from the east. It reached the battlefield and hovered, its downwash flattening the tall grass and creating waves on the river.

Killian Daley jumped up from the picnic table and whooped. His guard of warriors did too.

"Daley recognizes the bird so it's not Sexton," Loq said.

"It's Benjamin Lance, the lawyer," Carrie Horse said, joining them. "He's brought reporters with him."

She was smiling. "Now we can tell everyone the truth."

The helicopter flew to the parking lot and touched down. As the tail and main rotors slowed, the door opened. The man who stepped out was Loq's size with a shock of white hair. He wore a fringed leather jacket, bolo tie, and cowboy boots.

Ducking, he walked under the blades and picked up Carrie Horse and gave her a hug. Then he put both palms on Daley's shoulders and whooped. The two men began whooping together. Soon, everyone except Loq and Bina were whooping and trilling.

The helicopter's blades came to a stop and four passengers disembarked. One was shouldering a video camera and zooming in on Killian Daley and Benjamin Lance. Another snapped photographs. The other two scribbled in notebooks.

"There's no turning back now," Bina said.

"Let's talk to the lawyer and see if he has a death wish too," Loq said.

They went over and Carrie made introductions.

"My wife spoke highly of you when you were guests at our ranch," Lance said, his voice a rich baritone tinged with a country drawl.

"I heard a rumor—completely unsubstantiated and unprovable in a court of law that I had any foregoing knowledge or personal involvement whatsoever in its subject—that you were helpful in affording my clients the opportunity to travel to this taxpayer-financed public park that is open to all regardless of race, color, religion, and national origin. If accurate, then I extend my gratitude."

Loq looked down his high cheekbones. "FBI Agent Robert Sexton won't let lawyer talk stop him if Daley or anyone else raises a gun. It'll be a bloodbath and that blood will be on everyone's hands, yours included."

The lawyer harrumphed before guffawing. "You remind me of myself when I'm arguing a case in front of a judge who has a reputation for coddling corporate polluters and kowtowing to racists. I go right for the jugular from the start so there's no mistake who I am, what I stand for, and how far I'll go to protect my client and win their case."

"Then if you want to protect Daley and my sister, tell them to lock all their weapons in the back of one of those delivery trucks and have it driven far away."

Daley started to say something, but Lance held up his hand. "I don't *tell* my clients anything. I *advise* them. While I may agree that brandishing weapons could, and I repeat, could incite law enforcement to commit violence, I'd never advise them that they are any less entitled to own and carry firearms than the next person."

He squared his broad shoulders. "I fought long and hard for my clients at Alcatraz and Wounded Knee that they had equal rights under the Second Amendment of the US Constitution whether they lived on a reservation or not."

Lance's shock of hair crested like a foamy wave as he nodded at Loq and Bina's holstered sidearms. "I notice you two are exercising that right."

"We're both sworn law enforcement officers," Bina said.

"Enough talk!" Daley said. "Let us prepare."

As he led his lawyer and the reporters toward the three tepees, Loq and Bina held back.

"That settles it," she said. "We stay here and stick to our plan of talking to Sexton first."

"Mm, but I have a contingency plan if that doesn't work."

"What is it?"

"When the shooting starts, I grab Carrie and take her out of here."

"She'll resist and hate you for it."

"I'd rather have her mad than dead."

"Then I have a contingency plan of my own."

"What's yours?"

"I'll deal with CD Larchmont because he'll be here. You know he will."

Loq inhaled deeply through his nose. "He already is."

30

Powwow drums pounded. Wooden flute music floated light as a feather and then soared like the hawk at White Bird Canyon. Smoke from burning sage wafted on a gentle breeze that rippled the Big Hole River and the tall grass growing along the banks. A dozen men slow-walked in single file toward the left side of the largest tepee. Some shook rattles. Others chanted. A line of a dozen women did the same on the right side. Somewhere a youngster laughed. A baby gurgled.

When the first man and first woman reached the tepee, the two lines turned and faced each other, leaving a wide aisle between them. Carrie Horse emerged from the tepee and walked toward the waiting audience. Her lips were kissed with the juice of red huckleberries. A beaded headband graced her forehead and long porcupine quill earrings quivered from her earlobes. She wore Loq's blanket over her shoulders as a shawl.

The four journalists who'd arrived with Benjamin Lance were recording everything. A man wielding a movie camera and a woman holding a microphone attached to a boom had joined them. So had another woman who held a cassette recorder bearing the call sign of the college radio station in Missoula.

A second still photographer was there too. At first glance, Loq mistook him for Snaps because of the blue kerchief knotted on his head and the tendrils of long hair dripping over his collar. Two Nikons dangled from his neck. He even had on an army field jacket like the one Snaps wore in Vietnam, its oversized pockets weighted down with lenses.

When Carrie halted, the drum stopped beating too and the flute grew silent. She closed her eyes and sang a song about beavers swimming down the Williamson River at dusk, mist shrouding the crowns of firs, loons yodeling from the marshes on Klamath Lake, and old women preparing *C'waam*, the short-nose sucker fish sacred to her people.

The song over, Carrie opened her eyes. "My grandmother sang that to me as a child, the same as hers did to her and hers before. They sang it to teach Klamath children we live in a special place of beauty and are part of a great circle of living things. A verse my grandmother didn't sing was how the year I was born the US government took away our reservation and no longer recognized us as a people."

She paused while looking at her audience, their faces telling her they shared her pain.

"Seven years ago, I stood on a tiny rock in the middle of San Francisco Bay called Alcatraz. Seventy-five years before I did, nineteen Hopi fathers were imprisoned on it for refusing to surrender their sons and daughters to armed soldiers who'd come to drag their children off to federal boarding schools.

"Long before Alcatraz became a federal prison, it was home to the Ohlone. I joined others there to take it back. We even offered to pay the government for it. Twenty-four dollars' worth of glass beads and red cloth. We thought the price was more than fair. It was the same as was paid to the Lenape for a much larger island they called the place where we gather wood to make bows. Their word for it in their language was *Manhattan*."

Like the breeze on the river, laughter rippled through the crowd.

"Our occupation of Alcatraz was the joining of hands in an unbroken circle of common purpose to reclaim what has been stolen from all of us. Our land, our children, our sense of community, our traditions, our beliefs, our connection to the earth, our pride."

People grunted. Some shuffled their feet.

"I met an Oneida man there who'd traveled from his home in New York. He told me that both of us being on Alcatraz along with people from tribes who lived between the two coasts was proof that all of America was Indian Land. Once. Now. Forever."

The grunting turned into trilling, the shuffling to stomping.

"I could tell he was a spiritual man who had a great vision. He was also a warrior. But you already know that about him because it was Kills in Daylight."

Carrie had to wait until the people quieted down.

"After Alcatraz, I returned home to raise my children and help my community heal. But on a cold, snowy day in February four years ago, Kills in Daylight called me. He told me what was happening at Wounded Knee." She paused. "The second Wounded Knee."

"*A'ho* Russell Means and Dennis Banks," a man shouted.

Carrie said, "Kills in Daylight explained to me how a grave injustice was happening. He said, 'The Oglala Lakota are our brothers and sisters. They need our help. I need your help. Will you come and join us?'"

"Of course you went," a woman called from the crowd. "All women are warriors."

Carrie nodded. "Once again, Kills in Daylight proved himself to be wise and brave in spiritual matters as well as battle. Also at the negotiating table following the murder of two of our men by US Marshals."

She raised her chin. "Brothers, sisters, mothers, fathers, children, friends and honored guests. We are in a different place today than we were on Alcatraz, in South Dakota, in all the places where Kills in Daylight has valiantly fought in the name of justice so we can be who we are. Proud Indians. Proud Native Americans. Proud Indigenous People. But in the government's pursuit to silence him, he's being framed for crimes committed in Oregon."

The crowd groaned.

"Kills in Daylight did none of those things," Carrie said. "This I know to be true because I was with him in Washington State when the BIA office was bombed, when an FBI informant was murdered. When he went to meet with him in Warm Springs, the informant was already dead after having been tortured. FBI agents were waiting there to ambush Kills in Daylight."

She took a breath as she eyed the crowd. The photographers snapped her picture.

"The government refuses to believe the facts that prove Kills in Daylight's innocence. Why? Because they need to persecute him to try and silence all of us."

"It won't work," a man called out. "They'll hear our thunder!"

The drummer gave the powwow drum a few blows. People trilled.

"The FBI and Montana National Guard are on their way here right now," Carrie said. "They intend to arrest Kills in Daylight, to arrest me, to arrest us all."

Someone gave a war cry and waved a rifle.

Carrie shook her head. "No, brothers and sisters. That's what they want. A reason to fire on us. But we don't need to fight them with guns and bullets. We'll fight them with the truth. The reporters, photographers, and filmmakers here will spread it for us across the land."

The journalists all pressed forward. The video and movie cameras and tape recorders whirred. The still camera's shutters clicked faster than a machine gun.

"Who better to tell our story than the spiritual warrior who makes our unbroken circle even stronger," Carrie said, her voice rising like the flute music. "Who better than Kills in Daylight to tell the world we are not invisible. We are not divisible. We are a proud people. Proud of our traditions, our ancestors, our beliefs, our connection to the land. Our land. Our blood."

Bowing to the trills and whoops and rattles rattling, Carrie backed away as Kills in Daylight stepped out of the tepee. Still wearing the white buckskin tunic with the red blanket over his shoulder, he strode down the aisle formed by the lines of men and women. When he reached the audience, he hoisted his silver Winchester over his head with both hands and called out.

"Justice! Respect! Freedom!"

The powwow drum thundered as the crowd answered with the same three words. Some raised the clenched fist of the Red Power movement, others raised their eyes to the heavens.

Those who did saw more than the blue sky and sun above. An FBI helicopter was buzzing toward the battlefield flanked by two massive green helicopters whose rotors drowned the thunder of powwow drums and chants, and turned the laughter of children into frightened cries.

The piercing shrieks of sirens added to the din as a black sedan raced into the park at the head of a squadron of state trooper cruisers and county sheriff's rigs, all with their gumball lights flashing.

Shots rang out and Loq saw a muzzle flash from a raised rifle aiming at the helicopters. He charged and grabbed the barrel and wrenched it from the hands of the shooter.

"Stop. They'll cut us to shreds. Those Jolly Green Giants have .50-caliber machine guns and two dozen armed soldiers inside their bellies."

"Coward," the man spat.

Loq responded by hurling the rifle into the river.

Bina pushed through the crowd and joined him. "Willie Hawkfeather," she said, her breath coming in gasps. "He and two others are heading toward a spot overlooking the parking lot at the visitor's center. They're armed. Sexton's chopper is landing there."

"They start shooting at lawmen, there'll be no stopping a massacre," Loq said.

"I'll go after Willie. Maybe I can talk some sense into him."

"Be careful. He'll have his blood up."

"So will I."

"Wait, have you seen Larchmont?"

"Only briefly, but I lost him when the crowd started panicking. Are you going to get Carrie out of here?"

His long mohawk shook. "Not yet. I'll talk to Sexton first and then go look for Larchmont."

They both sprinted toward the visitor's center. Bina peeled off to the spot where she figured Willie and the others were headed. Loq kept going, reaching the parking lot as the FBI helicopter touched down next to Benjamin Lance's.

Agents Sexton and Tujunga hopped out while the main rotor continued to spin. Both held walkie-talkies. Loq raised his open palms and waited for them. The senior field agent's face flashed anger when he saw him.

"You're looking at twenty years for busting out of federal custody," Sexton said.

"You mean false imprisonment," Loq said. "Daley's lawyer is

here. He said you didn't read me my rights, didn't bring any charges. He says I can sue for what you did."

"Bullshit!"

"The only thing different today than what I told you is the battlefield. Daley and my sister are still going to surrender. Peacefully. There's no need for violence."

"Too late for that. One of the pilots radioed that bullets hit his bird."

"It was only a rabbit gun. I chucked it in the river."

"Well, I'm going to chuck in prison whoever helped you bust out."

"I picked the lock using the pin from Bina's barrette."

"More bullshit."

"We're wasting time here. National Guard teams are fast-roping from the Jolly Greens to secure LZs. One north of the clearing, one south. Radio the commander. Convince him to stay back. Keep the lawmen here."

Agents Aftershave and Bourbon ran up and made a grab for Loq. He ducked and spun away. Bourbon drew his weapon and jabbed it in Loq's face.

"Stand down, agent," Sexton ordered.

"No way," Bourbon said. "He made a laughing stock out of the entire agency. We'll see who laughs last."

Tujunga didn't hesitate. He karate chopped Bourbon's wrist, forcing him to drop the gun.

Bourbon yelped and then snarled at Tujunga. "You punk. I'm gonna tell everyone you struck a fellow agent. No one's ever gonna have your back again."

Loq said to Sexton, "Are you going to radio the Guard's commanding officer or not?"

"I can't guarantee he'll listen."

"Make him."

"Either way, you got three minutes to get Daley and Carrie to surrender. They don't, I'll lead the charge myself."

"And Larchmont. Order him to stand down too."

"Even if I could reach him, it wouldn't do any good. He's on his own."

"Give me one of your walkie-talkies. I'll call you when I'm with Daley and put him on."

Tujunga handed his over. Loq took it and raced back to the tepees.

31

Bina Mantioc wished she was riding Túxin as she ran up the trail to the hillock above the visitor's center. Umatilla history was full of stories of how their horse soldiers took advantage of speed, height, and the thunder of hooves to intimidate enemies. As she went after Willie Hawkfeather now, she only had herself to rely on.

Low voices came from the other side of the bushes. She stopped, rose on her toes, and looked over. Willie and two other teenagers were kneeling with their backs to her while sighting down the barrels of their rifles.

"I'll take out the one in the black suit," Willie whispered. "You guys get the trooper standing by his cruiser and the deputy in the cowboy hat."

Bina shoved through the bushes. "Drop your weapons right now! Do it!"

As the two other boys froze, Willie said, "Don't listen to her. She's not going to shoot anyone. Are you, Bina?"

"That's Officer Mantioc to you. And if your friends think I won't, tell them about the man who broke into Aunty Moon's house. He was dead certain I wouldn't shoot either. He got the dead part right."

The two boys dropped their rifles immediately. Willie held on to his, but moved his finger away from the trigger.

"Willie, stay put. You two, go back to the tepees and wait there. Go on. Now!"

The pair took off running. Bina sucked in her breath when they brushed past. Neither looked older than sixteen.

"Put the rifle on the ground, Willie. I'm not going to ask again."

"You might as well shoot me because I'm not going to jail. I'm a warrior and would rather die on a battlefield."

"Not on this one, you won't. No one's going to die here today."

"Tell that to the cops and army. They're going to gun down everyone."

"Not if Loq and I have anything to do with it."

"You're not in charge. Kills in Daylight is."

"We'll see about that. Now, drop the rifle."

When he did, Bina kicked all three guns into the bushes before marching the teenager back to the tepees. When they arrived, she found Loq huddling with Daley, Carrie, and Benjamin Lance.

"What are you doing with Willie?" Carrie said.

"Keeping him from making another big mistake. He and two other boys were drawing beads on law officers in the parking lot."

"They're our enemies," Willie said. "She kept us from taking them out."

"I kept you from committing murder. Theirs and everyone here because the National Guard troops would've responded with lethal force."

"She's right," Carrie said. "We can't win with guns. We must win it with words that speak truth."

Willie ripped open his shirt and exposed the fresh wounds from the Sun Dance. "Then why did I go through this?"

"To prove to yourself you have courage. To honor those who danced before you. To be part of something bigger than yourself."

"What?"

Bina said, "What you tattooed on your neck. *Wawáyak.* Spirit power. Indian spirit."

Loq held the walkie-talkie up at Daley. "What's it going to be?"

Daley glanced at his lawyer. Lance said, "Give it here. I'll speak to the agent on your behalf. We don't want anything said that could be twisted into self-incrimination later."

Loq handed it over. "Remember, Sexton won't be scared off by lawyer talk."

"We'll see about that."

The lawyer clicked the button. "Agent Sexton, Benjamin Lance, attorney-at-law. My client has authorized me to hear how you're going to have the National Guard withdraw its helicopters and troops posthaste. As soon as those war machines are gone, we'll communicate our terms for a strictly voluntary and nonbinding preliminary hearing at a court in a jurisdiction of our choosing."

He paused and then drawled, "Should I say *do you copy* or *over*?"

"Cut the good ole boy shit," Sexton said. "You're not on *60 Minutes* being interviewed about how a country lawyer beat the Supreme Court. Here's the way this is going to play out. You and Loq escort Daley and Carrie down to the parking lot. I Mirandize them and transport them to Butte for processing. Any of their gun-toting followers try to interfere, the deal's off. Period."

"But—"

"No buts. As for the National Guard, they answer to the governor of the State of Montana, not me. The way I hear it, he wants them staying put until every last one of Daley's followers has packed up and left the park. You think you can convince him otherwise, you're welcome to try."

Lance harrumphed and then laughed. "You know, Agent Sexton, you remind me of myself when I'm arguing a case in front of a judge who has a reputation for coddling corporate polluters and kowtowing to racists. I go—"

"'Right for the jugular to prove' blah blah blah. I heard you say the same thing to Mike Wallace when you were telling him how you represented a bunch of draft dodgers. You got one minute to bring Daley and Carrie Horse down here. I won't be able to hold back the deputies and troopers a second longer. They got about as much patience as a high school jock on prom night." He gave it a couple of beats. "That country enough for you?"

The lawyer harrumphed again. "I'll confer with my client."

"You do that. Clock's ticking."

Carrie put her palms on Killian Daley's cheeks and pressed her forehead against his. "You won. By getting here, by being here, by telling our story for the reporters and filmmaker at a place with so much history, we all won."

"But I haven't given my speech. No one's heard me," he said.

"They already have. They've been hearing you the entire time we've been making the journey. They heard you in Salt Lake City. They heard you all over the country after your news broadcast in Sheridan. Think of how many more people will hear you when you're on trial. You'll be quoted on the front page every morning, on network news every night."

"I was willing to die here today."

"No one will ever doubt your bravery. You faced down the

FBI and National Guard. You'll show your courage in the court fight ahead."

She let go as Daley looked at his lawyer, but a gunshot banged before either could say a word. People ducked, others who were armed raised their weapons toward the north side of the valley where the shot came from. Another shot echoed.

"Shooter on high ground. Eleven o'clock," Loq said without realizing it was an echo of what he'd said when Jack Candy was firing down on the ranch.

"Sounds like it's coming from the hill we were on yesterday," Bina said.

Guardsmen from the helicopter that landed on the north side started shooting back. The radio in Lance's hand squawked.

"What the hell's going on?" Sexton shouted.

"It appears to be gunfire," Lance said, "but that's only conjecture, not proven fact."

Loq grabbed the radio. "Single shooter. High ground above the north LZ. Got off two rounds. Guard returned fire. Hasn't been a third shot."

"Maybe they got him," Sexton said.

"It wasn't one of Daley's followers."

"Then who was it?"

"CD Larchmont."

"You don't know that."

"But I know him. He's playing at something. I recognized the sound of his rifle."

"Bullshit. Nobody can do that. Not even the FBI's lab has come up with a device that can."

"A man who fired the same weapon a lot can. It's an M70 sniper rifle, what Larchmont and I used in Vietnam."

"Doesn't matter who was shooting," Sexton said. "The Guard troops are already forming up. Tell your people to toss their weapons and get down on the ground."

"There's no need. Daley already agreed to surrender. Carrie too. They were just coming down." He held the radio out.

"It's true," Carrie said. "We surrender."

Daley looked at the reporters who were recording him. He took a deep breath. "For the good of my people, I lay down my arms here but will fight in the courts for justice forever."

"Too late," Sexton said and clicked off.

"White flags!" Carrie said. "Hurry. Make as many as you can." She turned to the reporters. "You wanted a story, this is it. You heard us surrender."

The electrical wire that had been laid earlier was quickly picked up and tied between the large tepee and a nearby tree. Anybody wearing a white T-shirt pulled it off and tied it to the line. Towels, dishrags, and cloth diapers were hung too.

Daley took off his white buckskin tunic and draped it in the center. He sat cross-legged beneath the line of white cloth that flapped in the breeze. "Come, everyone."

Carrie sat next to him and linked her arm with his. Loq sat next to her and linked arms. Bina linked hers to Loq's. Benjamin Lance plopped down on the other side of Daley and linked arms. Soon, everyone was sitting in a large circle with linked arms except for the reporters who were recording it all.

Daley lifted his face to the sky. "*Watkatanehelatu ka'ika wahnislate.*" And then he translated. "I give thanks for this day." He spoke in Oneida again and translated. "It is a good day."

"And I am glad that I am here," the others answered, either in Oneida or their own language or English.

Carrie leaned toward Loq. "A prayer we say each morning."

"Is he really Oneida?" Loq said.

"Yes, little brother."

"And do you really love him?"

"With all my heart."

Loq sensed movement and looked across the circle.

Helmeted guardsmen holding guns rushed forward but held their position just outside of the circle. He knew more were doing the same behind him. It was all he could do to keep from jumping up and grabbing one and wrestling his gun away.

Sexton and a lean man with a chiseled jaw and captain's bars on his uniform strode forward and joined the guardsmen. Sal Tujunga was right behind them.

Someone started chanting, another singing. Daley started reciting the morning prayer again.

"Sergeant Wilkinson!" the captain barked. "These people are supposed to be face down with hands clasped behind their heads. We need compliance here. Pronto!"

"Yes, sir."

The sergeant kicked the man sitting in front of him. "Git on your belly, chief. Put your hands behind you. All of you, do the same."

The man who was kicked linked arms even tighter. The humming and singing grew louder. So did the tension among the guardsmen. Especially when cameras kept clicking and tape recorders whirring.

The sergeant kicked the man again while yelling at him to let go and roll over. The people on either side of him squeezed their linked arms even tighter and sang even louder.

The captain ordered more of his men to force them to let go of each other and roll over. As the guardsmen started prodding backs with their guns and kicking at backs, a corporal scanning the perimeter through binoculars shouted.

"Sir, we got incoming hostiles."

"From where?"

"Twelve o'clock."

"Armed?"

"Look to be."

"On foot or in vehicles?"

"On horses."

"Say again?"

"They're mounted."

The captain snatched the binoculars while Sexton strained to see past the three tepees where eighty-nine once stood. A line of thirty or more horses and riders was coming straight at them. George Tahamtaham was in the middle on a Cayuse stallion. He wore his Umatilla Tribal Police uniform. Riding on Appaloosas on either side were uniformed members of the Nez Perce Tribal Police from the Lapwai Reservation.

Flanking them were tribal officers from the Blackfeet Reservation, Chippewa Cree from Rocky Boy's Reservation, Gros Ventre and Assiniboine from Fort Belknap, and Crow from their reservation outside of Billings. Each tribe was represented by a rider holding a flagstaff, their tribal flag snapping smartly as they rode. Other Indian riders carried US, military branch, and divisional flags, and had donned the uniforms they wore while serving in World War II, Korea, and Vietnam.

The photographer with the blue kerchief knotted on his head switched to a telephoto lens and snapped away. The filmmaker panned his movie camera from left to right, and then back at the captain and Sexton, capturing their reactions.

"What the hell? Intel didn't say anything about this," the captain said.

"What are our orders, sir?" the corporal said. "Should we prepare to engage?"

"Take up defensive positions, but hold your fire." Under his breath, he muttered, "I'll be damned if I'm going to be on the news shooting a World War II vet bearing the Stars and Stripes."

While half the guardsmen kept their weapons pointed at the circle of seated Indians, half turned theirs on the riders. The oncoming line formed a crescent moon around them and halted.

George Tahamtaham was closest. He nodded. "Agent Sexton, Captain."

"What do you think you're doing?" Sexton said.

"Our job," the police chief said.

"You have no jurisdiction here. None of you do. This isn't a reservation."

One of the Nez Perce tribal cops edged his horse closer. "No, it's the burial ground of our ancestors and sacred to my people." His eyes found the captain's. "US Cavalry soldiers also died here. Is this how you show respect to your fallen?"

The captain's chiseled jaw tightened. "Signaler, get me HQ on the line. Pronto!"

Sexton stomped over to Daley. "This doesn't change a thing. I'm still arresting you and Carrie Horse."

"Do you believe in anything, Agent Sexton?" Daley said.

"What's that supposed to mean?"

"Providence? God? Creator? Nature? Spiritual power? Anything at all?"

"Only the law."

The FBI agent moved to Loq. "You did this. I know you did. It's the same thing you did getting the Hmong and hill tribes to fight for us in 'Nam."

Loq looked down his high cheekbones. "You still don't get it. They never fought *for* us. They fought *alongside* us."

Sexton snorted. "Answer the damn question. Is this your doing?"

"The honor belongs to every rider who risked their life to protect others."

"Well, they're not going to protect anyone from being locked up, that's for damn sure. Not your sister and Daley, not you and your girlfriend, not anyone."

"Then you'll have to do it on your own."

"What makes you say that?"

"Because the captain is learning how fast political winds can shift."

Sexton looked over his shoulder and saw the chisel-jawed officer holding a shortwave radio handset to his ear. "Yes, Governor. Yes, sir. Right away, sir."

He handed it back to the signaler. "Sergeant Wilkinson! Order all personnel to return to the choppers. Move out. Double time."

"But, sir," the sergeant said.

"Are you questioning my order?"

"No, sir."

As soon as the captain turned away, the sergeant gave the man in front of him a final kick, which prompted a smile.

"What are you grinning about, chief?"

"How we kicked your ass without raising a foot. How when you walk past those Nimiipuu Appaloosas, they're going to kick it too."

32

T he giant green helicopters left as fast as they came. Agent Sexton and Benjamin Lance agreed that everyone but Killian Daley and Carrie Horse would be free to leave upon giving their name and address to a joint team comprised of a tribal police officer, state trooper, and county sheriff's deputy.

As people lined up to do that, Loq and Bina went searching for CD Larchmont. They soon found the spot he'd been shooting from, but there was no bullet-riddled corpse, no blood splatter on the bushes, no brass left on the ground either.

Riding back to the tepees, Bina said, "He must've stashed a vehicle on the other side of the river like we did. He's long gone by now."

"No, he's close by."

"Why do you think that?"

"Because Killian Daley's still here. Larchmont doesn't get paid if he doesn't deliver him to his father."

"I wonder why Sexton isn't taking Larchmont more seriously."

"Old habit. After giving him free rein in Vietnam so long as he delivered results and never burned him, Sexton learned to accept his methods."

They kept riding.

Loq said, "What's George going to do about Willie Hawk-feather?"

"Arrest him for breaking probation back in Oregon without telling anyone he knows about the murder. He'll take him back to the reservation and work with the tribal council on what to do with him. If anybody can rehabilitate Willie, it's his own people."

"What happens when the BIA investigates Candy's disappearance and finds out Willie killed him? Somebody's going to say something. It's not if, it's when."

"George knows that, but he thinks there's a case to be made that Willie wasn't in his right mind after seeing Candy murder his friend Freddy Salish and the Apache woman. He thinks Daley's lawyer might even consider taking the case. You know, Willie's a minor, no education, discrimination."

"Your boss is taking quite a risk doing that. He could be charged for concealing a murder."

"George has been taking them his whole life. Growing up on a rez, fighting in Korea, getting himself hired as a deputy in an all-White sheriff's department, and now being tribal police chief."

"You forgot one thing."

"What?"

"Hiring the first female tribal cop."

Bina smiled and then rode closer. "Are you going to tell me what your plan is for Carrie or do I have to be surprised like everyone else?"

"I can't tell you because it'd make you party to it."

"That sounds a lot better than saying you don't trust me."

"You know the answer to that."

"Yes," she said. "I do."

When they reached the tepees, they saw that the wraps had already been removed from the two smaller ones and tied in bundles.

Carrie came over. "Once Kills in Daylight blesses it, we'll unwrap the center one too. We're going to leave the poles—the bones—of all three as a memorial."

"That's a beautiful idea," Bina said.

"When is Sexton taking you to Butte?" Loq said.

"As soon as we're finished here. Benjamin convinced him to allow us that."

Carrie stroked the spotted pony's muzzle and looked up at Loq. "Don't interfere, little brother. It would only make matters worse. I've made my decision. I'm asking you to respect it."

Loq thought about how easy it'd be to grab her arm and yank her up while telling the pony to gallop. He'd race back up the valley, cross the river before anyone could get off a shot, and ride straight into the Beaverhead Mountains. They'd go where no vehicle could follow, stay in the trees where no helicopter could spot them. They'd live off the land while making their way home to Chiloquin like they used to do when going fishing for mullet or picking berries. He could see them riding up to their mother's house, see Carrie's two children running out and her gathering them in her arms and smothering them with kisses.

"Loq!" Carrie said. "Promise me you won't interfere."

He only nodded and turned his pony away.

"Men," Carrie said.

"Tell me about it," Bina said. She hopped off Túxin. "Here, I'll help you unwrap the big tepee."

Loq found Sexton and Tujunga talking with Benjamin Lance as the last of Daley's followers were giving their names to the cops in the parking lot. Vehicles were streaming out of the park.

"Bina and I couldn't find Larchmont, but you know he's still around, still going to do something," he said as he dismounted, but kept hold of the reins.

"Who's Larchmont and do what?" the lawyer said.

When Loq told him, Sexton said, "Don't listen to him. Loq and CD have a long history between them."

"Of bad blood?" Lance said.

"Broken blood," Loq said.

The lawyer turned to Sexton. "Now that I'm witness to the fact that you were warned about a potential threat to my client and everyone still here, I must strongly advise you to take steps to secure our safety."

Sexton remained blank-faced.

Loq asked him where the other agents were. "The one that smells like Old Spice and the other of cheap whiskey."

"Not that it's any of your business, but I sent them back to Butte to start the paperwork and put a chain lock on that holding cell. The built-in one looked pickable to me. Agent Tujunga and I'll transport Daley and your sister by helicopter."

George Tahamtaham joined them. He said the other tribal police officers were already riding across the Big Hole River to get their rigs and go home. He was about to do the same.

"Where did you leave your prisoner, Hawkfeather?" Sexton said.

"Handcuffed to the same tree where I tied my horse."

The senior agent all but rolled his eyes. "I can't wait to get back to civilization."

George asked Loq where Bina was. "I want to see if she's going to caravan back with me or if she and you ... well, if she's got other plans."

"She's at the tepees with Carrie. Probably going to help unwrap the last one."

"Not until my client is finished getting dressed inside and gathering his belongings," Lance said.

The clouds lifted and a thunderbolt clapped inside Loq's head. He clicked at the spotted pony. "Go!" And grabbed the saddle horn and ran alongside the sprinting horse before swinging aboard. "The tepee! Larchmont's hiding in it."

George Tahamtaham started running after him, not wasting time to stop and untie his horse. Sexton and Tujunga were close behind but quickly passed the older tribal cop. Even the lawyer broke into what amounted to a fast walk.

Loq neared the big tepee. The flap was open and he saw CD Larchmont just inside. He held a gun in one hand and the middle of a length of rope in the other. One end was slip-knotted around Carrie's neck, the other around Bina's. Both women were gagged. Daley was slumped in a daze. His hands were tied in front of him and blood trickled from his forehead where he'd been pistol-whipped.

Larchmont looked up at the sound of hooves. He yanked the two women in front of him and shoved his semiautomatic against Carrie's head.

"Keep your hands where I can see them, Loq. I'll drop both girls before you can draw."

"Sexton's right behind me. George Tahamtaham too. You can't take us all."

"Don't need to." He shifted the gun from Carrie to Bina. "Sexton and the lawyer aren't the only ones with birds. I got one picking me up any second now. Bird lands, your sister and girl-friend are my shield. You're going to help by bringing Daley along. Once I'm safely on board with these three, away we go. If the girls behave, I'll land and drop them off. If they don't, I'll just drop them."

"Away to where?"

"That's between me and Daley's old man and his checkbook."

Sexton and Tujunga arrived. Tahamtaham was only a few steps behind.

"What the hell are you doing, CD?" Sexton said.

"What I'm getting paid for. Reuniting a father and son."

"Daley already surrendered. He's under arrest. My arrest!"

"You're slipping. You forgot to cuff him. Now he's mine."

"Even if I let you take him, it won't change a thing. We'll arrest him at his father's. Arrest the father too for harboring a fugitive."

"Men like Daley Senior don't get arrested. You remember how it is, how it's always been. They buy and sell lawmakers like it's nothing more than picking up the tab at a bar."

Benjamin Lance finally joined them. "You're making a big mistake, sir, because you don't need to do this," he wheezed, trying to catch his breath. "As his attorney, I'll see that Kills in Daylight never spends a night in jail, much less ever gets sent to prison."

"Because you'll get paid for doing that. Guess what? I'll get paid even more for doing this."

Loq shifted his gaze from Carrie to Bina. Despite the gags, Carrie's eyes told him not to try anything. Bina's said she trusted him no matter what.

"You won't get away with it," Tahamtaham said.

"Of course I will. No one's going to care who gave the kid a ride home. His old man will make sure of it."

"He can't protect you for blowing up the BIA office and hurting the people inside or torturing and killing the informant at Warm Springs."

"Who says I did? Even if someone tries to frame me for it, I'll have enough money to disappear and buy a new life."

A helicopter thrummed in the distance.

"No one needs to frame you because you committed both crimes and I can prove it," Tahamtaham said. "Warm Springs tribal police did their own investigation. They lifted your prints there. I got an eyewitness of you skulking around the BIA office in Pendleton right before the bomb went off."

Larchmont snickered. "I'm like those new Teflon pans. Nothing's going to stick. Besides, I got an insurance policy. Right, Sexton?"

"I don't know what you're talking about," the senior agent said quickly.

The helicopter drew closer. The thrumming turned into thwapping.

"Time to go." Larchmont tightened his leash on Carrie and Bina. "Everybody drop their guns. Hop to it." He tapped his gun on the women's heads.

Loq slid off the spotted pony and unbuckled his holster. It clunked when it hit the ground. So did George Tahamtaham's. Sexton and Tujunga removed their weapons from their clip-on holsters and placed them on the ground.

"Okay, Loq. Come get Daley."

The helicopter was hovering above the clearing and started to land.

Loq stepped inside the tepee, slid his arm around Daley, and helped him to his feet. He wobbled, but Loq kept him from falling.

"Lead the way," Larchmont said.

As Loq half carried, half dragged Daley away, Larchmont stepped out of the tepee with his gun jammed against Carrie's head.

"Gentlemen, if you would." He chinned at them to step inside.

After they did, he closed the flap and pinned it. He dragged Carrie and Bina along as he trotted after Loq and Daley to the nearby helicopter.

The chopper's rear door was already open and the pilot back behind the stick.

"Daley boards first," Larchmont said. "Help him in."

Loq wrestled him inside and plopped him into a seat.

"Now move away."

Loq did. Larchmont maneuvered around so his back was to the open door. He let go of the leash and waved the gun at Carrie and Bina to stand near Loq.

"Change of plans, ladies. You get to stay and watch him die."

Larchmont swung his gun toward Loq. "You and your Indian ways. Always thinking you were better than me. A better soldier. A better shot. A better man. And springing me from that VC cage? Here's how I'm gonna repay you."

He started to squeeze the trigger. Carrie leapt without hesitation or impatience. The bullet struck her in the chest and knocked her flat, the rope yanking Bina down with her. Larchmont sneered as he took aim again. Loq reached for the skinning knife he wore at his back.

But it wasn't there to throw.

He looked at Larchmont. Killian Daley was right behind him, his bound hands clutching the skinning knife he'd slipped from its sheath when Loq helped him into the chopper. He plunged the blade into the back of Larchmont's neck.

When Larchmont slumped forward, his gun firing harmlessly into the ground as he fell, Loq nodded to Daley. It was a worthy kill. It was a kill in daylight.

Loq dropped to his knees beside Carrie, slid the noose from her neck, and removed the gag. Daley hopped out of the helicopter and knelt next to her too.

She smiled at them. *"Yayna sle-ok, ni cis gena.* Because of seeing the mountain, I went home."

And then Carrie's eyes turned to the sky and the path that would take her there.

33

Loq pulled the skinning knife out of CD Larchmont's neck and wiped the blade on the killer's clothes.

"I was wrong about you, Kills in Daylight," he said as he sheathed his knife. "Carrie told me she loved you and now I see what she saw. You are a true warrior. You are a spiritual man. The way you speak to people's hearts, the way you help them remember who they are, who we all are."

"And I see what she has always seen in you, my brother, and why she loved you so deeply," he said.

Loq picked up Carrie, and called to the spotted pony.

"I'm taking my sister to her children and mother so they can give a blessing and say they will see her again in the spirit world."

"I will help you."

Loq sat Carrie in the saddle on the spotted pony. Kills in Daylight held her in place while he swung up to sit behind her.

Bina reached up to Loq. "Here, the key to my rig. I'll get yours in White Bird Canyon."

Before he could ride off, the men in the tepee freed themselves. Robert Sexton scooped up his gun and came running. Tujunga, Tahamtaham, and Lance were close behind.

The senior FBI agent took it all in a glance—CD Larchmont's body and Loq on the horse with his dead sister.

"Put her down, Loq," he said. "This is a crime scene. She's evidence."

"It only is because you wouldn't stop Larchmont, just as you didn't in Vietnam," Loq said.

"Drop her body and get off the horse!" Sexton raised his gun.

Loq didn't blink.

Tahamtaham stepped in front of the FBI agent. "What kind of man are you? Can't you see his sister was just murdered by your hired killer?"

"I'm more than a man. I'm a lawman," Sexton said.

"No, you're not. You broke every law of human decency."

"Get out of my way, old man! I won't tell you twice."

Twice was the sound of two hammers clicking.

Sexton swiveled his head. Sal Tujunga was aiming two guns at him.

"Are you out of your mind?" Sexton said.

The young agent didn't waver. "Robert Sexton, I'm arresting you for conspiring to murder a paid FBI informant and concealing evidence of that crime and the bombing of the BIA office."

"What are you talking about?"

"What Larchmont said. You're his insurance policy."

"Bullshit."

"No, nor is the evidence I've been collecting at the request of the Office of Professional Responsibility. It's the reason why I was assigned to you. They've been investigating you for a year."

"You? You're a rat for that bullshit internal affairs department? DOJ only created it to cover its ass after Watergate."

The two guns remained steady. "That may be, but these

aren't bullshit, nor is what I'm about to say as witnessed by everyone here." He took a breath. "You have the right to remain silent. Anything you say can and will be used against you in a court of law ..."

Loq had heard enough. He tightened his arms around Carrie and tapped his heels. The pony didn't bolt, but began a slow walk. The tall grass swayed as they passed through it, the tips gently brushing horse and rider's legs.

They forded the Big Hole River and Loq pictured the Williamson River when he held on to his sister's ankles as she taught him how to swim. He pictured them riding double on a saddleless swaybacked horse along the Sprague River where they'd stop and fish for mullet using treble hooks weighted with old sparkplugs. They'd sell the fish for a penny a piece to elders and use their earnings to buy candy kept in big glass jars at the Chiloquin hardware store.

When he got to Bina's pickup, he sat Carrie in the front seat, folded his blanket into a pillow, and rested her head on it. After loading the pony into the trailer, he checked the sun before getting behind the wheel. It would take him thirteen, fourteen hours to drive home, plenty of time to come up with a good song about her to teach to her children.

It was past midnight when he crossed into Harney County on Highway 20, the two-lane he'd driven more times than he could count in the course of his job as a Fish and Wildlife ranger. When he was on the outskirts of Burns, the thought of taking the cutoff down to No Mountain and the Warbler ranch came and went. Though Nick Drake deserved to hear about Carrie's death in person, Loq knew he'd understand why he didn't stop.

The sun was rising when he reached Chiloquin. He slowed and glanced at Carrie before taking the road to his mother's house.

"I'm sorry I doubted you," he said. "I'm sorry I couldn't save you. I promise I'll never let your children down."

Gravel crunched beneath the tires of the pickup and trailer. He got out and closed the door quietly so as not to wake anyone inside the house. When he walked around to the passenger side, his mother was standing there wrapped in a blanket, her face etched with grief, her eyes swollen from crying.

"I knew Carrie had been killed even before she came last night to tell me herself," she said. "A mother always knows when her child dies because part of her dies too. That part of me is with her now in the spirit world. The rest will join her when I die and we will be together again."

Loq hugged her. "Part of me died too."

"I know, my son. I know."

"Are the children awake?"

"Not yet."

"I'll bring her inside."

"I've already laid out her clothes."

The next three days were a blur and a blessing. The house was filled with elders, friends, and family telling stories, singing songs, crying, laughing, and eating. Lots of eating. Everyone who came brought food. Casseroles, pots of stew, pots of beans, smoked fish, wild duck, wild rice, and *C'waam*.

Loq lost count of all the desserts, but was glad to see Carrie's children hadn't lost their appetite for sweets. And he was even gladder when Nick, Gemma, and their kids arrived. Hattie and Johnny swept up his niece and nephew and took them outside to play. The healing had begun.

Pudge Warbler and November also came to pay their respects. The Klamath elders greeted the famed Paiute healer by calling her by her tribal name, Girl Born in Snow. A new round of singing and chanting began both in Numu and Maklak.

Loq didn't say anything about the old sheriff's weight loss or sallow cheeks when he shook his hand and told him George Tahamtaham said to say hello.

"The feds don't always get things right," Pudge said, "but they sure did when they allowed the reservations to have their own police. The Confederated Tribes are darn lucky to have George as chief of theirs."

"Same as Harney County is having you as sheriff. I see you're wearing your uniform again."

"Yep. I started going back to work, except the week a month I get the chemo. Orville's done a heckuva job as Acting Sheriff, but I'm not ready to roll over yet. Besides, I'm drinking some tea November brewed up, and, well, it appears to be putting some giddyap back in my step."

Loq went outside to get some air. He was leaning against the fender of Bina's pickup when Nick came out carrying two mugs of coffee and handed him one. They drank without saying anything, not feeling like they had to because they knew any words would feel hollow compared to what they felt.

Finally, Nick said, "Whose rig?"

"Tribal cop from the Umatilla rez."

He waved his mug. "Is he in the house?"

"She's not here. We switched rigs and I drove hers down from Montana."

"She, huh?"

"Mm. Her name's Bina Mantioc."

"Pretty name."

"So's she."

They drank their coffee and watched the kids play.

Nick said, "When the time's right and if you want, we can talk about what happened at Big Hole."

"When the time's right. And you? Anything happen while I was away?"

"Something did, but we can talk about that later too because I'll need your help fulfilling a promise I made to Johnny."

"When the time's right."

After Nick and his family and the last of the mourners left, Loq saddled the spotted pony and rode down to the lake on a trail that was as familiar as his own skin. His heart was heavy and he wondered how it could feel that way since it was broken.

"Because it's so big, little brother. You've always been the big-hearted one in the family."

He looked over. Carrie was riding next to him on the horse she'd lifted over the finish line at the Fort Klamath powwow.

"And you've always been the smartest," he said.

"Don't forget the fastest too."

They laughed and kept riding, reminiscing about all the things they'd done growing up—the fun times, the good times, even the sad and bad ones.

The sun was starting its descent over the Cascades when Carrie said, "Race you to the lake?"

"Let's go!" And he urged the pony into a gallop.

The two horses ran neck and neck, their tails and manes flying, Carrie laughing and Loq laughing too. He wished they could gallop forever, but the finish line they'd always raced to came up too soon, and when they crossed, Carrie won by a head.

"I beat you again, little brother," she said.

"You're always first."

"And to the spirit world too."

She was smiling when she said it, and when the bright rays of the sun started to fade and her voice did too, Loq could still see her, still hear her. He always would.

He continued riding, losing himself in thought and memory, unaware of the sky's changing bands of color mirrored in the waters of the lake beside him. Hoofbeats brought him back to the moment, and he looked over his shoulder, expecting to see Carrie again, but it wasn't her.

Túxin nickered and the spotted pony whinnied back.

Loq slowed and Bina drew abreast.

"Your mother told me where you were," she said. "We talked awhile when I was paying my respects. She asked me if I cook traditional."

"What did you tell her?"

"That I'm too busy working and leave cooking to the men. It made her laugh. That's good, isn't it?"

"It is."

They rode a little farther.

Bina said, "Did you hear about Robert Sexton?"

"No."

"They're bringing him up on a bunch of charges. Sal Tujunga really was working for that Justice Department's special branch. I think it was one of the reasons why he was sending information along to Kills in Daylight and Carrie. Why he helped us break out of the cell in Butte. He was setting Sexton up for a fall."

"I said he was clever."

"The FBI thinks so too. They're giving him a promotion. He'll be in charge of any Indian-related investigations in their western division to make sure they're done honestly."

"What about Kills in Daylight?"

"I see you're calling him by that name now."

"The same as you just did. He earned that right."

"That he did. Benjamin Lance is working out a deal where all the charges against him will be dropped, including killing CD Larchmont. No one is going to file anything against his followers either."

"That won't silence Kills in Daylight."

"No, it won't."

"Good. Now when he speaks, he speaks for Carrie too."

"What are you going to do?"

"Take it one day at a time while the kids get settled here and go back to school in the fall. What about you?"

"George gave me a little leave to bring your rig down and drive mine back."

"The Umatilla's not too far away."

"Not if you don't want it to be."

"I don't."

"Me either."

"That's good. Better than good. Want to keep riding?"

"I'd rather dance."

"What kind of dance?"

"The Sweetheart Dance. Do you know the steps?"

"Mm, but let's teach each other new ones and make up more as we go."

Bina slipped off the roan mare and Loq jumped off the spotted pony. As they gathered each other in their arms, the first stars of the evening began to jingle.

ABOUT THE AUTHOR

Dwight Holing is the award-winning author of twenty books, including two bestselling mystery series: the Nick Drake Novels and the Jack McCoul Capers.

His Nick Drake mysteries have won the Silver Falchion Award for Best Western, the CLUE Award for Best Mystery & Suspense, and the Laramie Award for Best Novel with Western, First Nations, and Americana Themes. His short fiction was awarded the Arts & Letters Prize for Fiction.

Dwight Holing is a member of Mystery Writers of America, Western Writers of America, and Sisters in Crime where he serves on the board of directors of its Capital Crimes chapter. He lives beside a coastal river in California with his wife and two dogs who'd rather swim than walk.

ACKNOWLEDGMENTS

I'm indebted to many people who helped in the creation of *The Broken Blood*. As always, my family provided support throughout the research and writing process.

I'm especially grateful to John Onoda who encouraged me to feature Loq as the lead in a Nick Drake novel so that readers could learn more about him, his tribe, and see the world through his unique point of view.

I also want to acknowledge my advance reader team who read early drafts and gave me very helpful feedback. They include Gene Ammerman, George Becker, Jeffrey Miller, Kenneth Mitchell, John Onoda, and Haris Orkin.

A heartfelt shoutout to my friends Randy & Lorna Rigdon and Harry & Melinda Childers who generously shared their personal stories about growing up and living in Chiloquin, Oregon.

Thank you Emma Moylan for proofreading and copyediting. Kudos to design artist-extraordinaire Rob Williams for designing and creating the cover.

I humbly offer my respect to the Confederated Tribes of the Umatilla Indian Reservation, the Burns Paiute Indian Tribe of Oregon, and the Klamath Tribes, whose mission is to protect, preserve and enhance the spiritual, cultural and physical values and resources of the Klamath, Modoc and Yahooskin Peoples by maintaining the customs and heritage of their ancestors.

Any errors, regrettably, are my own.

ALSO BY DWIGHT HOLING

The Nick Drake Novels

The Sorrow Hand (Book 1)

The Pity Heart (Book 2)

The Shaming Eyes (Book 3)

The Whisper Soul (Book 4)

The Nowhere Bones (Book 5)

The Forever Feet (Book 6)

The Demon Skin (Book 7)

The Broken Blood (Book 8)

The Thunder Head (Book 9)

The Yellow Hair (Book 10)

The Jack McCoul Capers

A Boatload (Book 1)

Bad Karma (Book 2)

Baby Blue (Book 3)

Shake City (Book 4)

Novels

Hard Blue Empty: A Mystery

Short Story Collections

California Works

Over Our Heads Under Our Feet